Passage to Inis Mór

PASSAGE TO INIS MÓR

*

Brian O'Raleigh

Copyright

Passage to Inis Mór

O'Raleigh - Brian
October 2021

Dedication

I dedicate this book to my wife

Kadek

And my children

Chris and Liz - Kathleen and Sharon

There are four harbors between heaven and earth

Where souls are cleansed

The Paradise of Adam, Rome, Aran and Jerusalem

No Angel who ever came to Ireland to help Gael or Gaul

Returned to Heaven without first visiting Aran

Cormac mac Cuilennáin
King of Munster - Bishop of Cashel
Died 13th September 908 AD

Prologue
Ireland

The old man stared across at me, his eyes glittering in the firelight.

"So, you're thirty-eight years of age and your life is in tatters." He smiled. "You're a fortunate man."

"Fortunate? I lose everything I own, and you consider that fortunate? This is a catastrophe for Christ's sake!"

"Settle down now, boy, settle down." He leaned forward and placed another log on the fire, "Take a good look at yourself. You were sick of the job, it was meaningless, you said as much yourself. What have you lost? The marriage? It was no use to either of you the way it was. Sure, you were driving the poor woman mad with your advertising nonsense. The house in Australia? It wasn't even yours. The Mercedes? No, that was just arrogance on wheels."

Maybe he's mad. I thought. *Maybe that's why he's always alone.*

"What you lost was an illusion, boy, the illusion of being a big shot."

"You've no idea what you're talking about." My heart was thumping. "I worked my butt off in that business."

But he continued on as if I hadn't spoken.

"Your life fell apart through lack of meaning. What value was your work? To anyone but yourself, that is. And your marriage is in tatters because you put your career ahead of your family." He pointed the stem of his pipe at me, "But listen to me now, and listen well. With all your problems and all your woes, what you are now calling a *catastrophe* would be better understood as a *calling.*" He stared across, his dark green eyes clear and steady. "Do you understand that?"

"No, I don't!" I grabbed the poker and began stabbing at the logs, sparks flying up the ancient, soot caked chimney. "What are you saying? You think I'm working in the wrong career, is that it?"

"That's not for me to say." He took a sip of tea before going on. "But now you'll be forced to take a good look at yourself. *That's* why I say you're fortunate. Most of your kind stagger on for years in jobs they hate, ignoring their wives and families, trading their souls for an illusory sense of security while sinking deeper into mediocrity each year."

I tossed the poker back on the hearth.

"That might be fine for you, but some of us have to live in the real world too, you know."

But he just shook his head and continued.

"Others become addicted to the almighty dollar. Trapped in the delusion that fancy cars and inflated expense accounts will bring lasting happiness whilst they avoid doing anything of value in the world." He raised his eyes to meet mine, and I was struck by the fearlessness of his gaze. "Self-centered fools preying on a crippled planet."

"What did you mean by a calling?" I said.

"Your calling, boy. Your purpose in life. Your gift. Call it what you will."

"Who are you?" I said, "You're not from the island, are you?"

But again, he just ignored me, staring into the flames as if lost in a dream.

Chapter 1
Australia 2016

I'm not sure when first I realized that the life I'd been living was over, but when it came, it came clearly. An undeniable intuition warning me I was wasting the best years of my life.

And yet every time I thought of the island an irrational hope surged in my heart, some inner sense of longing drawing me backwards towards the unknown. Over a period of just a few months, memories and images came to me in a dozen different ways. Appearing in a newspaper article one morning, and then in a casual conversation with a stranger that same afternoon. The following week, I met a young woman from Inis Mór on a busy Sydney street, and then, a few days later, I ran into her again at a Halloween party. Synchronistic events that brought the island back into focus.

At first, I tried to dismiss it all as coincidence, but when I received a letter from my grandmother saying that she was dying and wanted to see me, I knew there was more to it than that. As I traced her spidery handwriting on the single sheet of pale cream foolscap, I felt a vague pang of remorse.

Dearest Conor,

I pray to God you might receive this letter in time. I have been ill for some while now and know I'm not long for this world. I have no fear of death, only some regrets that I need to address. If you are to read these words before I pass, please come home. There is something you must know

Grace O'Rourke.

As I stared down at the cryptic message, an age-old memory stirred within. A tall, handsome, grey-haired woman standing upright and alone beside a cottage gate, the sea behind her dark blue with white-capped waves.

I tossed the letter back on the table. The idea was ridiculous. I hadn't seen my grandmother since childhood, the memories tarnished by the bitterness of a long-standing family feud. But that night as I lay restless on my bed, thinking back to earlier, simpler days, the words of a poem began running through my mind. Not a poem that I knew, but a series of lines already formed, whispering up from some unconscious source, pulling at the edges of my mind, demanding and insistent as a child. The words spoke of the island, of going back, tumbling out across a mind unfettered by thought…

I lost my way long years ago, I faltered, and I strayed

I turned away from those I loved these choices I have made

But now at night I wonder, could I return once more?

Could I return to what I was by the cliffs at Inis Mór?

As the words faded, I was transported back to the last time I'd ever seen the island, falling away behind me in the mist from the deck of an ancient Irish ferry, on a winter's day some thirty years before, and I knew in my heart that my destiny lay there, whatever that destiny would be.

Chapter 2
Bondi Beach

The following morning my waking thought was my grandmother's letter, but I dismissed it immediately, dragged myself out of bed and headed for the bathroom. I turned the water on hot, hoping to wash away the demons that had been haunting my sleeping hours for months. As I stepped into the shower, I noticed Giselle's dressing gown hanging on the back of the door. *Put it away*, I told myself, but I told myself that every day. It was as if I kept it there as a talisman, hoping that one day it might somehow lure her back to me.

We tried counseling, but after eight hours of therapy and more than a thousand dollars' worth of cash, all we'd ended up with was a bunch of New Age tags to taunt each other with. I'd been relabeled an emotionally unavailable, borderline alcoholic, whilst Giselle was enabling my addictions with her co-dependent behavior.

When I told the therapist, I could have got that much and more free of charge from the Pop Psychology section of the Kings Cross library, she'd told me that her professional opinion was that as long as I continued to overwork and drink on weekends, I was wasting my money and her time and recommended a six-month period of total abstinence.

I did quit drinking eventually, but by that time Giselle had lost all faith in me, and when her mother had been diagnosed with cancer, she'd gone back to her family home in France, taking our eight-year-old son with her.

I'd driven them to Sydney International Airport that wretched day, immersed in a cloud of shame. Giselle staring out the side window, me looking straight ahead. The strangled silence threatening to choke me, my stomach muscles knotting up in a convoluted mix of despair and denial. When we arrived at the departure gate, I'd touched her arm.

"Call me as soon as you arrive," I said, but she'd just nodded and looked way. "Things will work out, Giselle,"

I knew she couldn't speak, afraid of breaking down in front of Tristan.

"Look after your mum, son" I'd told him, more to break the silence than anything. But then Giselle looked up, and for the first time that day, our eyes met.

"You were supposed to do that, John," she'd said, accusatory tears glistening on her cheeks, "not Tristan."

Her words had cut into me so deeply that I'd just turned and walked away. Stumbling my way back to the car in utter confusion, one part of me wanting to run back and beg them not to leave, the other part wanting to crawl away somewhere and die.

Halfway home I pulled over to the edge of the freeway and, amidst the thundering anonymity of a thousand passing cars, I broke down and wept.

I turned the water on cold. If I allowed myself to dwell on my wife for too long, I'd spend the rest of the day immobilized. *Positive, positive, positive,* I told myself. The Pepsi Cola account was ready to sign. The final meeting with their marketing people had gone well. This one account would swing us back into the black in a big way. *Every day in every way, I'm getting better and better.* I mumbled the mantra out loud repeatedly, as I shivered in the chilling flow, striving to ignore the voices screaming 'bullshit!' in the back of my mind.

I toweled off, pulled on a shirt, and went through to the kitchen. The day was sullen and overcast. The heat wave that had sweltered Sydney for days was all but done. As I opened the coffee jar, the bold aroma of La Esperanza came swirling up to greet me like a Genie from Aladdin's lamp.

I'd been hooked on Colombian coffee since spending six months in Bogotá as an exchange student. That's where I met my wife. She was studying fine arts at the university. Giselle wasn't what you'd call a beautiful woman, not in the conventional sense, but she had a way about her that had me intrigued from the very beginning. She was tall and graceful, with a tousled mass of jet-black hair and a lingering trace of a French accent left over from her childhood days in Brittany.

The first time we got together was on a weekend excursion the university had organized to a coffee plantation high in the hills above Bogotá. Giselle had been a coffee lover for years, whilst I'd never found my way past Nescafe. I'd only joined the outing because I knew she'd be there. We stayed with the group for most of the day, but as evening approached, we slipped away and found a little place to eat in a nearby village. Later that night, as the moon rose over the darkened hills, we sat around a flickering campfire and talked for hours about everything and nothing. The following morning, she gave me a discourse on Colombian coffees before introducing me to Esperanza. I'd been faithful to them both ever since.

I set up the percolator and flicked on the radio. The weather forecaster was warning that a southerly depression was heading for the Central Coast. Old news, my left ankle had been throbbing for days, an infallible sign that heavy weather was on the way.

I poured a cup and took it over to the bay window. Most days the beach looked like a cover shot from National Geographic, but today the sands were all but deserted, just a few old diehards jogging along in shorts and anoraks by the water's edge. Over to the south, swollen masses of slate gray cloud approached stealthily from behind the rocky headland that defines the southern extremity of Bondi Beach.

A sudden scream wrenched my eyes downward. Directly below, a group of teenagers in school uniforms were hassling a smaller boy as they waited for the bus to Dover Heights Primary. He was trying to fend them off, but the biggest lad, an overweight lout with spiky hair, was shouting and jabbing a finger close to his face. *Smack him in the mouth, son,* I thought, *one good punch and he'll never trouble you again.*

I hated bullies; I'd had too much of it myself. I turned eight the day we arrived in Australia and, after finding a small flat at Bondi, my mother had enrolled me at the local primary school. I'd arrived midterm with red hair, a gammy leg, and an Irish accent, and the first few months had been hell. But then my gym teacher had suggested I join the boxing team, and that changed everything. In the school tournament later that year, I landed a wild punch that put my opponent on the canvas for a ten count. Nobody had ever bothered me again.

As I finished my coffee, the school bus appeared and, just as quickly as it had begun, the bullying was over, the boys shuffling reluctantly on board for one more day at school.

* * *

Forty minutes later I was in the lift heading for my office on the 7th floor. The moment the doors slid open my secretary was striding towards me clutching a handful of mail.

"Good morning, John. Mr. Bannister called twice, he said it's urgent…"

"Slow down, Janine," I held up a defensive hand, "You know the routine. Breakfast first, the Bannister's of this world later."

"I'm sorry, but he's so insistent..."

"Don't take it on board; ok? If I'm not here, tell him to call back. If he wants to go beyond that, you can give him a dial tone with my blessings."

I watched as she disappeared down the hallway. She was young, fresh out of university, and the strain was beginning to show.

I sifted through the envelopes cautiously, then tossed them back on the table. The rain was still holding off, but the sky had taken on a heavy, threatening tone, and out across the water, wispy trails of low-lying mist were beginning to round and blur the edges of the Sydney Harbour Bridge.

'Please come home,' my grandmother had written, 'There's something you must know.'

I'd asked my mother on her deathbed to tell me what had happened on the island, but even then, she'd refused to discuss it.

"Stay away from Inis Mór," she'd said. "There's nothing there for you but grief." I'd heard that same line all my life. "Promise me you'll never go back there, son. Promise me you won't."

Janine was back. A take-away coffee in one hand, a white paper carton in the other.

"There were no croissants." She hesitated. "So I got a ham and cheese baguette instead."

"That's fine, Janine." I smiled, hoping she'd relax, "Keep the dogs at bay for a while, would you? I'll be taking calls later."

I was enjoying the second mouthful of baguette when Janine reappeared.

"I'm sorry, John, but Mr. Haines from Lend Lease is on line three. It's about the Mercedes…"

"And you told him I was in?" I regretted the words before they were out of my mouth.

"Yes, I'm sorry, I didn't know what else to say. He's called several times this week."

"That's ok, I'll handle it."

I waited for her to disappear before picking up the receiver.

"John Carlyle."

"Peter Haines from Lend Lease, Mr. Carlyle. How are you today?"

"I'm fine thanks, Peter. How can I help you?"

"Mr. Carlyle, you're five months in arrears on the Mercedes. Four thousand nine hundred and seventy-five dollars, to be precise. We spoke three weeks ago, as I'm sure you'll remember, and you assured me at the time that you'd be bringing the account up to date by the thirtieth of last month. To the best of my knowledge that did not happen."

I was juggling figures as he spoke. My credit cards were close to the max, there was six or seven thousand in my personal account, plus what clients owed me.

"My apologies, Peter. I'll have a cheque out to you before the end of the week."

"Thank you, but we'd prefer it if our courier could pick up a bank cheque tomorrow morning. Failing that, we'd have no option but to repossess the vehicle."

The contrived civility of his tone was infuriating, an ingratiating manner tainted with a subtle arrogance.

"That won't be necessary, Peter, you'll have your money in a day or two."

"I'm sorry, but you've already broken two agreements and I have my instructions. Those are our terms."

"Ok," I told him, "I'll see what I can do."

"Thank you, Mr. Carlyle. Our courier will be there first thing in the morning." He hung up.

I reached for the baguette, but my appetite had disappeared, so I dumped the remains in the rubbish bin. Lend Lease was a problem, although they had been patient. I'd have to come up with a solution quickly.

As I was finishing the coffee, my mobile rang. I checked the screen, a private number.

"John Carlyle."

"Paul Reynolds, John." My old boss's voice came across the line, as smug and patronizing as ever. "Is this a good time to call?"

"I'm busy, Paul," Reynolds was the last person I wanted to talk to, "I can't talk for long."

"That's fine," he sounded amused. "I just need a moment or two at most."

"What is it, mate?"

"Well, I thought you should be the first to know that my company signed off on the Pepsi Cola deal last night. All legal and binding. They liked your presentation, said it was quite brilliant, but just a little *too* daring, perhaps. Traps for young players, John."

"You arrogant bastard…" but he'd already hung up.

It took me a few seconds to fully grasp what he'd said, my brain battling helplessly with denial. I'd spent four hard months and a truckload of cash on that one account. Scriptwriters, storyboards, pilot videos, expensive dinners, tickets to shows and endless, endless meetings. I'd gambled everything on that one deal.

I felt like a punch to the gut, and I sat there for some time feeling physically sick. Finally, I got myself together, picked up the phone, called my accountant's office, and asked for Maurice Shaw.

"The Pepsi account's gone to Paul Reynolds." I told him. "He just called."

"Are you sure?"

"Of course I'm sure! He's not going to lie about a thing like that."

There was a pause.

"You needed that account, John."

"Thanks, Maurice, I am aware of that. So, what now? Any advice? Any words of wisdom?"

The cold, hard, steel fingers of stress groped at my heart as I waited for a response.

"You're behind on your mortgage and on the payments for the Mercedes. We received a call from Lend Lease yesterday."

"To hell with Lend Lease! I'm asking for advice, for Christ's sake."

There was another silence and then he came back, his voice cool and impersonal.

"John, it's pointless taking that tone with me. I advised against the leasing of that vehicle. I also advised against the purchase of the property at Bondi. That money could have been put to better use in your business."

"Maurice," my stomach was churning, "the last thing I need right now is another lecture, okay? Give me something positive. What about another loan? You know, just enough to tide us over."

He hesitated, considering his words.

"John, I know it's not really any of my business, but you're not drinking again, are you?"

"You're right," I'd cursed myself a dozen times for discussing my drinking problem with him. "It is none of your business, but for the record, no, I haven't had a drink in twelve months. Now get your accountant's hat on. There must be some way we can raise another loan."

He ignored the question and came back again in his professional straitjacket.

"You still have a few outstanding creditors, don't you?"

"Yes, but the total wouldn't amount to much. Ten… fifteen thousand dollars max."

"Who owes you the most? That Italian restaurant at Bondi?"

"Yes. Just short of five thousand. I went to see him a few days ago. He's broke, but he's genuine. He offered to pay it off in installments."

"Why don't you start legal proceedings? That should smarten him up a bit."

"No. Definitely not. He's got a young family, and he's in enough strife now without me suing the poor bastard. Come on, think, there must be some other way out of this."

"Well, the best advice I could give you would be to surrender the Mercedes. That would be a good start." There was another pause, but I knew what was coming. "The mortgage on the apartment is another unnecessary strain on the company, perhaps you should consider letting that go as well."

He stopped speaking abruptly, probably worried that he'd gone too far, and I sat there in the void staring out across the city. If I lost my home and the Merc, everyone would know I was on the skids. Paul Reynolds would see to that.

"My grandmother's dying in Ireland," I said into the silence.

"I beg your pardon?"

"My grandmother, my father's mother, she's dying. She's asked to see me."

"I had no idea you had family in Ireland, you've never mentioned them."

"No, we weren't close. She's from Inis Mór. One of the Aran Islands in Galway Bay."

"You're not considering going over there now, are you?"

"I'm not sure, she's the only relative I can remember."

"How long has it been since you were in contact with her?"

I could hear his training kicking in again, adding, subtracting, separating out feeling, emotion and humanity, replacing them with logic, rational thinking and common sense.

"I don't know. Not since I was a child. Probably thirty years or more."

"John, you've been under a lot of pressure recently and you have made some rather unfortunate decisions. But running off to some God-forsaken place in Ireland can only make matters worse. They'll bankrupt you, John, and..."

I stared at the wall as he continued. Listing the debts, issuing the warnings, stating the obvious in his pedantic, two-by-two makes four, schoolmarmish way.

"Hang on, Maurice," I cut him off, "my people are from Inis Mór, so I don't appreciate the God-forsaken bit. Okay?"

"Look, I'm sorry. I didn't mean to offend you. What I'm trying to say is that if you go over there now, you'll almost certainly lose control of the company. You have to act responsibly at a time like this." He hesitated again. "And whilst we're on the subject, you do realize that you owe us a considerable amount of money also, don't you?"

"We'll talk later," I told him, and hung up.

* * *

I spent the rest of the morning chasing debts. The excuses were endless, but they were all in the same boat as myself and I didn't have the heart to push too hard.

By 2.30, I needed a break, so I pulled on a raincoat, took a brisk walk up to Kings Cross, and found myself a table at the Tropicana. There were a few of the old hard heads from AA there, but nobody I wanted to talk to, so I ordered the special and scanned a newspaper to avoid eye contact.

The street outside was practically deserted. Just a few shoppers in flapping raincoats, hurried along like discarded newspapers by the rising wind.

"Spaghetti?" The waitress had more ink than the tattooed man.

"Thanks," I told her, studiously ignoring the flight of a red-eyed dragon emblazoned across her shoulders and cleavage, "and another coffee, if you would, please."

I drank the second coffee but couldn't bring myself to eat, so, after toying with the spaghetti for twenty minutes, I gave up, paid the bill and left.

* * *

I'd barely settled back into my office chair when Janine appeared.

"John," she was standing in the doorway, "Roger Bannister from Oztrak Cinematics is on line two."

As she reversed out of the office I picked up the phone.

"John Carlyle."

"Well, John Carlyle. I've been trying to get hold of you for days."

"Roger, how can I help you?"

"You know how you can help me. You can pay the $23,000 you owe. And I don't want to hear any more excuses. I'm giving you one more week. Seven days. If I'm not paid in full by then, I'll be serving a bankruptcy notice on you."

"Calm down, Roger," I said, "I fully intend to pay the account. I just can't do it right now. As I explained before, we're experiencing a temporary cash flow problem. As soon as we sign up for some new business, I'll be paying your account in full. You have my word."

"Your word," he snorted, "and what would that be worth?"

"Take it easy, Roger," a vein in my neck was starting to throb. "and a word of advice. Threatening me with bankruptcy will not help this situation."

"They warned me about you, Carlyle. I should have listened. You have seven days. If I'm not paid in full by then, you're a goner."

"That's nonsense and you know it." Don't react, be cool. "We're a solvent company with a temporary cash flow problem. But I warn you," stop talking, you're making it worse, "if you go about telling people we're bankrupt, I'll not hesitate to take legal action. Do you understand?"

"What!" He exploded. "You're threatening to sue me, you bastard? If you had any decency, you'd sell that bloody Porsche you ponce about in and pay your debts."

"It's a Mercedes, you bloody moron! And all you've succeeded in doing in this conversation is moving your bill to the bottom of the pile!" I slammed the phone down. *Jesus Christ, take it easy, man! That didn't help anyone. Breath in,* I told myself, *breath out, Breath in, breath out.*

As I sat there trying to calm down, I found myself studying a cluster of photographs on my desk. The largest was of Giselle, smiling into the camera on a beach somewhere years ago. The one in the middle was a professional shot of me in a boxing ring, crouched over in red gloves and black shorts. No designer stubble, no styled hair, looking young, dangerous, and ready to go. It was actually from a photo shoot we'd done for a sports company. They'd asked for a Russell Crowe look alike, but after sifting through dozens of images, the photographer decided that I looked more like Russell Crowe than any of them and so I'd ended up as the model in one of my own commercials. It was a bit of a laugh at the time, although I was an amateur boxer. My trainer believed I could have turned pro, but for the ankle.

"Give this lad a new hoof," he'd declare after each match, "and I'll give you the next middleweight champion of Australia."

The smaller one was of my son on his seventh birthday. I stared at his innocent face. I loved Tristan, there was no doubt about that. But I always seemed to be letting him down. I'd spent almost all of one session listening to the therapist talk about absent fathers. She'd gone on for so long that I'd felt obliged to point out that this particular absent father was working his ass off to pay the bills, including her $175 an hour counseling fee.

Some nights my hand would hover over the phone, wondering whether to call Tristan. But sometimes I just couldn't bring myself to do it. The pain of hearing the sadness in his voice was so intense it would depress me for days afterwards.

I checked my watch; it wasn't a good time, but I called anyway.

"Allo, Giselle…" Then the subtle change of tone when she realized it was me. The cautious, echoed silence as I told her of my grandmother's letter…

Her soft, quiet, guardedness like a stiletto in my heart

Reaching up inside me to tear my soul apart

Wondering how to reach her, praying she'd relent

Praying she could leave behind the hurt

And love me once again

Praying we could put aside the silvered shards of glassy words

We used to cut each other with

Praying that she'd turn again and bring me back the gift

The way it was before, no broken words, no lies

When I'd least expect it, turning into eyes that held no blame

Eyes that never harboured fear or shame

Praying she'd believe in me again...

"She's dying." Giselle's voice came back into focus, softer now, the lilting tones of her French accent, stirring the pain of the distance between us. "You must go to her, she's family."

"Look, Giselle, if I go to Ireland, maybe I could come over to see you in France afterwards...?" I waited for an answer, holding my breath.

"John?" Janine was standing in front of my desk, looking terrified. "Mr. Bannister's on line two again. I told him you were busy, but he said if you don't take his call, he will start bankruptcy proceedings today, immediately."

"Giselle, I'm sorry, can I put you on hold for..."

She cut me off,

"Don't bother! What a nerve! You wake me up in the middle of the night and then tell me you're too busy to talk? Nothing's changed, has it, John? Are you drinking again?"

The red light on line two was flashing.

"No. I haven't had a drink since you left and I don't appreciate you asking the same question every time we talk."

"Well, drunk or not, you're still the most self-centred person I've ever met in my life."

"Look, this is important, Giselle..."

"Important to you, not us," her voice was trembling. I didn't know if it was from grief or anger, "I was up till midnight last night looking after my mother and I'm not interested in listening to any more of your nonsense. You haven't even asked how Tristan is. So, no, don't even think about coming to Brittany. You're not welcome here, is that clear?" The line went dead.

The red light on line two had stopped flashing.

"Janine?" I called out, "Janine?"

I checked my watch, 4.50 pm. I buzzed the intercom. Nothing. I walked through to reception. Deserted. The note propped up by Janine's telephone informed me that she was sorry, but she couldn't take the stress anymore.

Back in my office I stood in front of the bar, an extravagant red leather monstrosity we'd inherited from the previous tenant. Giselle had wanted to pull it out, but I didn't want people thinking I'd turned into a puritan just because I was on the wagon.

A dozen or more bottles stood to attention across the mirrored shelves. Johnny Walker, Red Label, Bundaberg Rum, Vodka, Black Label, Gilbey's Gin. The one that caught my eye was a bottle of Krug Grand Cuvee, its long, graceful neck topped with bright gold foil. How could that do me any harm? I didn't even like Champagne. When I drank, it was whisky with beer chasers, a Drambuie tossed in now and again to speed things up a little.

A sudden flash of lightning startled me, and I crossed to the window. The horizon was obscured now, purple black clouds tumbling low overhead as the first deep rolls of thunder announced the beginning of the long-awaited deluge and, as I stood there mesmerized, the tropical downpour that had threatened all day, burst its banks and swept in torrents across the darkened city like a tidal wave unleashed.

My father had been killed on a night exactly like this, and my mother had been terrified of storms till the day she died. I slid open the glass door, stepped outside, and stood underneath the awning, peering at the city lights through the torrential rain. The storm was directly overhead; the rain pounding down like drum rolls on the sodden canvas above; the building quivering a little with each prolonged roll of thunder, lightning flickering over the Harbour Bridge.

A car horn honked in the street below, and I peered over the railings cautiously. Directly across the road, the lights of the Beef & Bourbon Bar & Grill glowed warm and inviting through the slashing rain. *Christ,* I thought, *I need a drink. Not enough to get drunk, just enough to take the edge off.* A taxi had pulled up outside the bar and a group of people were screaming and laughing as they ran through the pouring rain towards the glittering entrance.

Everyone's entitled to a few drinks. You haven't had a drink for over a year, you can handle it now. And besides, who would know?

You can't drink. You're an alcoholic... The judge had ordered me to attend a dozen AA meetings after my third drink-driving conviction. The guy running the meeting had given me a questionnaire listing twenty symptoms. First time I'd scored 100% in anything.

Three drinks. Three quick drinks and a bite to eat. Who would know? A few beers to unwind, then off home for an early night. What's wrong with that?

'You don't take the first drink,' that was the AA line. You heard it at every meeting. 'You don't drink for one day at a time.' What they didn't realize was that it was the drink that had saved me. It was the only relief I had from the feelings of loneliness and isolation I'd suffered from as far back as I could remember. The feeling that I was not enough, that something was wrong with me. Without the drink, I'd have probably killed myself years ago.

I stared down through the teeming rain. Seven floors below the concrete paving stones glowed dark and inviting. It would be over in a split second… over and done with. The voices were at me again. 'It's hopeless. You're an alcoholic, a loser. Your wife's gone. Your business is bankrupt. You're fucked. That's the way it is.'

Having a drink makes more sense than killing yourself. Even my therapist had agreed on that.

'Drinking's better than suicide,' she'd said. 'It's hard to come back from suicide, John.'

A few drinks, no more. A few drinks, then get out before the craving set in. As I stared down at the Beef & Bourbon, I realized that was exactly what I'd told myself just before the last bust. I'd been dry for three months that time and it hadn't been easy. My sponsor came to mind but couldn't bring myself to call her.

Roseanne was a hard-core AA member I'd met at my first meeting. I'd told her up front that I had reservations about labeling myself an alcoholic and as soon as I fulfilled the court order, I'd be out of there. She was a middle-aged, big-bosomed, foul-mouthed, ex-hooker with a wicked smile and a penchant for pithy one-liners. But she'd been sober since Bhuda was in daycare, and her no-holds-barred approach to sobriety attracted me.

"Reservations are for Indians, mate," we were at the Cosmopolitan Cafe in Double Bay, her favorite haunt. Tables out on the sidewalk, socialites wearing the latest fashions, greeting each other as if they'd just flown in from Hollywood. Roseanne, in a maroon velvet dress from the local second-hand shop, fake jewelry flung carelessly around her neck, a pair of oversized multicolored thongs gracing her feet, puffing on a black cheroot, oblivious to the curious stares. "If you want my advice, there are three things you need to do to stay sober. One, get your butt into a meeting every day. If you don't like the sound of that, make it two meetings a day. Two, put your cock in your pocket and leave it there, okay? You're a married man, stay away from the new women at AA. Half of them are neurotic, the rest are totally fucking insane. That means no coffees, no phone calls, and no cozy little chats about spirituality. Okay? No nothing. And three, if you feel like taking a drink, call me." She pushed a scrap of paper across the table. "If you've already had a drink, don't bother. All you'll get then is a dial tone."

* * *

Roseanne had helped me stay sober for a few months, but despite her help, and despite all the knowledge I'd gained from a dozen meetings, when the urge came, I'd pushed aside everything I'd learned and gone across the road convinced I would only have three drinks.

Those three drinks turned into a two-day bender, most of which I couldn't even remember. I woke up in a taxi outside my apartment at four thirty in the morning, no wallet, no keys, and no mobile.

Giselle paid off the cab and spent the rest of the day ignoring me. I tried to talk to her a dozen times, but she wouldn't even look at me. When I came home on Friday evening, she told me she'd booked tickets to France and was taking our son with her.

Standing there in the slashing rain, surrounded by the chaos of the raging storm, I realized for the first time how meaningless my life was without them. I went back inside, called a travel agent, and booked a ticket to Ireland.

Chapter 3
The Gresham Hotel

I flew into Dublin three days later, the last leg of my flight held up in London for seven dreary hours due to the atrocious weather conditions that had laid siege to half of Europe.

As the taxi swung away from the terminal into the storm-darkened streets, I stared out the window at the teeming rain, wondering what sort of madness had convinced me to return to Ireland.

"The Gresham Hotel it is then, sir." The driver was tossing comments over his shoulder as he wound his way through the evening traffic. "You've brought some fine weather with you now, as if we didn't have enough of our own."

"We've had a heat wave in Sydney for the past three weeks," I told him. "So you can't blame me for any of this."

"Jaysus!" he exclaimed. "Sure a good day's sunshine would kill half of us here. Now what in God's name would any right thinking man be doing in Dublin in winter time when he could be cavorting around on a sunny beach with some of those half-naked women you have over there?"

"I'm on my way to Inis Mór to see my grandmother. She's dying."

"Oh, my apologies," he said. "No disrespect meant to you now, sir, and none taken I hope."

"No, none at all. I hardly know her. I've been gone for years."

"Ah yes, but she's blood, and the islanders are a close lot. Half of them are mad, of course, and the other half are a long way from sane. They've been over there too long, I suspect. God alone knows what they get up to in the Winter."

"You know Inis Mór?"

"No, I do not. I've never set foot on the Aran Islands and never will. They're still living in the dark ages over there, or so I'm told."

The driver fell silent, weaving his way through the traffic, the vicious squalls and pounding rain bringing back memories that filled me with dread.

Twenty minutes later, he was swinging the cab into the curb in the city centre.

"There you are now sir, the Gresham Hotel it is; and good luck to you on Inis Mór."

Moments later, as I was going through the formalities at reception, a sombre looking manager approached.

"You have our sympathies, Mr Carlyle. They called from Cill Rónáin this morning. We had no way of contacting you."

He handed me an envelope, inside a message from my grandmother's brother informing me that she'd died in the early hours of that morning.

Christ, I thought as I followed the bellboy to the lift. What now? I would still be expected to attend the funeral. There was no way around that. How had I gotten myself into such a ridiculous situation? I could hardly remember the woman. My mother hadn't spoken to her since we'd left Ireland. A family disagreement that had never been explained.

As I unpacked, I realized with a start that my antidepressants were missing. I'd left them at home in the bathroom cupboard. Think it through, I told myself, it's not all that bad. The doctor told me months ago that it was time to get off them, and maybe I can get some more here anyway. It was doubtful, I'd tried Prozac and several of the others, but they hadn't helped at all. The only one that worked was a little known import from Switzerland, expensive and hard to come by in Australia.

I switched the television on. The evening news was running footage of a storm-ravaged England. Scenes of middle-aged women clutching scarves and shopping bags, wading through knee deep water in the Midlands and shots of children screaming and laughing as they played in rubber boots and plastic raincoats in the flooded streets of London. The capital had taken a severe battering and a bedraggled reporter, clutching a shredded umbrella in one hand and a microphone in the other, was telling the world at large that the gales were the worst in living memory.

The reporting then switched to Ireland. Dublin, Shannon, Galway and most of the other Irish airports had been closed until further notice, and gale warnings were current for the entire region. My flight must have been one of the last allowed in.

I switched the TV off. If this kept up it would be impossible to get to Inis Mór for the funeral. I should never have left Australia. The trip had turned into a complete fiasco. Grace O'Rourke was dead and I knew nobody else on the island. My accountant had been right; it would have been better to spend the money on the mortgage.

As I sat there I found myself gazing at a picture above the fireplace. A half-naked man, clutching a sword in one hand and a shield in the other, stood tied against a tall oblong stone, ropes slung around his body, a large black bird perched on his right shoulder. At first, I thought it was one of the ancient Greek heroes but then I leant closer to read the small brass plate set into the base of the gilded frame …

Death of Cuchulainn

The Hound of Ulster

The portrait gripped my attention, the faintest glimmerings of some childhood memory struggling to ascend to the light of day, and I was still studying the image some minutes later, when the phone rang.

"Hello?"

"Is that you, Conor?"

"Yes … Well, John actually."

"This is Lorcan Reardan, Grace's brother. She passed away at three o'clock this morning. God rest her soul."

"Yes, I got your message. I'm sorry to hear that."

"I was with her to the end. She hung on as long as she could." He was obviously upset. "She wanted to see you something fierce."

"I know," I said. "I did the best I could. I'm sorry."

He cleared his throat before continuing.

"She knew she was going. She was asking after you right up to the end."

"I'm sorry," I had no idea what else to say. "I couldn't get here any quicker than I did."

There was a long silence, and as I sat there on the edge of the bed, wondering what it was all about, I could hear him breathing heavily on the line.

"She wanted your forgiveness." He was speaking in the blunt, hard way the islanders have, lapsing into silence occasionally. "When she knew she was going, she asked would you go to the graveside to forgive her."

"Forgive her for what?" I said.

"I have no idea," I could almost hear him shaking his head, "she wouldn't say. I have charge of the Will. There are papers here for you to sign. I've to put them in your hand. I gave her my word. She's left you the cottage and the five acres. It's ready for you there now, and the boat too. She was clear on that. She was hoping you'd come home to stay. There's everything you'd need. It's tidy and clean, and there's a push bike there waiting for you. I saw to it myself."

"A cottage?" I said. "Whereabouts is it?" My head was racing. I had no idea what property was worth in Ireland but I'd read somewhere that prices had gone through the roof when the Celtic Tiger had revived the economy. A three bedroom cottage on five acres should be enough to get me out of my financial problems in Sydney.

"You don't remember?"

"No. I have a vague recollection of a white house with a thatch roof near the sea somewhere, but I could never remember where it was."

"That would be Tír na nÓg. It's up on a hillside overlooking the ocean. There are two bedrooms downstairs and an attic. Your father was born there, you know. It's been in the family for over two hundred years."

"And a boat? Not my grandfather's boat?"

"Yes indeed. We had her borrowed out here for years. She's a fine little sea-boat, although she may need some care."

He stopped, as if to consider his next words.

"Grace wanted you home, Conor, but your ma would have none of it. She was a good woman was your mother, but she had her heart broke when your da died. She was never the same after. She was in bits when she left here. The next thing we knew, she'd taken you off to Australia. People do the strangest things in grief …"

But then suddenly I couldn't hear him anymore, because the voices had begun again, the same ethereal voices as before, whispering up out of nowhere, pulling at the edges of my heart and soul …

I feared not life, I feared not death, I feared the place between

The place there is no passion, the place we lose our dreams

I know there is a meaning, I know that life holds more

I know someone is watching by the cliffs at Inis Mór

Night waves turning seeking, a half open dark door

Whispered lost memories from that hard, broken shore

Black waves rolling over me, dark down from the deep

Where lies my purpose, where will I sleep …

"Hello? Are you there, Conor?"

"Yes, I'm still here," I said, struggling to recall his last words. "I'll get a ferry across in the morning if they're still running."

"There won't be a ferry to these islands for days, m'boy. The seas are way too high. You'll not be here for the funeral, but you'll be with us in spirit, we know that."

After he'd gone, I peered out through the misted windows as rain swept in opaque sheets down the length and breadth of O'Connell

Street. Five acres and a centuries old cottage. I hadn't expected any of this, and for the first time in a long time, I felt a surge of hope.

The storm was intense, and I stood there mesmerized. This is how it all began. My father had taken me on a trip to Dublin to celebrate my seventh birthday, something that had haunted me for years afterwards. We'd arrived on a night exactly like this. Gale force winds had caused the accident, a massive two-hundred-year-old oak tree coming crashing down across the bonnet of my father's car like an executioner's axe, heavy branches smashing in through the windscreen, trapping us both in our seats. When I became aware of what was happening, my left foot was wedged up underneath the dashboard and people were trying to drag me free.

My father was pinned in the driver's seat, the steering wheel pushed up hard against his chest. He'd looked all right, except for a trickle of blood down one side of his mouth, and he'd kept on talking the whole time.

"See if you can't get that foot free, son. That's it, pull it free and get out of the car." But as the minutes passed, he got quieter and quieter and, in the end, he didn't speak at all. The last memory I have of my father is of a pale grey face staring at me fixedly as I was dragged free of the wreck.

I was in hospital for a week and all that time my mother kept insisting that he was all right. But as the days passed, she'd become more and more withdrawn until finally, on the morning I was released, she'd told me that he'd died alone in the car that night.

I asked her once, about a year after his death, if he would still be alive if it hadn't been for my birthday, but she didn't answer, she just smiled. A tight, brittle little smile, that showed all her teeth. Then she turned and left the room without speaking.

Chapter 4
Memories

I awoke while it was still dark the following day feeling tired and disoriented from the long flight. The conversation with Lorcan had brought back memories. Long forgotten images, like black and white clips from some ancient movie.

Snap out of it, I told myself. A three-bedroom cottage on five acres had to be worth a good bit. If I could arrange a quick sale, I should be back in Australia within weeks.

I'd always had a vague, mental image of a white, thatch-roofed cottage surrounded by grey stone walls. But anytime I'd asked my mother about it, her answer would be the same.

"Ah, that was a long time ago," she'd say, refusing to meet my eye. "I can hardly remember the place myself. Get on with your life, son. You're an Australian now. It's no use living in the past."

But what Lorcan had said was true, the accident had changed her irrevocably. Her way of coping with my father's death was to ignore it. His name was never spoken. There were no photographs of him, no mementos, nothing. It was the same with my grandparents, they were never mentioned. It was as if she wanted to erase all memories of Ireland from her mind.

Occasionally, a letter would arrive bearing our old name and some Irish stamps. But she never said who they were from and I never asked.

I'd dream of him sometimes in the months after the accident, but in the absence of his name, his memory dwindled, until finally one day, just a few years later, I realized with a shock that I couldn't remember his face anymore. I wasn't sure back then why this veil of silence came to be drawn across my father's life, but I knew from the time we arrived in Australia that we were not to speak of him.

My mother was a tall, proud, independent woman, introverted by nature and not one to discuss her feelings. But she had a natural grace, and with her long, flowing, dark brown hair, her slender frame and the elegant way she carried herself, she turned heads wherever she went.

I'd catch a glimpse of her in the evenings occasionally, gazing into the dressing table mirror as she brushed her hair. She confided to me once that my father used to brush her hair like that, and sometimes, when I was young, I'd wonder if she ever thought of him.

She wasn't a particularly gregarious person, but within eighteen months of arriving in Australia, she met a widower sixteen years her senior at an office party and, by the following summer, they were married.

Robert Carlyle came from an English military family and had served in the British Army before migrating to Australia. He was a tall, well-built man with a tight, military style crew cut, and an abrupt manner of speaking, a legacy from his days as a Regimental Sergeant Major. His first wife had died of cancer, the year before he met my mother, leaving him with two young daughters whose grief quickly turned to anger when he'd announced his intentions to re-marry. The girls were in their early teens by then, and from day one, they made it clear that I was not welcome in their home.

Christmas times were difficult, and my mother's awkward attempts to include me in the festivities only made things worse.

"This is Conor," she'd introduce me to the in-laws each year as if they must have forgotten me by then. "You remember Conor."

But Carlyle had lost a brother in the troubles in Belfast and any reference to Ireland, no matter how oblique, always served to irritate him.

"We call him John now, darling," Carlyle would chip in smiling, a firm hand on my shoulder. "You're a little Aussie now mate, aren't you?"

* * *

When I woke again it was eight o'clock and, after a quick shower, I dialed room service.

"Good morning, sir. Would you like breakfast?"

The deep, male voice had a strong Polish accent.

"Yes, please. I'd like some ham and eggs and brown toast, if I could."

"Of course. And will that be tea or coffee?"

"Do you have any of the Colombian blends?"

"I'm not sure, sir. I think maybe it's Brazilian …"

"Ok, if you don't have any Colombian coffee, send up a pot of tea please, and maybe some marmalade."

Breakfast was delivered on a stainless-steel trolley by a tall, thin, bespectacled Asian girl looking decidedly anorexic in a black and white uniform, accompanied by an elderly man, silver-haired and resplendent in a dark navy-blue suit, starched white shirt and red tie.

"Good morning, sir. My name's Patrick." Then in an aside to his assistant. "Over there, Molly. That's a good girl. Lay it all out on the table for the gentleman, that's it …" and then back to me again. "I took the liberty of bringing up the newspapers. As if the day's not depressing enough as it is. That's it Molly, serviettes too, if you would. That's right. She's in training, sir. I hope you don't mind. We all have to start somewhere. Now pour the tea for the gentleman …"

As I ate, I searched the TV channels for an update on the weather. The outlook looked grim, winds gusting up to one hundred thirty miles per hour had ripped roofs from houses on the outskirts of Dublin during the night and gale force winds had cut power lines to thousands of homes. As the reporter was about to conclude, a news flash informed us that Irish tug boats had been called out on an Air/Sea rescue mission and were battling enormous seas assisting a crippled, eighty-five thousand ton oil tanker with seven men on board that was drifting helplessly off the West coast.

Immediately after breakfast I decided to look around the city. My first stop was the concierge at the front desk, a large, well-built Irishman who looked as if he might double as a bouncer in his spare time.

"Keep your head tucked in under that, sir, and you'll be fine." He handed me a large umbrella emblazoned with the hotel's name before directing me along the street to the local supermarket. Ten minutes later, shrouded in a bright yellow plastic raincoat, topped by the hotel's green and gold umbrella, I set out to explore Dublin.

I had no real memories of the city, just vague, sepia-toned images from childhood of drab-looking streets, grey stone churches, old-fashioned buses, and middle-aged men in long, dark overcoats and black boots.

All that was gone now. In its place, a modern, bustling, metropolis reminiscent of London or New York. I'd read articles about the Celtic Tiger, but I was not prepared for the enormity of the transformation that had taken Ireland from abject poverty to one of the world's most talked about economic miracles in just twenty short years, and despite the recent meltdown of the financial markets, the city center was filled with people rushing along beneath oversize umbrellas in their camel hair coats and cashmeres. The coffee shops crowded to capacity with smartly dressed young business people, while the latest Mercedes Benz and Jaguars nosed their way through windswept pedestrians at every street corner and crossing.

In the very center of the city, a four hundred-foot stainless steel spire towered high over the historic post office like some gigantic exclamation mark, erected as if to emphasize Ireland's astonishing vault into the twenty-first century and beyond.

"I call it Ahern's hard on." A ragged little man, wearing a multicolored woolen beanie, and what looked like a World War I army greatcoat, was observing me cautiously from the shelter of a shop doorway. "It set us back four-million Euro and it's hard to see where it all went." He was gaining confidence now, smiling up at me like an old acquaintance. "You look a little lost, sir. Could I be of assistance?"

"I'm looking for a good coffee shop." I said, feeling a little embarrassed at the trivial nature of my quest. "One that carries a range of different coffees."

"Come in here now if you would, sir, out of the rain," he stepped to one side as I joined him in the doorway. "There's a shop like that over in Temple Bar I believe. Coffee World, it's called, or something like that. For connoisseurs they say, with the emphasis on the "con" part. The prices are fierce, or so I'm told. You must have money to burn, God bless you, sir."

"Is it far from here?"

"Temple Bar? No, not at all. A few minutes in a taxi would have you there."

He shuffled closer, a hint of defiance in his whippet-like features, and in the confined space of the doorway, I found myself caught up in his body odor. A vaguely familiar essence of life and death, of fear, futility, and failure. And I felt as if we were connected somehow, as if I knew him, as if he'd been there for years, just waiting for me to arrive, and it dawned on me with a shock that he somehow reminded me of myself.

His face was alight now, smiling up at me broadly, his happy go lucky impish grin a total contrast to every other aspect of his being.

"Now sir, could you think of any good reason at all why you wouldn't be offering me a few Euro for a drink?"

"I'll help if I can," I told him, fishing for my wallet, "but I've only got Australian money on me."

"Whatever sort of money you have would be a blessing to me right now, sir. I'm in dire need of refreshment."

I offered him a ten-dollar note.

"And what would that be worth?" He held it up to the light as if to make sure that it wasn't a forgery.

"The Aussie dollar's a bit less than the Euro," I said, feeling as if I were cheating him somehow.

"Well, you'd better be giving me another one then, just to be making up for it." He nodded approvingly as I reached into my wallet again. "You have a good heart, sir, don't let anyone tell you otherwise. But look out for those Bulgarian tinkers. They'd have the shirt off your back."

I pressed another ten dollars in his hand and left him there smiling to himself as I went looking for a taxi, rainwater cascading down from the gutters above, the Gresham Hotel's umbrella threatening to rip itself to shreds at every corner and shift in the wind.

The coffee shop wasn't hard to find, for as we turned into a small, cobbled lane off Marble Bar, the first thing that caught my eye were the words *Coffees of the World* emblazoned in large gold letters above an old fashioned, bright red shop front. And, after paying off the cab, I ran a gauntlet of slashing rain, buffeting winds, and flooded gutters before pushing my way through the front door and forcing it closed behind me.

The interior of the store was warm and welcoming. Softly lit oak-paneled walls, polished wood floors, a display of the latest stainless steel coffee percolators on a varnished mahogany countertop, the muted strains of Andrea Bocelli's *Time to Say Goodbye* filtering in from somewhere at the rear of the premises, the intoxicating aroma of a hundred different coffee's reminding me of Giselle and our student days in Colombia.

I walked across to the counter, my leather soled shoes heralding my approach across the hard, glossy floorboards. The shelves lining the walls were painted black and packed with a hundred different brands. Every conceivable type of coffee was there including many of the world's most revered names. It was a coffee lover's paradise.

I found the Colombian section and began checking the labels but, just as I was reaching out to examine one of them, a heavy Dublin accent, close to my left ear, startled me.

"Good morning."

I spun around. The biggest black man I'd ever seen was towering above me like a mythical warrior from the Arabian Nights.

"Jesus Christ!" I said. "You frightened the living daylights out of me."

"Ah now, don't be taking the good Lord's name in vain in my shop!" He was grinning down at me, his teeth a luminous white against jet-black skin. "I was out the back when I heard someone moving around. I thought it might be some of those little brats from the flats. They come sneaking in here occasionally for the craic." He straightened himself up to his full height. "So, what can I do for you? Or are you just in here for a smell? Some of them do that, you know. They can't afford the price of a decent coffee so they come in here for a free sniff. One old biddy used to come in every day with her dog and just stand around sniffing things. Now I didn't mind that so much until one morning Fido lifted his leg and let rip on a sack of Kenyan Mocha. I had to bar the two of them. Well, you should have heard the language! If I hadn't been born and bred in Ballyfermot myself, I'd have had no idea what she was going on about. Anyhow, I gave her a free sample of Arabica Light to keep the peace and told her to go off and snort it in the comfort of her own home. Serves her right. It's one of the world's worst coffees. Arabica *Shite* is what they should have called it."

"That was very considerate of you. I hope you didn't resell the Kenyan Mocha" We were both laughing. "Anyway, I'm looking for a particular brand. Do you carry Esperanza?"

"We do, of course, it's one of our best sellers. But we're out of stock at the moment. I ordered more last week. It should be here by Friday."

"I'm heading for Galway and then over to Inis Mór as soon as the weather clears," I told him. "Is there any place over there that I might get some?"

"You'd have no hope at all on Inis Mór. It's all black tea and whiskey over there. You could try Eyre's Square in Galway. You may find a decent coffee shop there." He took a miniature hessian sack down from the top shelf. "Have you tried the Colombian Breakfast Blend? It's similar to Esperanza." He lifted a flap and went behind the counter. "Why don't I make us up a brew now? It won't take a minute." And then over his shoulder. "What's your name?"

"John Carlyle."

"Wesley Thomas," he nodded without offering a hand. "This is my place. I live upstairs here."

I watched as he clattered about behind the counter, grinding the beans, measuring the coffee.

"You were born in Ireland?" I asked.

"Yes," he nodded, "my parents migrated to the UK in the sixties, but after the race riots in London they moved over here. They were among the first black people to settle in Dublin. I was born here; I'm an Irish citizen, and I speak fluent Irish. My big brother, and he is a big bastard, is serving in the Irish Army. So, I'm as Irish as Paddy's pig, as they say." He smiled, "You seem surprised."

"I am. I've never met a black Irishman before."

"Ah, don't be giving me any of that old racist shite," he was laughing openly now. "You Aussies have no respect for your own black people, that's well known."

"So, do you know Inis Mór?" I asked. "Have you been there?"

"Yes, I spent a long weekend over there a few years ago. I'd heard rumors about the island, and I wanted to see for myself. It's a strange place, John. One of a kind."

"What do you mean by strange? Strange, dangerous, or strange, weird?"

"No, it's not that. It's just that they have their own ways. Some call the place, 'Irish Ireland'. Try to keep an open mind when you're over there. There are some things we'll never really understand."

"I shouldn't be there too long anyway," I said, "I have to sell a cottage. As soon as that's done, I'll be off back home to Australia."

"You own a place on Inis Mór?"

"Yes, my grandmother left me a cottage in her Will. Do you have any idea what property prices are like over there?"

"No. None at all. They'd be high, same as anywhere else. My da bought this place years ago, so we're miles in front."

I spent an hour chatting with Wesley and left with a shiny new stainless-steel percolator, a sturdy German coffee grinder, a bag of Estrella del Sur that he'd recommended, and a promise that he'd forward my Esperanza to the Post Office at Inis Mór the moment it arrived at his shop.

Chapter 5
The Galway Express

When I woke on Friday morning, I was relieved to find that the storm had blown itself out. I packed hurriedly, called Rail Erin, and, two hours after checking out of the Gresham, I was ensconced in a comfortable compartment of a sleek new express train bound for Galway.

"It seems the worst of the weather is behind us." I'd exchanged greetings with the middle-aged man in the seat opposite as I'd sat down and been conscious of his appraising gaze ever since.

"Let's hope so," I said. "It was quite a storm."

"Well, it's to be expected at this time of the year." He smiled. "You're visiting Galway?"

"No. I'm headed for Inis Mór. My grandmother died there last week. I came over for the funeral, but with the weather as it was, I missed it."

"You have my condolences." He was aged around sixty, well-dressed in a dark green tweed suit and tie with a soft, slightly Americanized, Irish accent. "You're Australian?" he ventured.

"Yes, but I was born in Galway. We moved to Australia when I was eight. This is my first time back."

"Welcome home." He leant forward. "Dermot Casey."

"John Carlyle," I said, taking his hand.

"It's a long way back for a funeral, John."

"Yes. My grandmother contacted me a week or so before she died. There was something she wanted me to know."

"And do you have any idea what it was?"

"No, none at all." It must be an Irish thing, I thought, they all want to know your business, "There was no contact with the family from the day we left. Some sort of feud, I think. I never knew what it was about."

"An inheritance perhaps," he nodded. "Much of the bitterness within Irish families has to do with the land. Who inherits the farm as it were."

"No, I don't think it was that. My grandmother left me the family cottage and some land in her Will."

"That's strange. But then again, the islands are strange. Some claim they're haunted, there's still plenty of that old nonsense about in the West." He looked out the window. "But the islanders are a race apart, I'll give them that. There's more geniuses came out of the West than any other part of Ireland."

"So, you know the island?"

"I do, of course. Sure, I was over there many a time as a boy. I was born and raised in Galway, but my grandparents were from Inis Mór. We spent our school holidays there most summers."

"Do you have any idea of property prices on the island?"

"No, not really, but they'd be high. It's virtually impossible to buy a house over there." He frowned, "Will you not be staying?"

“No.” If it was that difficult to buy a place on Inis Mór, then it would be a seller’s market. That meant top price. “I’ll be selling the cottage as soon as I can and heading straight back to Sydney.”

“Well, if that’s the case, you won’t be too popular on the Mór. It’s unheard of selling the family home over there. I took some Irish American friends across there a few years ago and the next thing they wanted to buy in of course. Well, there was a house for sale that year as it happened,” he shook his head, “but not to strangers. The islanders won’t sell to outsiders, it’s an unwritten law. My friends were disappointed, offered all sorts of money, but that just made things worse. You know the type, Plastic Paddies we call them. They’ve a mental picture of Ireland as some mythical place where salmon leap from every stream, there’s a bottomless pint of Guinness to be had for a few shillings at the local thatched roof pub, and they dream of sitting there in the evenings gazing off into the sunset whilst Bing Crosby croons *Have you ever been across the sea to Ireland.* Well, all that old nonsense is dead and gone, if it ever existed at all.”

“Who’s Bing Crosby?” I said.

He stared at me quizzically for a moment, then burst out laughing.

“All right, so I’m exaggerating. But you do know what I mean.”

“No, not really,” I told him. “I’ve never had any wish to come back here. I’ll be selling the cottage as soon as I can and heading back to Sydney. How much were they asking for the place?”

“Around three fifty or four hundred thousand I believe.”

“Euro?” I felt a rush of excitement. Jesus! That would be more than enough.

“Yes, of course.”

"So, who'd buy a place like that?" I was doing the math in my head.

"Family, or maybe a close friend. You'd never hear the end of it if it were sold to an outsider. That's how it is over there."

"Well, that doesn't apply to me," I told him. "As far as I'm concerned, the best offer will decide who gets the place. I have no intention of living in Ireland."

"So, you've never considered yourself Irish?"

"No, not really. We'd all get ripped on Paddy's Day, of course, but everyone does that."

"Well, it's different in the USA. If you've Irish blood in your veins in America, it's something to be proud of."

"You said Inis Mór's a strange place. In what way?"

"Well, it's a fair enough question," he nodded. "You see, the islanders are different and always have been. I spent a few days on Inis Mór last year and it was like stepping back in time. The weather was bleak, but I don't mind that." His voice trailed off as if remembering. "They're a hardy lot, but once they get to know you, they'll take the time to stop and talk in the street. There's none of the haste that's overtaken the rest of the world, and they still hold true to a lot of the old ways. It's part of the Gaeltacht, so Irish is the first language. But there's more to it than that. I heard an old woman in a pub there one-night singing in the sean-nós, you know, the old way. Her voice rising and falling in some kind of lament. It has a haunting quality to it, almost as if it's from another world." His eyes had glazed over, held by the memory. "It conjures up an image of an Ireland that's probably lost to us all ..."

"Come on now, Dermot," I told him. "Don't go getting all misty eyed on me. You're starting to sound like one of those Plastic Paddies from America ..."

"Well, fair play to you," he was laughing again. "I asked for that one. Look." He was pointing out the window. "Over there. That's Galway there now, just coming into view ..."

Chapter 6
Rossaveal

I spent the night at the Skivington Arms, close to the centre of town. It was an old-fashioned pub with a welcoming staff and all the charm and hospitality the Irish are famous for. After signing in I was escorted to my room by a tall emaciated-looking man with large, prominent teeth, high pointed ears, red hair, and a wide, infectious smile.

"You're a fortunate man, sir. This is the only room we have left, and every other hotel in Galway is full to the brim." And then with a conspiratorial wink he confided. "That's not true of course, we tell everyone the same thing, in case you don't like the room and might be considering moving elsewhere." And then he was off back down the stairs, laughing uproariously at his own humour, like a slightly demented, oversized leprechaun.

I was up at six the following day and took a walk around the town center. I hadn't had much exercise for days and it was good to be out and about. The rain had eased overnight and the wind was now little more than a breeze.

I was back at the hotel before seven, eager to be on my way and, after a simple breakfast, I made inquiries at the desk and was directed around the corner to a small, stone-walled office at the end of a tiny cul-de-sac, a battered wooden sign bearing the words: *Aran Ferries*.

As I stepped in through the bright, emerald-green doorway, I was overwhelmed by a sense of *déjà vu*. I'd been in this very place some thirty years before. It was the same dusty old room, the same ancient odors of salt water, tar, and tobacco permeating the air. The same battered old wooden counter raked at an angle across the bare-planked floor, two tiny windows set into thick stone walls, peering out onto a rain-washed, cobblestone lane, an assorted collection of chairs pushed back against the once white walls.

"There's a ferry bound for Inis Mór at midday, God willing." The old man was looking anywhere but at me. "The seas are high and will be all week." He was glaring out through the rain-streaked windows, as if angered by his inability to control the elements. "We've been stranded here for days, there's people needing to be home." As I handed over the money, he pushed a ticket across the counter top. "Now, if she doesn't sail at all, you'd try again in the morning so." He pointed a bony finger. "There's a bus outside ready to go. If you miss that, you miss the ferry."

"Do I have time to run up to the shops?" I asked. "I need to get something."

"That's entirely up to you," he smiled a crooked smile, "but the bus is leaving now, so it'll be a choice between that something of yours, or the ferry."

Two minutes later, I was dragging my cases onto a crowded bus, ruddy-faced islanders talking and laughing as they crammed luggage up into the overhead racks. And then we were off, winding our way through the outskirts of Galway. The city streets gradually melding from a patchwork of cobblestones and tarmac into a single, stone-walled lane, meandering its lonely way through a rolling, rain-soaked countryside.

I stared out through the misted glass at the cloud-darkened fields, remembering my mother standing there in that same office, red-eyed from weeping, asking if there would be a charge for the coffin that lay waiting outside in a long, black, wide windowed hearse. Remembering the man with the big red face and his wife with her arms around my mother. The rickety old bus taking us all out to Rossaveal, and me looking back at the hearse trailing along behind. Still not believing he was dead, fearful that we might lose him.

We stood on the quay alongside the ferry, the shiny black coffin speckled white with snow. Carried up a shaking gangway by four straining men, breath hanging in the air, when my mother had refused to have him hoisted up in a sling. And then that final three-hour voyage to the island. Heavy grey clouds tumbling low overhead, sombre men in black greatcoats and pipes tugging silently at their caps as we passed by. And me propped up on crutches next to my father, his coffin tied down with rope against the rolling swell of the ocean, and my mother in a black hat and veil, staring endlessly away over to the north. Away from Inis Mór.

* * *

"You're in luck, folks." The driver was swinging the bus around into the terminal. "The ferry's boarding now."

There was a babble of excitement from the passengers and minutes later, they were streaming up the gangway, jostling and laughing, happy to be heading home. The rain had increased, so I followed them down below, crowding into the wood-panelled saloon, the odour of wet tweed and salt water mixing in with the bitter sweet smell of stale Guinness, the islanders laughing and chattering away in a language I hadn't heard since childhood.

On that final trip, my mother had kept to herself all the way across. She'd been a Protestant before they married and everyone had known that. It had set her apart, or so she'd imagined, and she'd never been easy on the island. The wake had gone on for two days but she stayed in her room all that time. My father was buried on a Tuesday morning and we left Inis Mór that same evening, my mother determined not to spend another night on the island.

Her family were middle-class people from Belfast, set in their ways and bitterly opposed to the marriage. Being a fisherman from the Aran Islands was bad enough, without being a Catholic as well. They had refused to go to the wedding, and finally, they just cut her off altogether. My father's people weren't happy with the union either and, after the marriage, my parents had settled in Galway where I was born.

The year before his death we'd stayed on Inis Mór for the whole summer. It is the only memory I have where my mother had seemed at peace on the island. We spent our days sailing and fishing and digging in the potato field close by the side of the cottage. Going down to the stony pebbled beach before dawn, collecting the kelp, slipping and sliding over the hard, shiny black rocks. Laughing as we slithered about, tossing armfuls of the dark green seaweed up into the wicker baskets before dragging them back to where the pony and trap stood waiting by the wall. Once it was loaded, we'd go trotting off to the field, a stone-walled patch of land no bigger than a building block. Spreading the kelp alongside the seedling potatoes that were set out in straight lines down the field, and then the digging. You couldn't just dig them in, there was a special way of doing it.

"There you go, Conor." Granda bent over, his big black boot on the top edge of the spade. "The first cut goes in there now, do you see? Then you turn the soil over like that, that's it. Now the second one goes over on top of that again, see that now? There ye' go. You need to cover the potato and the kelp. And then there's this little bit here, see that now? The smiley that's known as, and that goes up on top again, so! Now the second one, that's it, and then the smiley over on the top of that again. There now, sure it's in your blood. We'll make an islander of you yet, so we will."

Although my grandfather was married to the sea, he'd never learnt how to swim. It was the fishermen's way, a way that went back for centuries. "You're better off drowning quickly in these waters," he'd say. "You go overboard in a winter gale and you're as well getting it over with. You'd only have minutes left anyways."

He was a tall, lean, strongly built man, his face browned and leathered from a lifetime at sea. His dark green eyes pulled into a permanent squint from peering through too much sun and salt-washed spray. He must have been sixty by that time, but he still went out each spring looking for the first of the salmon if the weather was any way right. *Erin* was thirty-three feet long, built along similar lines to a Galway Hooker, and steady and graceful on the wind. He'd taken me up to the cliffs one day to watch my father sailing the boat offshore from Dun Aengus.

"He should never have left here." We were looking out to where *Erin* lay heeled over to a breeze, my father standing upright in the cockpit, waving up to us as he'd promised he'd do. "He's a seaman and always was." Granda was talking to himself, "Why in God's name would he want to leave all this behind?" My father was their only child, and it had been assumed that he'd follow in the family tradition. I'd sit there some nights watching them splicing rope in front of a flickering fire. Granda trying to persuade my father to return to Inis Mór.

"Why would you want to be over there in Galway, son," Granda was shaking his head, "when you could be safe and well here on the Mór with your own people?"

"Leave him be, Da," Grandma would cut in, "they're here with us now, isn't that enough for you?"

And the talk would move on to other things. Granda joking with my father, not wanting to spoil the evening.

"Sure Jaysus, son, you're slow as a wet week," he'd say. His hard, bent fingers pulling and twisting at the separate strands of hemp. The rope melding from a flurry of tasseled ends to a flowing, contoured entwinement as round and smooth and plaited as a woman's hair. "We can only pray to God above that you're having more luck over there in Galway than you're having with that poor skein of rope." And then they'd be laughing together, Grandma sitting there smiling in her chair.

My father loved the ocean too, and sometimes he'd take me out sailing with him in the boat. "Pull her over there now son, that's it. Hold her there now, hold her steady! That's it … hold her … be ready to miss that boom … right … let her go … let her fly … good boy." And the boom crashing across over my head, the sail flapping and banging as he let go of the anchor. The chain rattling away down over the bow. Down through the cold, clear water. The anchor breaking free of the early trailing bubbles, twisting and turning as it sank down towards the sandy, kelp-strewn bottom of Galway Bay.

"We'll come back here one day, son." We were sitting in the cockpit of the boat, relaxed and content after a long day's sail. "Your mother will come around." He was looking out across the water towards Cill Rónáin, lying there quiet in the evening light. "And then we'll all come back here for good."

* * *

We'd returned to our home in Galway after the funeral. At first, my grandparents used to visit every week. They'd wanted us to come back to the island to live but my mother was determined that we would not. "It's you they want over there, son, not me," she'd say. "I'll not have you brought up a fisherman. Not while there's breath in my body, I won't." But then, just a few months later, Granda was gone too. He'd become more and more depressed after my father's death and some said that he'd just stepped over the side of the boat. They'd found *Erin* offshore, her sails raised, the tiller lashed amidships, sailing along by herself to a breeze. Grandma never came to see us after that, and a year or so later we immigrated to Australia.

My mother cut off all ties with her past and the only time she ever mentioned Ireland was when she'd had a drink too many.

"We've a good life here in Australia now, John," she'd say. "You remember that. Forget about Ireland, there's nothing for you there but grief."

A sudden blast from the fog horn pulled me out of my reverie and I went up on deck. The ferry was handling the conditions well. White water spraying back from her bow as she plunged into some of the heavier swells. I walked forward, hanging on to the safety rails, then up a short flight of rusting steel steps, and then there it was in the distance, Inis Mór, rising to greet me from a low-lying, rain-soaked mist. The lighthouse on Straw Island standing like some grim sentinel, dark scudding clouds above, as the voices began again in my troubled mind, the words coursing up from a place deep within. Unfamiliar streams of poetry emerging from the very fabric of my soul. Choking off my breathing and bringing tears to my eyes …

I knew this island long before I ever came

Some hidden memory held in kind

Images of needing to forsake

An unused life in place

A turning from, a turning to

A knowing of the heart

A feeling to return unto that lonely dark

A memory of birth and death

And yet a singing lark

A wish set deep into the heart

A keening, keeling, wailing song

A grief that I was back

A heartfelt sense of age without a track

No words to speak the loss

The land from which she bore

The jagged rocks and sea scream birds that soar

Welcoming me, as they had before

Forgiving me my absence

As they waited by the shore

Returning to the rock and stone of Inis Mór ...

Chapter 7
Kilronan

I caught my first sight of the old man as we entered Killeany Bay. He was standing at the far end of the stone jetty that juts out from the harbor wall at Kilronan, staring towards the incoming ferry. It was his stillness that drew my attention. A solitude that set him apart from the crowd as he gazed seaward through the drizzling rain. He was tall for an islander. Tall, broad-shouldered, and straight, with a bearing that could have suggested arrogance.

And then we were alongside, rolling and straining against the battered old tires slung from the boat's gunwale. Men casting out ropes to waiting hands. Seamen lowering a gangway to the stone-cobbled quayside below.

As I struggled with my suitcases down the rickety gangway, I glanced across to where the old man had been standing, but he'd disappeared, swallowed up in the confusion of the milling crowd.

"Taxi?" A small, thickset, red-haired man, his face twisted into a crinkled smile, was peering up at me from beneath a tweed hat. "Pat Donovan at your service, sir. Where are you headed?"

"Kilmurvey," I told him. "Is it close by?"

"Sure, everything's close by on Inis Mór." I followed behind as he wobbled away, legs bowed by the weight of the two cases. "The island's two miles wide and eight long. You'd fall off on a foggy day if you weren't careful." He came to a halt alongside an old London cab and hoisted the cases up into the luggage bay. "Jump in there now, sir, if you would. We'll have you in Kilmurvey in no time."

He slammed the doors, and we were off, weaving our way past a clutter of whitewashed cottages scattered along the front street, groaning up a long, winding, stone-walled road heading inland, away from the quayside. He was talking to me from the front seat, but I couldn't make out a word he was saying.

"I can't hear you," I called out.

"How's that?" He slid open a small window and shouted back over the roar of the engine. "I was asking would you be up for a quick pint. To welcome you to Inis Mór as it were. There's a great little place just along the road here."

"Not for me, thanks," I told him. "I want to get to the cottage and get settled in."

"Huh," he grunted, "more's the pity. Another time perhaps. So, where are you from, sir? Australia by the sound of things."

"I lived there for years," I told him. "Irish family."

"Ah, you could have saved your breath on that last bit. No offence to you now but you have a fine big Irish head on you." The taxi was running along through narrow laneways, glimpses of the ocean now and again at a crossroads. "Sure Jaysus, wasn't I in America myself for ten years and you could pick Paddy a mile away in a crowd. Big turnip heads on them. Strolling down Broadway with the gimp, as if they're still pulling their boots out of a potato field."

He was still laughing when I spotted the old man again. Striding along by the grassy edge of the lane, quick and purposeful. A seaman's cap pulled low across his eyes; a black walking stick clutched in his right hand.

"Who was that?" I said.

"Who was what?" The driver glanced at me in the rear vision mirror.

"The old man." I turned and looked back but he was gone. "The old guy we passed just now. Do you know him?"

"No idea," he shrugged, "One of the villagers, I'd imagine. Or maybe one of those German tourists. Sure Jaysus, they're everywhere, hiking up and down the length and breadth of the island, ranting on in Prussian, frightening the cattle. They're obsessed with the place. God alone knows why, there's nothing here but rock."

"So, what brought you back, Pat?"

"Well now, isn't that a question I ask myself every day of my life and I've yet to hear a good answer to it. Apart from not wanting to be anywhere else, there's no good reason for me to be here at all." We were running along by the shore now, the lane winding past a small inlet, the ocean a swirling mass of dark green, white-capped waves, pounding endlessly into a black pebbled beach, pristine white seabirds wheeling overhead. "It's something deeper, I suppose." He went on. "I've never known what. The island has a way of holding you." His voice had changed, the banter giving way to the man. "It's not a place you can leave behind for long." We were approaching a cluster of cottages set by a curve in the road. "So," he grunted, "there you are now, take your pick. Which one would you like?"

"Grace O'Rourke's place," I told him. "Do you know it?"

"I do, of course. Don't I know every house on the island? It's a little further on."

A few moments later he brought the taxi to a halt outside a neat little house that stood alone in a field overlooking a small, horseshoe shaped bay. The walls were freshly whitewashed, the roof thatched, the doors and windows picked out in a brilliant shade of red.

"That's it there now, and a lovely little cottage it is." He was peering back at me, eyes narrowed in the mirror. "You were related to Grace?"

I was staring at the cottage, transfixed.

"Yes,"

"You're an O'Rourke." He sounded doubtful. "From where?"

"I was born in Galway. My father was Con Rua O'Rourke, Grace's son."

"Holy Jaysus!" he exclaimed. "You're Con Rua's boy. Why didn't you say? And here's me treating you like a stranger. Welcome home to Inis Mór, m'boy. It's great to have you back."

"Thank you ..." he was still talking,

"... Ah, she was a grand old woman was Grace. Sure, the whole island was here for the wake." He was pointing towards a distant rise. "She's up there on the hillside now. You'll find her easy enough."

After he'd gone, I stood silently in front of the cottage. It had been there unchanged all this time, and now here I was, thirty years later, an unknown intruder from a foreign land. As I turned the handle and stepped inside, my heart was thumping.

Going through the door was like stepping into a by-gone era. Half remembered artifacts from a past life appearing before me as disjointed and ethereal as dreams. A thick, stone doorstep, hollowed down with the passage of time. A solid wooden slab above a fireplace darkened by smoke and age. Windows set into the three-foot thick walls, each divided into four small square panes of glass. Heavy black wooden beams that had once held fishing nets supported a high set, off-white ceiling, the centuries-old stone floor wrought smooth and shiny from generations of bare feet, a battered old bicycle propped in the hallway.

A cluster of photographs, set in pewter frames, was perched on a sideboard and I went across and peered in at the faded images. The largest was of an elderly couple I took to be my grandparents, leaning against a stone wall. The second was of the old-fashioned family type and a group of sepia-toned people in 1950's style clothing peering silently back at me with fixed, unnatural smiles, as if embarrassed to be dragged so far into the future by a stranger's inquiring eye.

The last photograph was of a young boy dressed in black, propped up on crutches outside an old stone church. For a moment, I was puzzled, but then I realized with a start that it was a photograph of myself on the day of my father's funeral. I studied the face as you would a stranger. The boy looked pale and drawn but there was no expression there at all, no sorrow, no pain, nothing.

The house was smaller than I remembered, the ceilings low, the hallway narrow, and it was hard to believe that it was the same place I'd known as a child. But then, as I climbed the steep wooden staircase to the tiny room above, it all began filtering back. This was the room I'd slept in that last summer on the island. The room I'd stayed in with my mother at my father's wake.

After returning downstairs, I checked out the facilities. The bathroom was a primitive, cold-water affair, built as an afterthought outside the kitchen door, and as I looked over the ancient plumbing, I thought back to the black marble spa I'd had installed in my apartment at Bondi.

I spent the rest of the day unpacking. Grace's brother had left a carton of groceries on the kitchen table with enough bread, eggs and ham to feed six people, along with a note welcoming me to the island, apologizing for not being there to greet me, and suggesting I visit them for lunch as soon as they returned from Galway.

I was too tired to cook so, after settling into one of the overly stuffed armchairs with a roughly hewn ham sandwich and a mug of black tea, I looked around. The cottage was in good shape, it was on a nice piece of land, and the views were fantastic. I could see it being worth the three or four hundred thousand Euro Dermot had mentioned.

But he'd also said that prices had fallen, so what about Sydney? I owed a ton of money to others, besides Bannister. The unit was mortgaged up to the hilt. I was more than five thousand behind on the Mercedes. I'd taken out three separate personal loans in the past twelve months, and I owed friends a bunch too. If there was any holdup in selling the cottage, I knew Bannister would go ahead with his threat to bankrupt me.

My pulse was racing, my mind skipping from one bleak scenario to the next. Calm down, I told myself, at least there's a way out now. Yes, maybe, but what if I can't sell the place? What if there are problems that I don't know about? It could all fall through. I pulled myself up out of the armchair, unable to stop the negative voices. To hell with it, I said out loud, I'm going to bed.

Chapter 8
The Old Man

I came to early the following morning feeling washed out and exhausted. I'd had a troubled night as the issues I was trying to leave behind returned to haunt me. Bits and pieces of things drawn together by some dark hand, destroying any possible chance of rest. Instinctively I reached out for my pills, before realizing that I'd left them at home. Then came the anxiety, the nagging feeling that I couldn't handle the day without them. This was why I took anti-depressants; they kept the worst of my fears at bay.

I tried to go back to sleep, but it was futile, my mind constantly dreaming up new scenarios that all ended up in disaster. So, when the first, faint traces of dawn began chasing shadows around my bedroom walls, it was a relief to pull on a tracksuit and fumble my way downstairs.

After showering, I made coffee and went out to the yard and, sitting on a crumbling stone wall overlooking a brilliant blue ocean, I took my first exploratory taste. Wesley was right, the Estrella del Sur was obviously one of Colombia's better coffees.

The taxi driver had said that the graveyard wasn't too far, so, after a second cup, I changed into a heavy wool sweater and corduroys, pulled on a brown leather bomber jacket and headed off out the door. It was a crisp, cold, winter morning, the wind running in from the west kicking up whitecaps on a still troubled ocean. My ankle felt strong and as I strode off up the hill away from the village, I walked briskly, trying to keep warm.

I saw the old man as I came up to the top of the first rise. He was sitting on a low stone wall by a crossroads looking out to sea, both hands resting on the head of a black walking stick. He was dressed in the same way as he had been the previous day and, once again, I was struck by his size and stillness. His back was to me but as I approached, he turned.

"Good morning," he smiled. "I took notice of you yesterday by the ferry." His voice was deep with a soft Irish accent. "You'd be Grace O'Rourke's grandson, no doubt."

"Yes, I am."

I was surprised for a moment, but then I realised that with less than a thousand inhabitants, the island probably thrived on gossip.

"Sit you down there now," he gestured. "You were not at the wake?"

"No, I was held up in Galway with the weather."

"You were gone a long while," he said.

"Yes, we moved to Australia years ago. My mother remarried. This is my first time back."

From where we sat, I could see the ocean in the distance. The fields running down towards the beach covered in lush green grass, crisscrossed on all sides by endless grey stone walls.

"So," he nodded, "you're Grace's grandson. Which would make you the only son of Con Rua O'Rourke, the Seanachaí."

"Seanachaí?" I said,

"Your father was a Seanachaí," he said, "a storyteller. You didn't know that?"

"No, I've never really known much about my father. I was seven when he died. My mother always said he was a fisherman."

"No," he shook his head, "God forgive her, but that is not true. His family was fisher people. Con Rua was a Seanachaí. He was known as that throughout Ireland and beyond. The Seanachaí of Inis Mór," he nodded again, as if satisfied. "And your name?"

"My name's John … John Carlyle. My mother remarried."

"So you said." He stared out to sea. "Con Rua O'Rourke, his stories are told in some parts to this day."

He seemed to be talking more to himself than to me, and I wondered if he lived alone.

"You knew him?" I asked.

"Ah, sure everyone knew Con Rua. He had the gift."

"How do you mean?"

"Well," he shrugged, "it's a simple enough thing. Sure, we all have a gift. Isn't that what life's about?"

"And my father's gift was storytelling?"

"Your father was a Seanachaí. He brought hope to many a hopeless cause."

"I'm not following you," I said. "What do you mean by that?"

"The Seanachaí is a lot more than a storyteller, boy. Seanachaí carried our language and our culture when it was forbidden by the stranger to do so. They wandered the length and breadth of Ireland, telling stories of Cúchulainn, Ferghus mac Rhoich, Conall the Victorious and all the other Irish heroes. They spoke only in the tongue in the old days, although it was a hanging offence to speak Irish, reminding our people of a noble heritage, reminding us of who we are. Many of them were hung for their troubles. The strangers weren't happy with them at all," he nodded. "But it was their gift, something they had to follow."

"A dangerous gift by the sound of it."

"It can be a lot more dangerous not to follow your gift, for that's how you lose your soul."

"You believe that?"

"I do, of course. I wouldn't doubt it for a moment." The old man glanced at me sideways. "So, what about yourself, what's your gift?"

"I have no idea. I'm not sure that I have a gift."

"Sure, we all have a gift, there must be some direction to your life."

"I'm in advertising, I have my own agency in Australia."

"And that's how you spend your days?" He raised his eyebrows. "Advertising?"

"Yes. I've done it for years. Creating ads, running campaigns, that sort of thing."

"And you draw satisfaction from that?"

"Yes, I enjoy it." But then I paused, remembering the row with Bannister and the mayhem I'd left behind, "What I should say is that I used to enjoy it. Things have been difficult recently."

"So, you're tiring of it?" He was studying my face.

"Well, no, not really. Although I have been getting a bit sick of it lately." I felt confused, unsure of where we were heading, "I've got a few problems, nothing I can't handle. I'm just not sure where I'm going at the moment."

The old man was staring out to sea.

"For a ship without a destination, no wind is the right wind." I was feeling irritated that the conversation had become so personal so quickly, but then without meaning to, I blurted out:

"My wife left me last year; my company's almost bankrupt. I owe money everywhere."

As I said the words, I felt an overwhelming sense of guilt and shame, but a relief somehow too, as if it had needed to be said. It's true, I thought. You've been on the rocks for a long time. Borrowing more and more money. Refusing to accept the simple fact that you've failed. Failed in more ways than one. Giselle had said as much during that final row. "I don't know who you are anymore," she shouted. "We hardly ever see you. Your own son is a stranger to you! What's our life about? An advertising agency. That's all you talk about, morning, noon, and night. Pepsi Cola, Australian Lager, Marlboro cigarettes, how much money you're going to make. Work, work, work, seven days a week! You've broken every promise you ever made to Tristan. We can't believe anything you say anymore. All you're interested in is drinking, drugs, and bullshit! What happened to you?"

"What are you talking about, drugs?" I shouted back, "I have a few drinks on the weekend and a joint now and again like everybody else in the world. Don't give me that crap!"

"Like everybody else in your world, John, not mine. You get drunk at least twice a week and you can't get out of bed in the morning without swallowing a handful of antidepressants. Hello! Anybody home? Wakey-wakey! They're drugs! You're obsessed with being a big shot and you're relying on drink and drugs to prop you up every step of the way!"

I slammed out of the apartment, stormed down to the beach, and sat there with my head in my hands, my stomach churning. I was angry, incredibly angry, furious because somewhere in my heart I knew that at least some of what she was saying was true.

You've got to get off the drink, I told myself. *Even for just a year or two. Use your willpower. You can do it.* Trouble was I no longer believed that. There'd been too many promises and too many failures. The old man was watching me.

"I may be able to save the company," I said, "Grace left me her cottage and there's a boat here somewhere. I have no idea what they're worth but, if I can sell them quickly, I should be able to keep going."

The old man stood up. He was even taller than I'd realized, his broad shoulders suggesting that he may have been an athlete in his day.

"Keep going where?" he said, and once again I was struck by the depth of his voice.

"Keep the company going, I mean. I could still pull it off with a bit of luck."

"You may want to give that some thought." He was peering down at me. "As you said, you have no real idea as to their worth. That cottage has sheltered the O'Rourke's for generations and *Erin* was one of the finest sailing boats on the West Coast of Ireland."

"Well, there's no rush." I'd regretted using the word bankrupt, I didn't want word getting around that I was broke. "I'll be staying on for a week or two, so I don't have to make any immediate decisions." And then, in an attempt to change the topic, I added: "So, where do you live?" He ignored the question and turned away, looking out across the ocean. "You are from the island, aren't you?" I ventured, but again he didn't answer, and I wondered if he might be a little odd. His clothes were unusual, the black coat way too long. The seaman's cap tilted at a peculiar angle and he spoke in a strange, old-fashioned way. One of the local eccentrics, I thought, not really crazy, just a little weird. He didn't move for several more minutes so finally, into the awkwardness of the silence, I said: "Well, I'd better be on my way." There was still no response so I stood up. "Nice to have met you," I said. "Good luck."

I'd only gone a few paces when his voice came booming out behind me. "So, you have no idea at all as to what your life is about?"

I turned back,

"How do you mean?" I snapped.

"Well, it's a simple enough question," he said. "I know what my life is about for example." And then he just turned and strode off down the hill, walking quickly and confidently as a man with a purpose in life.

* * *

The graveyard was set in a slight hollow overlooking the ocean, and as I walked in through the wrought iron gates I was captivated by a sense of antiquity. Celtic crosses from ages past stood everywhere above the silent graves. Mute testimonials to the Christian beliefs that have held sway over these islands for centuries. Several of the gravestones were relatively new, the names clean-cut into the stark grey stone. Others were older, the lettering blurred from the passage of time. Some of the oldest were entirely devoid of markings, their inscriptions stripped away by the coursing winds that have swept summer rain and winter snow across the face of Inis Mór for thousands of years, the Celtic crosses above them leaning forlornly over their anonymous inhabitants. Their identities secreted away for all time in the memories of their long dead friends around them.

I found my grandmother's grave at the far side of the cemetery. A simple mound of earth, the flowers still fresh, a temporary wooden cross erected whilst her headstone was being prepared. I approached cautiously, unsure of what secret we shared. My mother had never spoken of Grace, but I'd known all of my life that trouble lay between them. Forgive you for what? I thought as I stood beside the freshly turned earth. I have no idea what this is about, Grace, I told her silently, but for what it's worth, I forgive you.

As I turned to leave, I noticed the monument standing directly behind her grave. Its tall black marble Celtic cross casting a shadow over me as I moved closer to read the inscription …

Con Rua O'Rourke

The Seanachaí of Inis Mór

1940-1978

As I took in the words, I felt myself tremble, as if some cold hand had reached up inside and brushed icy fingers against my heart. I stood there for a long time, confused about what I should do. I hadn't been near a church in twenty years. Should I kneel, say some sort of a prayer?

I looked around. An elderly woman, riding past on a push bike, was watching me over the low stone wall. I waited for a few moments until she'd disappeared, then I made the sign of the cross on my forehead, turned, and walked back down the hill.

Chapter 9

Lorcan Reardon

The following morning I awoke at seven, the sound of the waves below my bedroom window calling me up from a restless night's sleep. I'd spent yet another troubled night, tossing and turning, thinking over what the old man had said. My mother had told me little or nothing about my father but since my own son had been born, I'd found myself wondering what sort of man he'd been. I'd gone to her many times but her answer was always the same.

"Leave him be son," she'd say, shaking her head. "For my sake, leave him be."

I never questioned that, but watching Tristan grow and change had brought him back to my consciousness, and now here I was meeting total strangers who had known him well.

Finally I stirred myself and went down below. The kitchen was freezing, the fire reduced to just a few red embers glowing softly in folds of grey ash in the grate and, as I shaved, I made a mental note to bank it up each night before going to bed.

After coffee, I fried the remaining eggs and then spent two hours rearranging the cottage before dragging the battered old bicycle out of the hallway and headed off towards Cill Rónáin. It was a cold, grey day, the wind sweeping in across two thousand miles of pristine ocean. The sun breaking through the low scudding clouds occasionally, scattering intermittent patches of sunlight over the fields. A dark blue, white-capped Atlantic glittering in the background beyond.

The ride into town took fifteen minutes. The winding lanes running between centuries-old stone walls, the bemused cattle huddled behind them peering out in wonder as this stranger from another world went rushing by.

My ankle was feeling strong, and I pushed myself hard, standing up on the pedals like a schoolboy, panting and straining up the hilly bits, gasping for breath as I neared each rising crest before cruising gratefully down the slope beyond. It was tiring but I enjoyed it, realizing before I was halfway there, just how much out of shape I'd allowed myself to become over the last few years.

As I arrived at the top of the final rise, the mobile rang in my pocket, startling me as I pulled the bike over to the edge of the narrow lane.

"John Carlyle."

"Maurice Shaw." His voice came across cool and clear. "Where are you, John?"

"I'm in Ireland. How are things over there?"

"Not good. Do you realize there's nobody answering the phone at your office?"

"Yes. Janine bailed out. The stress got to her."

"Well, it doesn't look good. You need to get back here as soon as possible. There are decisions to be made and papers to be signed. We can't hold off your creditors forever."

"Look, my grandmother died here a few days ago. She left me a cottage on five acres. If I can sell the place quickly, I should be able to pay all the creditors outright, including the Mercedes."

"I'm afraid it's too late for that. They took possession of the car yesterday."

"Oh Christ, Maurice, you should have stopped them! You know how important it is to me. Look, contact them now. Tell them I'll be paying the contract out in full in a month or two."

"I'm sorry, John, but we can't get involved in that type of thing." He was speaking briskly now, back in his accountant's armor. "As for the cottage, how much would it be worth on today's market?"

"I'm not sure. It's over two hundred years old. Property prices aren't all that good on the mainland at the moment, but you can't buy anything on Inis Mór so it should still fetch a good price. At least two hundred thousand Euro, probably a fair bit more. Almost certainly enough to get me off the hook in Australia."

"Perhaps it will, but all of that will take time, and your creditors are taking legal action now."

"Tell them to wait. Talk to them for Christ's sake, that's your job! If they bankrupt the company, I go too. You know that. The apartment was used as security on that last loan. Do it, talk to them. We only need another month or two at most. Who's talking about legal action, Roger Bannister?"

"Yes. Him and the people who did the video presentation."

"Oh, Christ," I said. "Bannister's a friend of Paul Reynolds. He knows I can't pay right now. Reynolds is behind the whole thing."

"I can't comment on that," he said, "but you do owe them a lot of money, and it is six months overdue."

My head was beginning to ache.

"Look, Maurice, there must be some way out of this."

"Voluntary bankruptcy would be one way out. There are plenty of people who had to go bankrupt, John." I sat there in despair, staring out across the stony fields, listening to him going on, business as usual. "How can I contact you in an emergency, John? Do you have a landline there?"

"No, but you can always contact me on this number. Look, see if you can put off any court action, would you? Talk to them. I'll have the money soon. I should be able to borrow against the cottage even if I can't sell it immediately."

"I'll do the best I can, but Bannister's pretty angry,"

*   *   *

By the time I reached Cill Rónáin, it was almost midday. Lorcan Reardon had drawn a little map on the bottom of the welcome note, and I found the cottage without any trouble, a small brass plaque by the side of the gate bearing the single word, *Erinmor.* As I arrived at the front door, there was a low growl. Just to one side of the path, squatting in the shadows of a bush, a jet-black bull terrier, bulging eyes and lolling red tongue, was observing me impassively. As I hesitated, the door opened, and a short, stocky, elderly man was peering out at me over the top of a tiny pair of gold rimmed glasses, his blue eyes friendly and inquiring.

"Conor O'Rourke, unless I'm very much mistaken? Pay no heed to Boson, he's the best watch dog we've ever had. Sure, he'd sit and watch you all day long." He smiled. "Pat Donovan called in earlier and told us you'd arrived. We were just about to head up to the cottage to see you." He held out a hand. "Welcome home to Inis Mór, Conor, Mary's dying to meet with you."

"It's John actually," I said, taking his hand. "John Carlyle, my mother remarried."

"You'll be Conor O'Rourke to me till the day I die, m'boy," he said cheerfully. "I could never call a son of Con Rua's by any other name. Sure, Grace would turn in her grave." He stepped to one side. "Come in here now and meet Mary. You're welcome in our home but don't be after telling her you're a John Carlyle. She had a great affection for your father."

As we were talking, a small white-haired woman approached, wiping her hands on a brightly colored floral apron.

"Holy Mother of God," she was staring at me as if I were a ghost. "Aren't you the living image of your da?"

"I don't recall much about him," I told her. "I remember him being very tall with red hair, that's about all. I guess you knew him well?"

"Ah, sure everyone knew Con Rua." She put a hand on my arm. "There was many a night he told his stories in this cottage. He was a rare kind of Seanachaí was your da."

"So I believe. I met an old man outside of Kilmurvey yesterday. He was telling me the same thing."

"And who might that have been?" Lorcan asked.

"I didn't get his name. He was an old guy, probably around eighty or more. Very tall, broad shouldered with a long black coat. He was wearing a seaman's cap. You know, the type with a little peak at the front. A bit of a local character, I suspect."

"That's not anyone I know from the island," Lorcan looked puzzled. "Where did you say you met him?"

"I met him near the graveyard, but I first saw him down by the ferry the day I arrived."

"Ah, he'd be from Galway so. Over for a day or two on the boat, no doubt."

"No, I don't think so. He was there when the ferry arrived. I think he's an islander."

"Not from that description he's not." He glanced across at his wife. "Unless it was Colm … Colm Feegan?"

"Sure, Colm's still short of seventy." Mary was shaking her head. "And he's not all that tall that you'd mention it." She turned to me again. "Could you be wrong about the age?"

"I don't think so. This guy would have been eighty at least. Probably more like eighty-five."

"Well, whoever it was, we can work that out another time." Lorcan was lifting a cardboard carton up onto the dining room table. "Sit you down there now m'boy and I'll run through Grace's Will with you." He was rifling through files in his makeshift cabinet. "I was a teacher over there in Galway for half my life, but I've been retired these past ten years. I still do a little tutoring on the island. Irish history mostly, nothing much now. More of an encouragement for some of the slower ones." He was pulling a folder out from the rest. "Here we are now, Grace O'Rourke, God rest her soul. She was a fine woman. She had no fear of life and no fear of death. She said as much herself right at the end."

"What did she say?" I said, remembering the lines that had run through my mind in Dublin.

"Ah, she was almost gone. It was something like, 'I feared not life, I feared not death.'" He shook his head. "I don't know about the rest of it, she was very weak."

"So what is that?" I said. "Is it a poem or something?"

"I'm not sure what it might have been. A dying woman talking to herself, I'd imagine. I believe there's something like that to be put on her stone. Here we are now." He'd taken a single sheet of paper from a cream-colored envelope and was adjusting his tiny gold rimmed glasses right at the tip of his nose. "The last Will of Grace O'Rourke." He coughed to clear his throat. "It's as simple as you'd like. Her solicitor in Galway drew it up just to make sure it was legal, but they're her own words." He cleared his throat again before continuing.

"I, Grace O'Rourke, knowing that I am dying and wishing to set some things right, am leaving all of my earthly belongings, whatever they may be, to my grandson, Conor O'Rourke of Sydney, Australia. I leave everything I own to Conor. The cottage, Tír na nÓg, along with the five acres that it stands on. *Erin,* the boat his grandfather built as a young man. Whatever money there may be in my account, and any bits and pieces of things he may choose to retain from my possessions. These things being his birthright and inheritance. There is only one request that I make binding. That the cottage is not to be sold, borrowed against, rented, or lent out in any way, or otherwise encumbered until at least two years past the time of my death. If these conditions are not acceptable to Conor for any reason, then the cottage, the boat, and everything mentioned above would go instead to my brother, Lorcan Reardon and his wife Mary, or their next of kin. Any other remaining property that Conor has no need of would also go to the Reardon's to use or dispose of as they will."

As he finished reading, I felt my hopes dying. She'd left me the house, but I couldn't sell it for two years. By the sound of things, I wouldn't even be able to borrow against it.

"There now." Lorcan slid the Will back into the manila folder and handed it to me. "That's a copy. Des Keegan has the original. He's the family solicitor, so if you have any questions, you should direct them to him."

"Is there any way I could sell the cottage now?" I asked.

"Sell it?" He looked up quickly. "Sell it to whom?" He glanced at his wife and then back to me. "Grace wanted you home, Conor. Give yourself a chance here, your family has lived on Inis Mór for generations."

"I'm sorry Lorcan but I live in Sydney. I have a business there. I can't stay on here indefinitely just to please my grandmother."

"Well …" He stood up. "… that's up to you now but the Will is clear. You can't sell, rent, or loan the cottage out for two years. I'm not sure what you want to do now, but she was firm on that."

"There must be somebody on the island who'd want the place," I said. "Maybe I could raise money by selling an option to purchase? Would you be interested? If the price was right, I mean?"

He was looking at me fixedly, and when he spoke again, it was clear I'd upset him.

"There wouldn't be a soul on this island that would go against my sister's last wishes, let alone myself." He paused. "Think it over, Conor, or John if you like. Just be aware that the Will is not in your name, and that could cause problems enough now under Irish law without wanting to deny Grace her dying wish."

He glanced at his wife.

"I'm not able to stay for lunch, but I'll be home before dark." And then turning back to me. "We'll talk another time. Mary will show you the rest of Grace's things. Good luck."

"I didn't mean to upset him," I said when I heard the front door slam. "But I'm in a bit of a spot financially and I have no intention of living in Ireland."

"He's in grief." She was fussing about in a cupboard, dragging out cardboard cartons. "Himself and Grace were very close." She lifted one of the smaller boxes up onto the table. "These are her belongings. I'll make us some tea whilst you look through it all."

Grace had spent the last six months of her life at the Reardon's cottage and most of her personal effects were there. I went through the jewelry, more to be polite than anything. But when Mary came back in with the tea, I told her that I thought my grandmother would probably have wanted her to have it all.

"That's kind of you, but Grace would have expected most of the jewelry to go to your wife. But wait, there's something she asked me to put in your hands." She'd opened a small wooden box and was holding up a gold ring. On the front, intricately inlaid in silver, an ancient looking Celtic symbol. "This was your father's. It's the sign of the Seanachaí, or so they say. Your father was given it by an old man here years ago." She was frowning. "She wore it herself; you know. Only ever on the one night of the year. Every Halloween from the day your father died." She looked away and I wasn't sure if she was angry or upset. "Don't you dare let go of that now. Not ever, do you hear. It was on his hand the day he died."

But then she softened and put a hand on my arm. "You were gone a long time, Conor, and you've learnt different ways. But we have our own ways here on the island, and you must learn to respect that too."

Chapter 10
Dun Aengus

Dun Aengus stands at the top of three hundred foot high cliffs close by the village of Kilmurvey, a formidable stone fortress that has, for over two thousand years, dominated the hauntingly lonely, starkly beautiful, island of Inis Mór. I'd gone up there after a late lunch with Mary, confused and depressed by the terms of the Will and drawn on by the enigmatic solitude of the place.

I approached the old fort slowly, passing first through the chevaux-de-frise, a formidable barrier of three foot high sharp edged stones, set close together to impede any frontal attack. And from there across to the next line of defence, stooping low, as an invader would have had to do, to pass underneath the narrow arched stonework then on to the main entrance set deep in the ten-feet-thick walls.

As I walked through into the inner keep, I saw him standing alone by the cliff-top, dangerously close to the edge. His seaman's cap pulled low across his eyes, the long black coat-tails flapping around his legs, the stick clutched in both hands behind his back. It startled me for a moment and I almost called out. But then, as I drew closer, he turned as if sensing my presence and stepped towards me, away from the edge.

"Good evening." He smiled a greeting. "I like to watch the sunset." Then, as if reading my mind: "The heights trouble you? I've walked these cliffs since I was a boy."

"This sort of height troubles me," I said. "I'd imagine a few people might have gone over the edge here."

"They have indeed," he nodded. "The gateway to Tír na nÓg, the Land of Youth, or so legend would have us believe." He turned back towards the ocean. "Some went over by their own hand, more were thrown. The penalty for invasion."

"You mean the English?"

"Ah now, we had the Vikings raiding these islands long before the stranger ever set foot on Irish soil." He was gazing out across the ocean, his eyes narrowed against the setting sun. "Some conquered Inis Mór, others died trying. The English were here for a long while. Not so much on the islands, they left us alone for the most part. The main garrison was over there in Galway."

"You remember that?"

"They come and go," he said. "Like men everywhere, there was good and bad among them. We've had invaders on Inis Mór for over two thousand years and yet the island goes on." He turned back at me. "So, have you worked out why you came back?"

"No, not really. I think I needed a break more than anything."

"A break from what?"

"Just a break. You know, time out."

"Time out from what?" he persisted. "From life?"

"I guess so."

"Time out would suggest a return. Why would you go back to something that's already done with?"

It was put so simply that it stopped me for a moment.

"Well, I can't just drop off the end of the earth," I told him. "I do have responsibilities back there."

"Do you now." He sat down on a stone ledge, gesturing for me to do the same. "And what would they be?"

"What are you suggesting? That I stay on Inis Mór? Some of us have other things to do with our lives, you know." His simplicity was irritating.

He fell silent for so long then that I wondered if I'd offended him. He was sitting facing me as we spoke, but I could no longer make out his features. His head and shoulders, a shadowy silhouette against the last traces of sunlight fading out across a darkening ocean.

"Why did you come back?" he demanded suddenly. "What caused you to return?"

"I told you, I needed time ..."

"No. That's the excuse." He cut me off. "I'm looking for the reason. What brought you here?"

I stopped for a moment, confused. And then for some reason I said: "Poetry, I guess … voices in my mind."

"Of course," he spoke the words softly. "Carried by the gift. I should have known."

"Known what?" I said, but he was off on a different tack.

"Some come here from a book they read or a moving picture. Others come through a dream or the voices. Intuition you'd call it now." He stood up abruptly, tall and straight. "Your responsibilities are to your own soul. The life force moves forwards not backwards. What went before is done. To go back there now for you is to die, be it mental or physical, no matter. Forget about the past, your life lies ahead of you." He moved closer and, for a moment, I caught a faint whiff of tar and tobacco. "You have returned." His voice was deep in the evening quiet. "There's no shame in leaving behind an unworthy cause. Your old life is finished. You'll have to accept that before you can move on. Nothing can change until it's allowed to be." He nodded. "Your first task will be to remember who you are."

And then suddenly he turned and was gone. A black coat melding into a shadowed night. A walking stick carried like a sword. A cap tilted at a rakish angle, and an easy, swinging gait, unnatural in one so old.

Chapter 11

Going Down

My mobile began shrilling at one o'clock the following morning, dragging me up from a restless sleep.

"Is that you, John?" Maurice Shaw's voice was urgent in the early morning stillness. "Is this a good time to call?"

"It's the middle of the night, Maurice. What is it?"

"They've started bankruptcy proceedings against you. There was nothing I could do. When will you be back?"

"Who's pushing the bankruptcy, Bannister?"

"Yes. Him and two of the others. They had a meeting yesterday. I tried to talk to them, but they're not interested. You don't have much time. If you could make a reasonable payment, that might hold them off for a while."

"You know I can't do that. Not unless the bank could extend the overdraft a little?"

"Impossible, John. There's no chance of that." His voice was taut. "I spoke to the manager yesterday. They're more interested in calling in the loan on your apartment. You'll have to let the place go or they'll sell it out from underneath you."

"Giselle's not going to agree to that," I told him. "Things are bad enough now without a forced sale on the unit."

"She's already agreed. The bank couriered the papers to her in France two days ago."

I was struggling to control my anger.

"They can't sell my home out from underneath me just because we're a few months behind on the payments. Get the solicitors on it!"

"John, you're seven months behind on the mortgage payments. They have a perfect legal right to sell the apartment." He paused. "Look, word has obviously got out that you're in trouble. The bank wants their money now before you're declared bankrupt. You can't blame them, it's business."

I sat upright on the edge of the bed, peering out the window, a heavy grey blanket pulled around my shoulders, the ocean a black, gently-heaving mass as far out as I could see. Flashes of white-capped waves occasionally as flickers of moonlight found their way through the dark, low-swept clouds above. Below me, as they had for a thousand years, the waves surging endlessly against the dark pebbled beach.

"Maurice, if you could hold them off for another few weeks …"

"You're not listening. You don't have any more days left, let alone weeks. Look, I'll be blunt. The bank wants you to sign the unit over to them now, immediately."

"Are you serious?"

"It's your only way out."

"So, I surrender the unit. They do a quick sale. The bank takes all their money plus costs and anything that's left over gets snapped up by Bannister and his mates? Is that what you're offering me?"

"I warned you about that apartment."

The muscles in my stomach had contracted into one large knot.

"And Giselle's agreed to this?"

"Yes."

There was another long silence and I sat there in the dark, wondering how it had all come to this.

"What's the bottom line? Tell me the truth."

"Look, I'm only trying to help …"

"Tell me the truth, Maurice." I told him again, "What's the bottom line?"

"Look, you're in a hopeless position. Your business is on the rocks. You have no apparent income. Your outgoings continue, and at least three independent companies are instigating legal proceedings against you. You're bankrupt now, John. The declaration will be a mere formality."

I stared out across the ocean. The same dark ocean I'd stared at the night of my father's wake. The same sickening sense of dread sapping my strength and draining my energy.

"What about the cottage you mentioned?" He was back again. "Could you flog it off quickly? Did you get an evaluation?"

"We'll talk later," I told him.

* * *

After hanging up, I called Giselle in Brittany. Her version was a little different to Shaw's, but the end result was the same. The bank had pressured her into agreeing, telling her that as a director, she could be held jointly responsible for the company's debts.

"I'm sorry, John, but I have to think of Tristan and I don't need any more problems in my life right now. I hated that apartment. We should never have bought the place. And John …" She paused but I knew what was coming. "I've been talking to a solicitor and I think it's time we went ahead with the divorce."

I stood up and went to the window, peering into the darkness, seeking escape.

"Giselle, don't do anything just yet, please. Wait till I come over to Brittany."

"No." Her voice was firm. "I've made up my mind. We only hear from you once a week and even then it's all about you. Your son's growing up without you and you don't even seem to care."

"Look, once I get things sorted out in Australia, it'll be different. I'll have more time. The company's finished anyway."

"So that's what it takes for you to see your son? You have to go bankrupt first? He asks about you every night and all I can tell him is that you're too busy." She paused before the final thrust. "Too busy being a big shot, that is."

"Please, Giselle, I love you both. You know that. As soon as I finish here …"

"No." She cut me off. "Don't make any more silly promises. I'm sick of them. If you loved Tristan, you wouldn't treat him the way you do. As for loving me, well, they're just words."

"Don't say that, Giselle. Is he there now? Can I talk to him?"

"No. He's asleep and I don't think it would be a good idea anyway. It upsets him too much. Can't you understand that? He's a child. He believes everything you say. No, it's better if you don't talk to him for a while. Write him a letter, but don't make any more silly promises. Send a letter. At least that way, he'll have something he can hold onto." There was a pause. "And, John … I am going ahead with the divorce. I want to get my life back on track. I don't want to argue with you, so I think it's best we talk through our solicitors from now on."

The line went dead. I tried calling back but there was no response. Just a friendlier version of her voice asking if I wanted to leave a message.

Chapter 12
Songs

I awoke again at nine thirty, rain pattering softly against the windows, the horizon leaden, the room cold and dank. The conversation with Giselle had destroyed any hope I had of a reunion, and I lay there feeling lost, trying not to let the depression overwhelm me.

What were my options? Did I have any? Perhaps I could raise a loan from one of the Irish banks, maybe offer them a higher interest rate. That wasn't very likely. Maybe I could get a loan in Australia? Would they accept the cottage as security? Not much chance of that. It wasn't even in my name.

Then there were the Reardon's. If I upset Lorcan too much, God knows what he'd do. The Will was in the name of Conor O'Rourke. I'd probably have to prove who I was legally. How long would all that take? It went around and around until finally I dragged myself out of bed and fumbled my way downstairs to the bathroom.

"Not so sure of yourself now, are you?" I stared at an ashen face in the pock-marked mirror. "You're a disaster." This was what the antidepressants were supposed to keep at bay. They weren't actually voices, more like echoes of some distant despair from a long, long time ago. "You're gone this time. No more loans. No more cozy little chats with your bank manager. They have you by the balls and they know it."

I eased myself sideways into the tiny shower, the white plastic curtain clutching at my shoulders like a shroud. "You've blown the whole thing. Your marriage, your home, the business, the Merc." A rusting enamel water heater hissed asthmatically on the wall. "You don't even know how much this place is worth." The shower was cold, but nowhere near cold enough to block the voices. "Even if it is worth something, you still can't sell it. You're bankrupt. The whole thing's a fiasco. You can't stay here for two years. Go back to Australia. Face the music."

Why would she insist on me staying for two years? Can people do that? That's probably where to start, I thought, find out if the Will's legal. People can contest Wills, that's not unheard of. Not here though, I thought. I'd have to be careful. I'll make some calls to Galway.

As I waited for the coffee to brew, I took another look at the Will. It was a simple, one-page document and I mulled over the words, searching for loopholes:

There is only one request that I make binding, that the cottage not be sold, borrowed against, rented, or lent out in any way, or otherwise encumbered until at least two years past the time of my death. If these conditions are not acceptable to Conor for any reason, then the cottage, the boat and everything mentioned above would go instead to my brother, Lorcan Reardon and his wife Mary or their next of kin.

"*There is only one request …*" that didn't sound very binding. A request is just that, a request. How could that be binding? There must be some avenue of appeal. The cottage would have gone to my father if he were still alive and then later to me.

I called inquiries and, a few minutes later, I had the numbers of three solicitors in Galway. The first two had no interest at all in the matter but the third, a Mr. James Farrell, listened attentively as I read out Grace's Will, asking me to repeat a sentence now and again before offering his opinion.

"Look, time's money and I've yet to be paid for one of these random calls." He had an abrupt, almost abrasive manner. "But I'll tell you this much free of charge. What your man Lorcan told you was right. The Will's not in your name and that could cause problems enough under Irish law. Second, if I was a bankrupt in Australia, I'd be staying quiet about any inheritance I'd come into in Ireland. And third, you're playing with words, John. Your grandmother stated, and I quote, "There is only one request that I make binding." So, it's a request right enough, *but she made it binding.* You want my professional opinion?" He didn't wait for an answer. "You may contest the Will if you like, but I guarantee that you'd live to rue the day."

By the time I got off the phone, it was after one o'clock and I wandered around the cottage feeling trapped. The rain had eased but the day was still bleak, a bitter wind buffeting the windows and rattling the kitchen door.

I ate a meager lunch, thoughts of Giselle swirling around in my mind, robbing me of my appetite and pushing me deeper into despair. By four, I couldn't put up with my head any longer so I pulled on a sweater and leather jacket and headed off out the door, hoping a hard walk would give me some peace.

At first, I headed towards Kilmurvey but, when I spotted a sign to Dun Aengus, I turned and headed towards the cliffs once again. The wind was pushing in from the west, tugging at my clothes and stinging my eyes as I strode quickly along a muddy track, trying to shrug off the negativity.

"Leave now, while you still can." I increased my pace, striding up the slope towards the main entrance. "You were never a logical person, lots of talk but not much substance." The voice was relentless. "You were promising for a while but that's all it was, just promises." I turned into a gap in a low stone wall. Dun Aengus lay directly ahead in the fading light. That's what they'd all said, that I had promise. So what went wrong? Not enough willpower? It wasn't that, my therapist insisted that I had too much willpower. "Not enough feeling," she'd said. "Too much intellect, no real feelings." To hell with that, I thought, they sit there psycho-babbling on about feelings as if they have a monopoly on them. Trotting out all the therapeutic, touchy-feely bullshit they love to wallow in. I'm not beaten yet. I've come back from worse than this. I was feeling more confident as I strode through the entrance. I didn't owe Lorcan a thing. I'll find the toughest solicitor in Ireland. Grace left the cottage to me. A good legal man would sort all that out in no time. I'll be the one making the decisions then.

I walked across to where the cliff fell away and peered over the edge. Three hundred feet below, huge, white-crested waves crashed in against the limestone rocks, seething and boiling as they hurled themselves against their age-old nemesis.

"The decisions have already been made." The voice was firm, and my heart sank again. "The Will is quite straightforward and it's legal. You can't sell the house and you can't borrow against it for two years. Grace made that quite clear."

I looked out to the west. The next landfall was America, two thousand miles away. I've never worked in America, maybe I could start again over there. "There's no hope of that, you're a loser. You'd be a loser there too." I stared down at the seething ocean. A small white seabird was sweeping in and out of the towering swells, seemingly oblivious to the dangers around him. One wrong move and he's dead, I thought, one wrong turn.

Every few moments, a tremor ran through the rock underneath me as another wave thundered headlong into the base of the cliff below. I looked down. As each wave receded, the stark, rocky ledges were revealed for a moment or two. The area was strewn with boulders, torn from the cliff face over the centuries by the endless raging seas.

Maybe it will collapse again. Maybe it will take me with it. I felt a movement inside, not fear, not regret, almost relief. That would solve everything, I thought, and it would be over. I stepped backwards, "If you'd have stepped forward, it would be over already." I felt a chill go through me. "Giselle will be okay; the insurance will look after her. Tristan too, he'd be better off without you anyhow. This is the way out. Do it, it would be best for everyone." I stood there in despair. It's over, I thought, you played a game and you lost. You're bankrupt, everything's gone. Nobody can help you now.

I moved back to the edge of the cliff and stared down. What's the point? Are we supposed to keep playing the same miserable role over and over again? Just watch on passively while those closest to us lose their faith, their hope and their trust. Are we supposed to ignore all the defeats, all the heartbreaks, all the hurt and just keep on trying? Is that the noble path? Is the other path any less noble? Is there no point at which we're allowed to say, enough … thank you … but I've had enough?

Mountainous waves were thundering into the rocks below, withdrawing for a moment or two, then smashing back in again. Nothing could survive down there. I'd be dead the split second I hit the rocks. No more misery, no more pain. "This is the way to go." The voice was softer now, quieter, but more insistent. "It's over. You tried. You did the best you could." What about Tristan? How will he take it, no family, no father? "He never had a father, you ignored him all his life. Giselle will marry again. Go on, get it over with."

I stared out to sea. It was almost pitch black. Endless banks of storm clouds wiping out the last faint traces of daylight on a distant horizon.

I closed my eyes. No tears, I told myself, no self-pity. This is how it's meant to be. And suddenly, I knew that it was time for me to go. I began to sway, backwards and forwards, rocking gently, heels and toes, more and more. I could feel the spray from the ocean running down my face, preparing me, blessing me. "This is not wrong," the voice had softened, "this is an accident, people will understand." The wind was rising and falling. "Don't worry," it was close now, almost touching me, "when you hear the roar grow louder it will be over." The wind whistled in my ears. "God help me," I whispered …

"You're very close to the edge, boy." A deep voice shattered the trance and I spun around, almost stumbling over the brink as I did. The old man was standing directly behind me. "I've been watching you," then a hand gripping my arm, firm and strong … "I wasn't sure if I should intrude …"

"Oh Jesus Christ …" I was totally confused. "I'm sorry. I was thinking of my son."

"Yes indeed," he nodded, "we tend to think of our families at times like these." He was still holding on to my arm. "I was about to build a fire." He nodded. "Would you care to join me?"

I glanced back down at the ocean, seething and raging between the rocks below, and suddenly, I felt sick.

"Yes."

I followed him across to a group of boulders on the edge of the clearing, shaken and unsure of myself.

"You appear troubled." He was arranging small pieces of kindling in a circle of stones.

"We're losing our home …" I paused, unable to say the words. "And my wife's divorcing me."

"I see." He finished his preparations and put a match to the paper. "So, your life is in tatters?"

"Yes."

"That can be difficult," he nodded. "When everything about us is falling apart, we end up wondering who we are at times."

"That's about where I am now," I said.

"What you're experiencing is not uncommon, boy. Every human being goes through times like this." He was adding lumps of wood from a Hessian bag, building up the fire inside a loose circle of stones. "Listen now and I'll tell you a story about how things used to be. You see, in ancient times when someone lost their way, the whole tribe would be there to support them. If the problem was bad enough, they'd take them out to one of the sacred circles ..."

As he rambled on, I sat there watching him, wondering who he was.

"You see," he continued, "tribal people revered the circle and many of their rituals were performed in them. They were sacred places, well away from the villages, often by a fork in a river or perhaps up on top of a hill."

"Like churches?" I asked.

"The ancient Celts worshipped the life force itself." He'd taken out a pipe and was packing tobacco into the shiny brown bowl. "The circles were our churches, the rivers, fields and animals, our teachers, your ancestors saw God in all things." He paused to put a match to the pipe, and I watched as he puffed it into life before continuing. "You see, a long, long time ago, long before the Christians ever came to Ireland, it was believed that every newborn child carried a gift. In some of the Celtic tribes, when a young woman fell pregnant, the old women of the village would take her out to one of the circles on the eve of the next full moon. They would sit her in the center of the circle and then they'd gather close around ..."

"What was the ..." I began.

"Whish now." He was holding up a hand, gazing into the fire as if remembering. "They would sit there silently and listen. Sometimes it came quickly, sometimes slowly, no matter. When one of the women heard the baby's spirit calling, she would begin to sing." He was peering into the fire now, eyes fixed and intense, oblivious to everything around him. "Answering the infant's soul, welcoming it to the world."

The fire was burning strongly, long orange-red flames crackling up into the timber in the gathering dark, the old man's shape shimmering in the haze between us, the firelight casting flickering shadows across his face.

"Before long, some of the other women would hear the baby's call and they would begin singing too, until finally, all the women of the tribe would be singing as one." He paused and took a long pull on the pipe, the pungent aroma of the tobacco swirling around us both as we sat in the gathering gloom. "When the child was born, it was taken out to the circle by its mother and all the women of the tribe would welcome it to the world by singing the newborn infant its song. Well, that same ritual was repeated at all the high points of that person's life: puberty, initiation, marriage, and so on."

He was squinting at me through the trails of smoke, his dark green eyes bright and alive.

"Later on, if you broke one of the tribal laws or if you lost your way in life as we sometimes do, the old people, both the men and the women, would come and take you back out to the circle. They would stand you alone in the very center and then the whole tribe would gather around and sing you your birth song. To remind you of who you were." He nodded. "To remind you that you carried a gift. A gift that the tribe still needed." He fell silent then, sitting there quietly as if in meditation.

"And that would pull them back into line?" I asked.

"Not always …" He shook his head. "Some would be so set in their ways, there'd be no shaking them. So caught up chasing money or power there'd be no bringing them back. If they persisted on that path, then they would be banished from the tribe. You see, boy, the gift is for the people. It's not to be used selfishly."

"They didn't punish them?"

"Punish them? Sure, there's punishment enough in not knowing who you are. That's punishment enough for anyone. Have you not had enough of that yourself?"

"You think I've lost my way?"

"Well, what do you think? You've been gone for thirty years. You have changed your name. You're separated from your wife and child. You've lost your home, and you have no real purpose in life. You're entirely lost. I will sing you a song."

And suddenly he was singing, singing to me in Irish. His head thrown back, his eyes closed, his deep voice rising and falling, reverberating all around me as in some ancient chant, sweeping and soaring over the ruins of Dun Aengus.

It startled me at first and, for a moment, I felt absolutely ridiculous but then as I listened, it took hold of me somehow as I recognized a word now and again. My own name, Conor, came into it repeatedly and Giselle and Tristan. I heard the word *Erin*, the name of my grandfather's boat, and my father's name, Con Rua O'Rourke, over and over again as if he were attempting to bring him back from the dead. And then suddenly, as I sat there across from this strange old man, his deep voice booming out without guise or pretense, rising and falling across the keep, reverberating somewhere deep inside me, I broke down and wept. A helpless, shaking sobbing that tore at my heart and soul, for although I barely understood a word he was saying, I knew better than I'd ever known anything before in my life, that this strange old man, whose name I did not know, was singing me the song of my birth.

Chapter 13

Sisters

The following morning, I rose to consciousness slowly, reluctant to leave behind the dreams that had filled my sleeping hours. I lay there motionless under the blankets, warm, cocooned against the world and unwilling to emerge. Untroubled for the first time in years as to what lay ahead. The only sound, the muffled, rhythmic, thump of the ocean on the pebbled beach below my bedroom window.

I'd dreamt of my grandfather's boat. Her long sleek hull, white and shining, her topsides dark green, her brass portholes glinting like gold in the morning sunlight, her sails filled and pulling, white crests rushing past her bow, her ropes creaking and straining against wind and water, my father sitting in the cockpit, talking and laughing, his hand on the tiller, and my grandfather too, winking across at me as if the dream was a secret thing between the three of us.

It had been like that sometimes when the wind and sea were right. We'd go down to where *Erin* lay to her moorings, transfer the food out of the rowing boat up into the cockpit and then my father would raise the mainsail and we'd slip out of Cill Rónáin to a breeze. We'd sail off to one of the other islands, or sometimes as far away as Galway, where we'd spend the night moored in the river close by

Spanish Arch, returning on the high tide the following day. It was always an adventure, my father tacking the boat offshore. *Erin* healed over to the wind, her sails raised, full and taut. Cutting cleanly through the dark blue waters, flurries of spray flying up over the bow as she drove herself along. Waves slapping against the hull sending shudders throughout the planking. The tiller trembling like a living spirit beneath my father's hand.

I went downstairs as if in a dream. The events of the previous evening seemed surreal in the morning light but then I remembered the old man, his head thrown back, his eyes closed, his deep voice rising and falling, and I smiled, for suddenly, it all seemed quite natural and right.

As soon as the coffee was ready, I took the percolator out to my rocky outpost overlooking the ocean. The day was clear, the ocean calm, the repetitive, even swells rolling in a rhythmic unison towards the island before breaking softly on the pebbled beach below.

I sat there for a while thinking about the old man, then I went back inside and toasted the remaining bread. It was a miserly breakfast, the food stocks were exhausted, so I wrote out a list of everything I needed, pulled on my leather jacket and headed off in search of the local store on my bike.

* * *

"You'd be Con Rua's boy, would you not?" The woman behind the counter was the oldest woman I'd ever seen. Her skin, worn smooth from years of mist and rain, the texture of fine, soft leather, her hair the color of arctic snow. "Sure, I knew who you were the moment I laid eyes on you. You're the image of him, so you are." She was smiling up at me, her eyes as bright and inquisitive as a cat's. "You must be a great one for the boats altogether, coming all the way back from America to take charge of Grace's hooker."

"I'm from Australia," I told her, "or at least, I lived there for most of my life."

"Is that you, Con Rua?"

An even older woman had appeared from behind a curtain, a walking stick clutched in a pale, bony hand as she moved slowly towards me across the bare planked floor.

"Go back in there now, Brigid, you have no right to be out here in the cold. Don't you be worrying your head about Conor, aren't I looking after him myself?"

"Is that you, Con Rua?" The older woman was moving closer, one hand outstretched.

"It's his boy, Brigid. Con Rua's dead these thirty years. Go back inside there now in the warm. You'll catch your death of cold out here."

"You are Con Rua, are you not?" She'd taken hold of my sleeve and was peering up at me. "They said you'd be back, and I never once doubted them."

"I'm his son," I told her. "I came back for Grace's funeral."

She was staring up at me as the blind stare, unblinking, unseeing.

"You were talking to the fili, were you not?"

"Come on Brigid, back in there now and finish your breakfast." Her sister had taken her by the arm. "You know what the doctor said, you've no right to be out of your bed on a day like this."

"Away with you, Madge!" The older woman spun abruptly, pushing her sister away with a sudden burst of energy. "Away with you now or I'll take my stick to you!" Then she turned back again, leaning towards me in a conspiratorial curve. "Ask him what happened to his boat." She whispered. "Ask him what happened to them what sailed on her. Go on now, ask him to tell you a story about that, if he will."

"She's not herself." Madge was steering Brigid around by the shoulders, guiding her gently back towards the faded curtain like some malfunctioning marionette. "She never was. She sees things. It's a gift and a curse. She's been that way from the start. There's nothing can be done about it now."

I watched as she led her sister away, stooped over and complaining, looking back at me occasionally, tossing comments over her shoulder.

"Ask the fili about the boat, Con Rua," she was cackling away like an old witch as she disappeared from view. "Remember to ask him what happened to the young lads what sailed with him now, won't you?"

Madge was back a moment later.

"Pay her no heed, sure she's mad as a March hare."

"What did she mean about the fili? Who is that?"

"Ah, pay no attention. Sure the faeries stole her brains the day she was born. People say she's possessed, but we all have our problems, do we not?" She straightened herself up, running her fingers through her white hair. "So, what is it that you'll be needing from us today?"

Chapter 14

Erin

After an early lunch, I jumped back on the bike, turning up the collar of my jacket against a probing westerly as I rode up the hill towards Kilmurvey. It was a clear, cold day, the sun shining down from a cloudless sky as I left the roadway and stuck off down a stony path heading for the cliffs once again.

Fifteen minutes later, I was standing on a rocky ledge looking out over an ocean glittering like a million golden sequins in the brittle midday sun. Out towards the horizon, a magnificent square-rigged sailing ship was forging her way through the dark waters, heeled over on a port tack, her sails filled, a flash of white foam at her bow occasionally as she ran into some of the heavier swells.

The cliff tops were a sanctuary for seabirds, climbing and reeling up above where I stood before coming swooping back down towards the cliffs, disappearing into the rocky mass beneath me. I watched them for a while then got down on my hands and knees and peered cautiously over the edge. There were hundreds of birds nesting in the nooks and crevices in the rocks below. Tiny flowers grew everywhere on the cliff face, surrounding the nests like bouquets. Many of the young had already hatched and they were peering around, open mouthed and expectant, squeaking for the scraps of food their parents brought back from each foray to the ocean far below.

I'm not sure how long I stayed there, but just as I was easing myself back from the cliff edge, the mobile rang in my pocket.

"Hello," I said reluctantly.

"Maurice here, John. How are things in Ireland?"

His voice came across sterile and cold, like an alien entity from another world.

"What is it, Maurice?"

"Good news. We've received an offer on the apartment."

"Who's 'we'?"

"Well, I meant the bank. We are all working on this together, you know. Look, the offer's very generous under the circumstances. It protects both you and Giselle and there may even be a little money left over. Ten or fifteen thousand dollars, perhaps. Although I can't guarantee that."

I was standing close to the cliff edge. A large albatross, his wingspan dwarfing all other birds nearby, was cruising along silently above the cliff-top, his majestic head and piercing eyes studying me, aloof and dispassionate.

"Is there any way we can hang on to the apartment?"

"No, of course not." He sounded irritated. "That's out of the question. Be realistic, John. You can't afford a place like that right now. Believe me. This is the best solution for everybody."

"So, I lose my home, my business, and my car and you see that as the best solution?"

"Look, I'm trying to help you here. This is the only possible way that you can walk free of all your debts without going bankrupt."

The albatross had circled and was returning along the cliff edge, its wings motionless, eddies of wind rising from the cliff base holding it to its steady path. Its head was lowered to one side, craning down to get a better look at this solitary intruder into its peaceful domain. It went gliding past in slow motion, its bright clear eyes piercing back into mine, open and accepting, curious and unafraid.

Maurice Shaw's voice was still running on in the background. "They could actually do all of this with just Giselle's signature, you realize. Technically, you're an absentee debtor. Or if you like, you could fax me a power of attorney over your affairs; that would speed things up a lot. I really think we should grab this offer whilst it's still on the table. The legal people can work out the details later. I'd advise you to ..."

I'd taken the phone away from my ear and was watching the albatross. It was a huge creature, its wingspan at least five feet across. It had turned for a third time and was cruising back towards me once again, even lower this time, its tail feathers twitching occasionally as it approached, its wings stable and steady as any airliner.

Shaw's voice was going on and on and I looked down at the phone. It was as if he were speaking a different language. A language I no longer understood. Then suddenly, the voice became sharper, the urgency of it pulling me back to the moment.

"Are you there, John?" He was angry. "Can you hear me?"

I didn't realize I'd thrown it until I saw it up in the air. The latest state-of-the-art Samsung, twisting and turning above the cliffs of Inis Mór. It seemed to rise in slow motion, its silver casing glinting and turning in the morning sunlight, pausing for a moment as it lost momentum, then plunging back down into the rock-strewn ocean below.

The albatross swung high and westwards, back out towards the open seas, and as I watched him disappear, I knew it was time to seek out my grandfather's boat.

I wheeled the old bicycle out to the road and set off into town. The Reardon's had told me that *Erin* had been taken out of the water a few years before for repairs so, as I swept down to Cill Rónáin, I wasn't sure of what to expect.

The first person I spoke to directed me to a shed close to the end of the main jetty.

"Grace's boat?" He was peering at me through glasses so thick, I could barely make out his eyes behind them. "She's over there in the shed," he pointed, "over by the end of the jetty."

I rode across to where a ramshackle structure leaned precariously over the water's edge at the shore end of the jetty. It had originally been built from timber, added to over the ages by bits of corrugated iron and plywood. The windows were obscured by old newspaper, stuck onto the glass from the inside and impossible to see through. I walked around the side and discovered two large barn style doors, the heavy iron chain between them coated in dense scales of rust. Set in to one of the doors was a small wicket gate. I pushed it open and stepped inside.

A dilapidated old sailing boat stood forlornly in the half-light, her long straight keel resting on a makeshift cradle slumped against two of the wooden poles that supported the sagging corrugated iron roof, high above. I walked around her slowly. She looked terrible. Her once proud paintwork faded and stained, the mast gone, her round brass portholes corroded and dull. It crossed my mind for a moment that perhaps it was the wrong boat. but as I came around to the stern, I saw the single word: *Erin* carved deep into her transom.

I stood there for a long time peering up at her, wondering just how far gone she was. She'd been built over sixty years ago, a piece of our family history now degraded and abandoned. There was a makeshift ladder propped at her stern and I climbed it carefully, unsure of my footing.

The deck area was even worse. Ropes rotting in the cockpit, mildew and dirt everywhere, her bronze deck fittings, which had once shone like gold, now tarnished to a dirty shade of green.

I forced the hatch open and peered below. In the musty half-light filtering in through the grimy portholes, broken equipment and rubbish lay scattered everywhere. The starboard bunk was buried underneath a pile of old sails, the tiller from the cockpit lying on top of the mildewed canvas. The other bunk was covered with coils of rope, a thick stack of newspapers and nautical charts, a circular red lifebuoy, an old brass compass and, incongruently, an ancient, battered, shopping trolley, minus its wheels, the name *Woolworths* stamped in red plastic on its side.

I stepped down into the cabin cautiously. Inside, the air was stale and dank. The galley to my left was filthy, the gimbaled brass stove creaking eerily in the gloom each time I moved. On the right-hand side was a chart table, the surface slanted like a school desk, pencils and a ruler sitting in a dust-covered wooden rack, patiently awaiting some guiding hand.

I picked my way carefully through the junk on the cabin floor. Bits and pieces of brass fittings, empty whiskey bottles, a coil of rusted galvanized wire, an upturned toilet bowl, cracked and useless, and a clutter of tin cans, many of them devoid of labels. I worked my way cautiously to the forward cabin and peered inside. It was dark in there but, as I looked closer, I saw a small V shaped bunk tucked right up into the bow and immediately memories came flooding back. This had been my place in the boat, a hideaway where I could sleep or read or just dream the hours away. I remembered lying there under the blankets, the water slapping gently against the hull, listening to them talking out in the main cabin, my father's voice rising and falling, and people laughing occasionally.

Directly above my head, a heavy wooden beam spanned the width of the underdeck. I reached up instinctively and ran my fingers along its length and there it was, my name, Conor, carved into the wood for all time. I'd cut it into the timber one day as my father had sat out in the cockpit steering. And then suddenly, the voices began again. The words whispering up inside me like some long-forgotten part of my soul, abandoned for too long … demanding to be heard …

The heart will hold the meaning that reason fell before

Spirit rising upward, a broken swung half door

A memory lost; a memory held in store

Angels weeping by a well, a father son no more

Passages behind another, faces by a door

Shadows moving ever, a cold stone splintered floor

Memories of childhood, wanting nothing more ...

As the words began to fade, I slid down onto a pile of mildewed canvas sails, half-formed images of my father's face rising up to meet me like ghostly reflections in a clouded mirror. A smile without features, a thrust of red hair, a pain in my heart, tears in my eyes.

Oh Christ, I thought, I should never have come back here. This is madness, some aberration from childhood, something I should discuss with a therapist when I get back to Sydney, or maybe something that would level out once I got back on the anti-depressants.

As I sat there with my head in my hands, I noticed a shaft of diffused sunlight close by the keel, letting me know that the boat was incapable of sailing. I stared down at the hole for a long time, thinking about my grandfather and how he'd built the boat and sailed her all his life. I thought of my father and how we'd watched him that day sailing *Erin* offshore from the cliffs at Dun Aengus. A ghostly hand waving back across thirty years of silence, and suddenly, in one of those irrational flashes of insight, I knew that I had to stay on the island until the boat was right. Even if I were to sell her, I could not abandon *Erin* this way.

Chapter 15
The Cottage

Later on that evening, as I sat by the fireside watching a DVD on my laptop, there was a loud knocking on the front door.

"Good evening." He was standing there smiling, the stick held in both hands across the front of his greatcoat. "Forgive me if you would but I was passing by and noticed a light. May I?" He was already walking past me into the house. "It's been many a long year since I stood in this cottage," he declared. And once again, I was struck by the depth of his voice.

"You weren't here for the wake?" I asked.

"Grace was a fine woman, respected by all." And then, turning back to me. "Am I disturbing you?"

"No, I was just watching an old movie, but I've seen it a dozen times already. Would you like a cup of tea or something?"

"A cup of tea would be grand." He smiled. "And a place by your fireside, as they say." As I walked out into the kitchen, he called after me. "Just black now, no sugar. I'm a simple soul."

When I returned, he was sitting in the armchair. He'd taken off his cap and for the first time I noticed his hair, a thick, white shock of it, sweeping back from his broad forehead, giving his face an even greater sense of authority.

"Who are these people?" He was leaning forward, peering at my laptop. Bruce Willis was threatening John Travolta with an evil-looking Uzi.

"It's *Pulp Fiction*," I told him, "an old favorite of mine. You don't know John Travolta?"

"No," he shook his head.

"There's your tea,"

"Any news of Sydney?"

"Yes, my accountant called. We've had an offer on the apartment. I'm going to have to let it go."

"So, you're thirty-eight years of age and your life is in bits." The old man was staring across at me, his eyes glittering. "You're a fortunate man."

"Fortunate? I lose everything I own, and you consider that fortunate? This is a catastrophe for Christ's sake!"

"Settle down now, boy, settle down." He leant forward and placed another log on the fire, "Take a good look at yourself. You were sick of your job, it was meaningless, you said as much yourself. What have you lost? The marriage? It was no use to either of you the way it was. Sure, you were driving the poor woman mad with your advertising nonsense. The house in Australia? It wasn't even yours. The Mercedes? No, that was just an arrogance on wheels."

Maybe he's mad, I thought, *Maybe that's why he's always alone.*

"What you lost was an illusion, boy, the illusion of being a big shot."

"You've no idea what you're talking about." My heart was racing. "I worked hard in that business."

But he continued on as if I hadn't spoken.

"Your life fell apart through lack of meaning. What value was your work? To anyone but yourself, that is. And your marriage is in tatters because you put your career before your family." He pointed the stem of his pipe at me, "But listen to me now, and listen well. With all your problems and all your woes, what you are now calling a *catastrophe* would be better understood as a *calling.*" He stared across at me, his dark green eyes clear and bright. "Do you understand that?"

"No, I don't!" I grabbed the poker and began stabbing at the logs, sparks flying up into the black, soot caked chimney. "What are saying? You think I'm working in the wrong career, is that it?"

"Well, that's not for me to say." He took a sip of tea before going on. "But now you'll be forced to take a really good look at yourself. *That's* why I say you're fortunate. Most of your kind stagger on for years in jobs they hate, ignoring their wives and families, trading their souls for an illusory sense of security while sinking deeper into mediocrity each year."

I tossed the poker back on the hearth.

"That might be fine for you, but some of us have to live in the real world too, you know."

But he just shook his head and continued.

"Others become addicted to the almighty dollar. Trapped in the delusion that the fancy cars and inflated expense accounts will bring them lasting happiness whilst they avoid doing anything of value in the world." He raised his eyes to meet mine and I was struck by the fearlessness of his gaze. "Self-centered fools preying on a crippled planet."

"What did you mean by a calling?"

"Your calling, boy. Your purpose in life. Your gift. Call it what you will."

"Who are you?" I said, "You're not from the island, are you?"

But again, he just ignored me, staring into the flames as if lost in a dream.

We stayed that way for a long time, each in our own separate worlds, and when he finally began again, he spoke without looking up.

"You were at the boat today?"

"Yes, I was down there this morning. She's a mess. I'm thinking of getting someone to fix her up. It wouldn't feel right selling her the way she is."

"Fix her up." He turned. "And who would do that for you?"

"I'm not sure. There must be somebody on the island that can fix boats."

"What about yourself?"

"Me? I don't know anything about boats."

"You're an O'Rourke. Your people have built boats on this island for centuries. All you'd need to do is to replace one plank and tidy up the rest. Sure Jaysus, you could do that standing on your head."

"I'd like to, I guess. I just wouldn't want to make a mess of it, that's all."

He was watching me.

"Are you willing?"

"I guess so … if it were possible."

"Are you willing or not, yes or no?"

We stared at each other for a long moment.

"Yes, I'm willing." I told him. "How did you know it needed a new plank?"

"She was holed the day they pulled her up out of the water. That's nothing. We'll bend a new plank around her in no time."

"You've done that sort of work before?"

"I have, of course. Some of my happiest days were spent that way."

"Repairing boats?"

"Yes indeed. I'd find them up on the hard somewhere. All they ever needed was a little hard work and a bit of love."

"How much do you think it would cost? A rough idea, I mean. I don't have much money."

"We'll work something out. Money would be the very least of my worries." He was peering into the fire, shadows flickering around his head. "The voices you spoke of, say more about them." He was talking directly into the rising flames. "Were there words?"

"Yes, but nothing that made any sense. It was like bits of poetry. I didn't understand any of it. It just started up one day and then I got a letter from my grandmother saying she was dying. That's why I came over here."

"She was sung to, you know. Warned of a loss to the family. Your father died not long after. That confused everything."

"How do you mean, sung to?"

He studied my face for a long moment and then he closed his eyes and settled back in his chair. He stayed that way for so long that I began to wonder had he dozed off, but then he spoke again and, as he did, I felt a chill run through me.

"When voices rise within you, the Calling as it's known
Open to the Mentor, turn your face toward the Crone
Your life was shaped to Purpose, a Gift with you was bore
The life force gathers closest by the cliffs at Inis Mór."

"That's a bit like what I heard," I told him. "What is it, an old poem or something?"

"What does it matter?" He looked across at me. "You listened, that's the main thing. Most people ignore those voices and end up missing their lives. Their real life that is. The life they could have lived. Some would call it intuition. Some talk of a still, small voice. Others talk of a quickening or a calling. It's the soul, of course, calling us to meaning. These things have been known to the Celts for thousands of years. The knowledge was passed from the Druids to the Bards and from the Bards to the Seanachaí. It was done over the centuries through the oral tradition. Our ancestors refused the written word."

"Where did you learn all this?" I said but he just ignored me again, carrying on as if I hadn't spoken.

"There's work to be done, work that will give meaning and purpose to your life." He'd taken up the poker and was stirring it into the flames. "*Erin* will be grand. Her mast is up above her in the rafters. It's nearly new. It was made up in Galway just a few years ago. They stripped off the bow fitting and chain plates and had them re-galvanized. They'd be around the shed somewhere, no doubt. Her hull's sound. Not a patch of rot in her anywhere. We'll bring her back every bit as good as the day she was launched."

"You knew *Erin* then?" I asked.

He glanced across at me.

"Much will depend on you, of course." He smiled. "On how committed you are. I'm here to help but you must be willing to work. My best days are behind me."

"You built boats?"

He was looking around.

"Is there more tea?"

When I came back in from the kitchen, he was still sitting in the armchair.

"There you go," I said.

He didn't stir for a long moment, locked in some dream with the fire, but then he roused himself and reached out a hand for the tea.

"That was how it all started." He murmured. "With a boat."

"A boat you sailed on?"

"A boat I built." He was still staring into the fire and I could see the reflection of the flames flickering like dreams in his eyes. "I was her master. I was a young man then. About your own age, ambitious, determined."

"So, what happened?"

"Boats have a soul of their own." He was speaking as if in a trance. "It's a mixture of many things. Part of their soul comes from the materials they're built from. The trees are the boat's ancestors, their grandmothers and grandfathers. The oak, the ash and the pine that gave their wood so that the boat might be, each had a soul of its own. The soul of a boat is a reflection of the men that built her. Their integrity or lack of it. Their dreams, their hopes and aspirations. *Erin* is no different. Your grandfather built her sixty years ago in that same old shed. He was a decent man, so her soul is sound." He put the cup back down on the hearth. "She was rented out for a long while, so she's had some abuse. When people have lost connection to their own souls, how could you expect them to honor the soul of *Erin*?"

He stood up suddenly,

"But we can change all that, God willing. Why don't you go down there in the morning and take a look around? Clean out that shed, you can't expect men to work right surrounded by filth. You must clean out the rubbish of the past, boy, that's the new beginning right there."

"Hang on," I said. "The shed's buried in rubbish. It would take days to clean out."

"So?" he demanded. "Clean it out the same way as it arrived. One piece at a time, one day at a time." He was heading for the door. "I have every faith in you. I'll drop by in a day or so and we'll take a look over *Erin* together."

I replaced the poker in its stand and followed him out to say goodnight, but he'd disappeared. I walked to the front gate and peered up the laneway but there was no sign of him, just the full moon shining down brightly across the fields of Inis Mór.

Chapter 16
The Boatshed

The following morning dawned cold, grey and ominous. The clear blue skies of previous days replaced by dark scudding clouds sweeping in low across the island, driven on by a stampeding westerly that rattled the cottage windows.

I rode down to Cill Rónáin after breakfast, an assortment of tools I'd unearthed in the kitchen cupboards slung in a brown leather bag over my shoulder, my ankle protesting each thrust of the pedal.

As I wound my way along through the narrow lanes, the wind was increasing, sweeping in boisterously across a troubled ocean, tugging possessively at me on the open stretches, battering my face each time I swung to the west and threatening to overwhelm me at every corner and turn.

The rain began pelting down as the boatshed came into view. Icy shards of water whipped sideways by a spiteful wind, driving into my face as I sprinted the last few hundred yards to the wicket gate and the shelter of the gloom beyond. Once inside, I paused, taken aback, the place was in a disgusting condition, far worse than I'd realized. The odor of stale urine just inside the door was overwhelming and some of the other areas smelt even worse. The floor was littered with bottles and it was obvious that the place had been used for drinking sessions for years.

There was rubbish scattered everywhere and water was dripping from the rafters as the rain found its way through holes in the corrugated iron roof. I looked around dismayed. I'd gone to bed the previous night feeling good about the project, but standing there now in the gloomy half-light, the rain hammering remorselessly on the roof above, I was beginning to have doubts.

I limped around the shed slowly. A solid brick fireplace stood in the middle of the floor. A rusting drainpipe commandeered as a makeshift chimney rose precariously upwards in a drunken curve to protrude through a rough-hewn hole cut high in the roof above.

In front of the fireplace, drawn up close as in any conventional home, a three-piece lounge suit held pride of place. The sofa was in tatters, its arms slashed and torn, bits and pieces of off-white stuffing squeezing out from the dark brown leather as if struggling to be free of their long dead host.

But the two armchairs were in better shape and I sat down in one of them wondering if there was any point going on. It would probably make more sense to sell her as she is, I thought. Sell her to one of the islanders. Someone who could fix her up properly.

I got up and went around to the far side of the shed. The place really was in a mess. Years of accumulated junk piled high against the side wall almost covering a workbench and circular saw. In the far corner stood a mound of bottles, some broken, others intact, all apparently thrown from the sitting area by drunken revelers. Paddies Irish Whisky, the ubiquitous brown labels of the Guinness clan, Heineken and Strongbow, along with a dozen other brands, competed for supremacy on the shattered pile. I picked up one of the bottles: "Guinness Is Good for You!" declared a discolored promotional label, and I couldn't help wondering just how much good it had done its purchaser on that particular evening.

Jesus, I thought, this place is too far-gone. It's one thing sitting up in front of a warm fire talking about renovating a boat, but in the cold light of day, the reality was something quite different. I'd been flattered in a way that the old man had thought that we were capable of resurrecting the boat together, but looking around now, I realized that it was an impossible dream. I stared at the boat as if in a trance. The rain had increased, the thundering, drumming noise hypnotic in its intensity, insulating me out from the rest of the world, cocooning me into a time warp in which only I existed.

Nothing I'd ever known had prepared me for any of this. I was completely out of my depth. Nobody could blame me for walking away. Why should I be the one to clean it up? I thought. The people who made the mess should be clearing it up or maybe some contractor who did that type of thing.

"Rory, will you get a grip there now, for Christ's sake!"

The voice came from somewhere nearby, dragging me back to the moment. I went across to a window, peeled back a corner of yellowed newspaper and put an eye to the hole. Outside on the wharf, a small group of men were catching lines from a battered old trawler just back from the ocean on the high tide. They were fishermen, dressed in heavy oilskins. A flash of yellow lining now and again as they moved about. Woolen beanies pulled low across foreheads. Rain streaming down their faces as they struggled with the ropes, dragging the boat ever closer, as she rolled and surged against the rising swell, laughing and joking, oblivious to the elements raging around them.

As I watched, wooden crates were tossed across the divide and then almost immediately the men were heaving them back up onto the cobble-stoned quayside above. The silver black fish still dancing and twisting, fresh from the sea, and it came to me as I stood there watching, that *Erin* had been that way once. Men working around her with hearts and hands. I turned back to the boat. What had the old man said? "You'll get rid of it the same way it arrived. One piece at a time, one day at a time." And it dawned on me that I'd been walking around the shed for an hour thinking of all the problems I'd have cleaning the place out when all I needed to do was to make a start. I began tearing at the remaining newspaper then, and as I ripped it from the windows, I could feel my energy returning.

When I'd finished, I stood there looking around. Just the simple act of letting in some daylight seemed to have broken the spell. *Erin* looked different already, the dark red Plimsoll line on her faded white hull now standing out clearly, reminding me of the days when I'd helped my grandfather paint her bottom as she'd lent up against the harbor wall in between tides.

I started in on the rubbish, dragging pieces to the far end of the shed close to the big doors. The pounding rain adding a drumming urgency to the work. There were all sorts of things there, discarded by people over the years, old tables and chairs, a single mattress, a few packing cases, splintered fish boxes, bits and pieces of offcuts of timber, coils of rotting rope, newspapers in piles a metre deep, a broken oar, an old wooden rowing dinghy cut in half through the middle for some unknowable reason, and an ancient box record player complete with a megaphone-type speaking horn that I put to one side to examine later.

My ankle nagged at me constantly as I worked, but I was enjoying the sense of purpose, and I was still slaving away hours later. when the wicket gate opened and Mary Reardon stepped through, followed immediately by Boson, sniffing at the floor and peering around suspiciously with his huge goldfish eyes.

"Holy Mother of Mercy!" she exclaimed. "What in God's name are you up to in here?"

"I'm cleaning out the shed," I told her, "and the boat too. I can't sell her in that condition. I'm thinking of doing her up a bit. How did you know I was here?"

"Ah sure, you won't be doing much on Inis Mór without me knowing about it. I was waiting for a break in the weather to come over. It's our shed, you know. We'd have it pulled down years ago if it wasn't for *Erin.*" She was looking around. "There's been people in here that had no right to be, but you know how it is. They have a few drinks and then they want a few more."

"What about the rubbish? Can I burn it out in the yard?"

"You can, of course," she smiled. "It'll be a blessing to be rid of it. I don't know how you'll open those doors mind. The place was locked for years and the keys are lost. You might have to take a hacksaw to it. The weather's starting to clear out the back of the island. This rain won't last; it came on too sudden." She was looking around. "There should be plenty of good timber in here somewhere. Lorcan was to fix the boat years ago but nothing ever came of it." She paused. "Grace had new sails made up over there in Galway, new rigging too. They're up at the cottage. They cost a small fortune. The mast itself is only a few years old. We had a man working on her for a while but that all came to a stop when Grace fell ill. *Erin* was built in this very shed, her timbers bent over the fireplace there."

"Yes, I know. The old man told me."

"Which old man would that be, now?"

"The old guy I told you about. He's a boat builder, or he was. He knew my grandfather apparently. He's going to help me renovate her."

"Well isn't that grand," she was smiling. "Did you get his name?"

"No, I didn't," I said, feeling a little foolish. "I'll ask him next time."

"There's tea there now and a bite to eat." She put a reed basket on the bench by the side of the boat. "Lorcan asked would you like to come over for dinner sometime. There are still a few things for you to sign to do with the Will." As she stepped back out through the gate, she paused. "Your grandfather would be proud of you, Conor, sure *Erin* was his life."

I sat there on the sofa after she'd gone, Boson at my feet, a steaming mug of black tea in one hand, a thick beef sandwich in the other, and for the first time in a long time, I felt a sense of peace, both within myself and with the world around me.

* * *

After lunch, I turned my attention to the double doors. The padlock was rusted up solid and, after wasting an hour oiling it and trying out the various keys I'd found, I took a hacksaw to the chain and, after a few minutes of furious sawing, the lock joined the rest of the junk on the rubbish pile. Then I oiled the hinges, gave the doors a shove and watched as they swung open without further ado.

Erin stood like a prisoner released. Rays of sunlight infused with tiny golden specks of dust streaming in through the open doors, playing around her silent hull like long-lost memories returning, her graceful flowing lines offering hope and a promise of better things to come.

"Conas atá tú?" I turned to find one of the islanders standing by the wall, a pony and trap behind him on the quay. "You'd be Con Rua's boy. Mary said I'd find you here." He was leaning forward, both arms resting on the stone wall. A thickset, strongly built old man.

"Colm Feegan." He nodded. "I knew your father and his father before him." As I took the outstretched hand, he added, "And you're Conor?"

"Yes …" I said, "Conor O'Rourke." It wasn't something I'd planned or even thought about, but as I spoke the words, something fell into place inside me.

"Now there's a sight for sore eyes," he was peering up at *Erin.* "She was a fine little sea boat in her day. You're about to set her right, I believe?"

"Yes, as soon as I get the shed cleared out, we'll be starting in on the repairs."

"Good man yourself," he smiled. "Welcome home, Conor. It's grand to have an O'Rourke back here working on a boat."

* * *

The following morning, I strapped a yard brush to the crossbar of the bike and rode off down to Cill Rónáin, the head of the broom trailing out behind me like a chimney sweep on his way to work. The weather had eased and bursts of sunlight were breaking through the clouds occasionally as I rode along, streaming down across the island, playing over the rocks and fields and sparkling like a million scattered jewels over the dark blue waters beyond.

I pedaled through the winding lanes thinking of the tasks ahead. It was simple work, but enjoyable, and I was looking forward to getting started on the boat itself. Bosun was waiting by the big doors as I arrived, his stumpy tail quivering with anticipation as he commenced his welcome rhumba.

I began clearing out the inside of the hull immediately, tossing everything over the stern, sweeping down the decks and then cleaning out the cockpit. As soon as the boat was clear, I climbed back down the ladder and began trundling loads of junk over to the far corner of the yard in a wheelbarrow I discovered at the back of the shed. It was a long day but, by eight thirty that evening, the whole place was free of rubbish and swept clean, the cobble-stoned floor wet and shining black after I'd spent the last hour hosing out the final traces of dust and dirt.

I stood there for a while looking around, then I put away the tools, closed the main doors, pedaled the old bike back home and fell into bed, too exhausted to even think about food.

Chapter 17
Patches

The following morning, I was up at dawn and, after enjoying a coffee perched high on my rocky throne, I went inside and ate a huge breakfast of sausage, bacon, eggs, and toast before jumping on my bike and heading back into town.

The day was perfect, clear blue skies with a gentle breeze, and as I strained hard against the pedals outside of Kilmurvey, I realized that muscles I hadn't used in years were coming back to life.

As soon as I arrived at the shed, I lit a fire in the grate, then climbed up the ladder and began cleaning out the inside of the hull. It took me all morning. Crawling around on all fours, brushing out between the heavy wooden ribs and stringers, taking the tops off the bunks to swab out the storage space, scrubbing away the grime and mold that had accumulated over the years.

When the job was completed, I made a pot of tea, grabbed a few biscuits and then went back up again and sat in the companionway peering down into the empty hull. She was spotless. I felt a great sense of satisfaction followed immediately by doubt. What now? I thought. Cleaning out a boat's one thing, renovating a boat is something entirely different.

I had no idea at all as to where to begin. There was the obvious damage to take care of and, from where I sat, I could see the hole in the planking. The timber had shattered right through, splintered shards of wood reaching up like tortured fingers inside the empty hull. I studied the hole from the companionway as I drank my tea. Maybe I could repair it myself. I could remove the damaged part, cut a new length of timber to replace it, glue a piece of plywood over the whole area to make sure it didn't leak and then run a coat of paint over the patch to hide it, that would be a quick and easy way of fixing it.

"So! You've made a start."

The mug of tea went crashing down into the boat as I spun around. He was standing like a statue in the cockpit. The cap, the coat, the walking stick.

"Who are you?" I blurted out. "I don't even know your name!"

"You didn't know your own name," he smiled. "How could you possibly have known mine?"

"You frightened the life out of me," I said. "I didn't hear you come up the ladder."

"You've made a difference." He was looking around. "And below?" He indicated with his stick. "Are you finished below decks?"

"I've finished the cleaning part. I was just working out how to fix the hole."

"Show me," he indicated again with his stick.

I moved aside, then followed him down below, his eyes roaming around the hull, probing, evaluating.

"There's a few weeks work here," he declared at last. "Two or three months would be more like it."

"But the hole's the main thing, isn't it?"

"No." He was back to his blunt way of speaking. "The hole's the simple part. Most of the work will be in stripping her back to bare timber."

"Why would we want to do that? Can't we just paint over what's there now?"

"*Erin* is very old." His voice was deep and resonant inside the empty hull. "She's been painted over a dozen times already. Mostly by people who had no respect for her at all." He pointed to a plastic tabletop that had been screwed on to the forward bulkhead. "All that old rubbish will need to come off. We'll take her back to bare timber and check each nail and fastening."

"How long will all that take?" I asked.

"It will take as long as it takes," he said. "Look now, if we're to do this at all, then let's do it right." He removed his cap. "Why don't we take a look at that hole and see if we can't make a beginning. Pass me that crowbar there, if you would."

As I handed him the crowbar, he went down on his knees and, before I could stop him, he was prizing off the damaged plank.

"Hang on," I said. "We can save that plank. It's only broken in one place."

He turned.

"And how would you have me save it?"

"Well, all we need to do is to remove the broken piece, maybe a foot long, and then put a new piece back in. We could nail it and glue it, and then put a plywood patch over the whole thing to make sure it's waterproof. After it's painted over, you wouldn't even know it was there."

"I'm not in the habit of patching things up. That is the problem, not the solution," he nodded. "Look at *Erin*, look at the state she's in. Patched up and painted over. Shoddy repairs to a once noble vessel." He turned back to me again. "*Erin* is a gift boy, a gift from those who went before. When you pass her on to your own son, what condition will she be in?" He shook his head. "She'd need to be in better condition than she is now. That's the obligation right there. No, we're not here to patch things up, we're here to find out what's rotten and remove it. That's what happened over the years. People patching her up. Covering things over whilst the real troubles went unattended. Too greedy looking after their own interests to consider *Erin's* future. Would your grandfather have patched her up?" He pointed the hammer at me, looking like a giant in the confines of the cabin. "No. Anything that's rotten comes out, boy. Let us seek out the problems and address them."

He went back to work.

"I hope you know what you're doing," I said. "Are you sure you know how to replace that?"

"Go down below and help ease it off the last two frames. Work it off gently now. No sudden jerking or you'll damage her ribs."

I went down below and soon we were prizing a twenty-foot plank off the hull, leaving behind a gap that I could hardly bear to look at. When I went back up, he was still on his knees, scraping away at the edges of the newly exposed timber with a small, dagger-like knife.

"Just as I thought," he murmured. "Not a trace of rot. The fastenings are sound too, although we'll still check all the rest." He was smiling up at me. "After we're done, she'll be good for another sixty years. That's the test right there. Ask yourself that question. How will your decisions affect generations yet to come? The grandchildren you may never meet. How will they speak of you and what you left behind? When your own grandson is sailing this boat a hundred miles offshore, beating into a westerly gale and praying to God above to spare his soul, he wouldn't want the additional burden of having to worry about whether his grandfather's little patch of plywood and paint was about to stay true to him or not now, would he?"

Chapter 18
The Captain

"People are like boats." The old man was sorting through a pile of timber stacked up alongside the shed wall, pulling out a plank now and again, holding it up to one eye and squinting along the length as if taking aim down the barrel of a rifle. "If there's no respect, their lives soon fall apart."

He separated out three of the longer pieces. "Take those over to the bench there now, if you would, and bring that bag of tools along with you. We'll make a final decision when we have them tidied." Minutes later, he was clamping one of the planks in a vice on the bench top. "Now, let's see what we can do with this one."

I watched as he ran the plane up and down the length of wood. The long smooth strokes, steady and even, his body swaying like a dancer. A faint hissing noise as he stripped away the outer layers, the heady aroma of new cut timber swirling around us like a genie freed from a bottle.

"There you are now." He handed me the plane. "Let's see what you can do with that."

I hesitated for a moment, and then took a sweep at the plank, but the tool jammed immediately, the blade cutting deep into the timber.

"Imagine yourself skating over thin ice. There you go, not too much weight, just skimming over the top." I took another sweep at the plank and to my delight, the plane sailed across the surface smoothly, long slivers of shavings curling up like feathers around my hands. "There you are now." He was smiling. "There you have it!"

Soon I was swishing away, backwards and forwards, the wood changing from a dusty, rough-hewn length of timber to a fresh, clean cut plank before my eyes.

"When did the job in Sydney begin to go wrong?" He was standing off to one side, watching.

"I'm not sure. I guess I finally realized just how pathetic my job was. You know, writing jingles, dreaming up meaningless slogans, selling rubbish to people who should have known better. I just got tired of the whole thing. It was only the money that kept me going."

"And the trouble between yourself and your wife. When did that start?"

"It's hard to say. We had a big mortgage. I was working long hours and she was always going on about me not spending enough time with Tristan. I tried, but by the time I got home most nights, he was either asleep or on the way to bed. We argued about the job a lot and finally she just refused to work in the business at all. I felt betrayed. I guess that's when we started drifting apart."

"But you still love her?"

"I've always loved her," I turned back to the bench, "but I guess she's given up on me."

There was a long silence and I kept working away on the plank, turning it over occasionally to dress the other sides.

"She believed that you were ignoring your son?"

"Yes, that was part of it, but there were other things too. We were in the middle of a major advertising campaign for one of the big tobacco companies when a good friend of ours died of lung cancer. That's when my depression started. The doctor put me on Prozac but that didn't help much. I tried positive thinking and all that other stuff, but none of it worked for long. Then she went off to Brittany to look after her mother."

"The light's getting away on us." He nodded towards the hearth. "Why don't you put the kettle on, and we'll call it a day."

By the time I'd organized the tea, he was sitting in the armchair, his leather pouch open on the table beside him.

"Depression can be a terrible thing," he said. "But there's no great mystery as to its source. It's the soul calling out to us, unhappy with the way we're conducting our lives. All the pills in the world won't fix that. The only solution is to change the way you're living. Listen now, if you would, with an open mind." He shifted back in his chair and closed his eyes, his voice calm and deep in the quiet of the shed.

"When the life force withers in you, when your Spirit dwindles low

Seek you out that ageless source from whence all power flows

When did you lose your meaning, where abandoned you your gift?

What hope to find your Purpose, with Soul now cast adrift?"

I sat there in the silence after he'd finished. The words had touched something inside me, like a half-forgotten dream waiting to be known.

"Where's that from?" I asked.

"From the spoken tradition, taken from the Irish."

"What does it mean?"

"You don't know?" He looked up.

"It's suggesting that we all have some sort of gift, I guess. Do you believe that?"

"Every human being comes to earth with a gift. That's been known throughout the ages. If that gift is not used, then that life is wasted. Or if we misuse the gift, as many do, then it will wither within us. That's often the cause of depression. You see, if we're to concentrate our lives solely around our own selfish ends, what hope is there for our children, or indeed for our world?"

He'd taken his pipe from the pouch and was tamping tobacco into the shiny brown bowl.

"Most people are bred away from their gift by well-meaning parents. Or sometimes by a teacher trying to mold and shape them into something they're not. Ignoring the innate gifts and talents that were given to the child at birth, condemning them to a miserable existence by guiding them away from their true purpose in life." He put a match to the pipe and took a few puffs before continuing. "Look, I'll tell you a story now about how this happens and listen well. This is a true story, although it would be better if it were not."

He paused again before settling back in his chair.

"A long, long time ago, but then again in some ways, not so long ago at all, in a place known to few, yet frequented by many, there lived a certain ship's captain. Now he was a decent enough man, faithful to his wife and a good father to their only son. Hard in some ways, as captains were in those days, but a fair man, a man respected by all who knew him. He'd risen from a cabin boy of fourteen to become master of a square-rigged sailing ship by the age of twenty-one. Before he was thirty, he'd sailed every ocean known to man. His knowledge of the sea and the trading ports of the world was unrivalled but, although he served in the employ of just one company for many years, he was an ambitious man and he yearned to be master of his own vessel."

The old man took a few long puffs on his pipe before continuing.

"Well, the son was a shy young dreamer of a boy, fascinated by music and storytelling and on the evening of his twelfth birthday, he asked his father would it be possible for him to bring back a violin from abroad for he'd been told the best were not to be found in Ireland. The captain had listened quietly but after hearing the lad out, he took him by the shoulders and looked him in the eye. 'You're to be a seaman.' he told him. 'Like your father and grandfather before you. You may play the violin but always remember that's what it is, boy … play. You're to be a seaman, that is your destiny.' Well, within two years of that date, the captain had raised money enough to build his own ship. One hundred and forty feet long and forty-five feet in the beam, she was one of the fastest vessels afloat and within months, she was plying the trade routes of the world. The ship was sound and her captain fearless and soon they were bringing home tea, cloth, and spices from the Indies and the islands beyond."

The old man was gazing into the fireplace as if in a dream.

"That Christmas was the happiest the captain's wife could remember. The family was together for the first time in years and their business was prospering. The son was fourteen by then, a tall, dark-haired, sensitive young lad, highly regarded in the artistic circles of Galway. Well, towards the end of that spell away from the sea, the captain's wife had brought the boy to him one evening in his study. She told her husband that their son had a request and the captain listened quietly as the boy began. The lad was nervous at first, but as he warmed to his story, he told his father that he had a passion for music and storytelling and asked his permission to pursue his studies in that direction. The captain listened carefully, encouraging the young man to express himself, but feeling a rising anger within. He felt betrayed by what he heard. He felt that in his prolonged absences, his wife had filled the young lad's head full of silly dreams. 'And what of the sea?' he'd asked when the young lad had finished. 'What of your heritage?' The mother had spoken then. 'He fears the sea,' she said, 'and has no desire to be a seaman. God has given our son a gift, let us be thankful for that.' The captain had sent the boy from the room before turning to his wife. 'My son does not fear the sea,' he told her. 'How could he? He has never known the sea. He knows only what you have told him of the sea. He fears the stories that you have bred into him, and he fears the unknown."

He threw a fresh log on the fire and spent a few moments poking at it before continuing.

"Now the captain had always tried to be a good father, but he knew the ways of the world and he knew that young men needed discipline to prosper, so he'd summoned the boy back into the room. 'You're to accompany me on my next voyage,' he told him. 'We sail within the week. You will sign on as cabin boy as I did at your age, and you will be allowed a small cabin, but you will be treated like any other member of the crew. We'll be gone for more than a year. You may bring your violin with you, but you will work each day as a seaman.'"

The old man paused again and took a few puffs on his pipe, blowing the smoke out slowly as if remembering.

"The captain told his son that if he gave of his best whilst they were away, he would be allowed on his return to choose freely whether it was the sea or the arts that he would dedicate his life to. The mother protested but the captain was firm. 'He's a sailor,' he told her, 'or soon will be. People are shaped by circumstance, not dreams.' Those were his final words and nothing she said afterwards could shake him. Well, the son obeyed, although he dreaded the sea. He'd spent his childhood watching his mother's face as the winter gales had lashed their home. He'd seen her on those stormy mornings staring out across the wild, grey ocean, wondering whether or not she'd ever see her husband again and he'd felt all his life that the sea held some unfathomable terror."

He was peering into the fire fixedly now, lost in the story.

"They set sail in February, bound for Australia around Cape Horn. He'd gone the other way many times, but time was money, and the Horn is quicker if the weather is any way right. At first the voyage seemed blessed. The seas were calm, the winds blew true, and the captain watched with pride as his son worked at his daily tasks. The other seamen accepted the lad readily enough, they knew he was not one of them, but he had no arrogance about him, and he did his work without complaint.

"Well, the early days of the voyage were grand. They ran before favorable winds out of Dublin before swinging the ship south, down into the Roaring Forties in preparation for rounding the Horn but, as they approached the dreaded Cape, the weather began to deteriorate. The wind and seas rose higher each day and as they did, the captain watched in dismay as he began to recognize the first signs of fear in his son's face. He noticed a hesitancy as the boy came up on deck. A half-concealed eagerness to return down below when his duties were done. A look of dread in the young lad's eyes as he watched the mountainous seas rearing up at their stern, and the way he gripped on to the ship's rails as he stood each watch.

"At first the captain was unconcerned, convinced that his son would rise above it all, but then the boy fell sick and as the days wore on and he stayed below decks, a certain tension grew between them. The captain talked to his son each morning, encouraging him and telling him stories of how he had been sick himself on his first voyage."

The old man paused for a moment before going on.

"The truth was the young lad loved his father and dreaded the thought of letting him down, but as the tension between them grew, the lad found it difficult to express himself. He'd brought his violin along with him and sometimes at night, he would play, hoping that his father might hear him and know that he was trying to be brave. The captain did hear but, as he stood there listening to the strains of the music rising up above the sounds of the wind and water, he began to wonder how it was that the boy could play his violin for hours on end and still be unable to meet his duties on deck. The music began to haunt the captain and soon he found himself wondering if the boy was simply malingering ..."

His voice trailed off and I wondered if he was upset, but then he seemed to pull himself together and he took up the story again.

"You see, what the captain did not understand was that the young lad played to give himself heart. That violin was the only thing he had left. He played it to stay in contact with his soul, for everything else he had known in the world had been stripped away ..."

He broke off the story again and went over to the half open door of the shed. I could see him fiddling with his pipe and when he returned to his chair a few minutes later, I sat there watching as he drew it back to life.

"It all came to a head the night they were approaching the Horn," he began softly. "The barometer was falling. The weather was intense. The men hanging on to rope handrails as they fought their way through each watch. The boat rolling her gunwales under as each successive wave swept on past them into the blackness ahead. The wind howling through the rigging, rain beating down ceaselessly. White water boiling along her decks, the ship's planking straining and groaning like condemned men's souls as they ploughed their way through the heart of the storm."

When the old man spoke of the sea, I could almost hear the winds howling, and I sat there mesmerized.

"Now the captain had no fears for the vessel, or his crew, and it came to him that night that, if he could convince his son to spend an hour or two up on deck, he might well come to terms with his fear and break the hold it had on him." The old man shook his head. "Well, he'd gone down below decks with the best of intentions, but the boy was playing the violin as he walked into his cabin and the captain snapped. He told his son that he was a disgrace to the family and that he was ashamed of him. He told him that the agreement between them was broken and that he would never be allowed to play the violin again, and finally, in his rage, he'd snatched the violin away from the boy and smashed it to the floor, stamping it to smithereens as his son looked on."

He stopped speaking for a moment, and just sat there as if remembering. When he began again, his voice was softer.

"The boy came up on deck an hour or so later of his own will. 'What would you have me do, father?' was the only thing he'd said. But the captain, ashamed of what he'd done, had been unable to speak and had taken him instead to the bow of the boat where the boson stood watch. 'Keep an eye on him,' he'd told the boson quietly. 'Put a rope around him if it gets any worse.' The last he saw of his son as he went below to rest, he was standing on the foredeck, staring fixedly into the foaming waters."

The old man turned away slightly, and I thought I caught a glint of a tear in his eye.

"They woke the captain an hour later to tell him that the lad was missing. They searched the ship, but to no avail. It was then that the captain gave the order to come about, to turn back." He was shaking his head. "An impossible task, boy. Square-riggers around the Horn when the storms are raging? There is no turning back. Not for man, nor for God above. Well, the men protested, for they knew the task was hopeless, but the captain insisted, and by pure force of will, they obeyed him. As they turned beam on to the gale, the boat began to founder but still he pressed on. The ship staggered up once, twice and three times, but she was being overwhelmed by the sheer weight of the seas and the men knew that soon they would all be lost. Finally, they rebelled and, after a terrible struggle, they overpowered him, locked him in his cabin and swung the ship back on course."

"So, they mutinied?"

"That's not mutiny, boy." He spoke the words softly. "If a skipper is incapable of carrying out his duties, the crew has the right to replace him." He paused again for a long moment before returning to the story. "Some said the boy went over the side by his own hand, others said he was washed from the decks by a wave. Whatever the cause, he was never seen again. Legend has it that by the time they put into Val Pariso, the captain's hair was as white as snow. What is known is that the moment they docked, the crew deserted the ship."

The old man went quiet again and he just sat there for a few moments without moving.

"And that's how it ends?" I asked. "The captain never went back to sea again. Is that it?"

"Oh no." He looked up. "That's not what happened. You see, the boson stood loyal, he blamed himself for the loss of the boy. The ship's cook stayed on too. He'd lost a son of his own to the sea and he'd cared for the lad during his sickness. They scoured the waterfront for crew. The captain told them they'd be sailing to find a lost boy but by that time, the story had got out and he was considered insane by many. Only a handful of men signed on. He found them in the drinking holes along the waterfront. Drunken men, lonely men, failed men, and every one of them had lost a son or a daughter. They were lost souls themselves and yet somehow, they understood the need for this hopeless mission. He set out with a ramshackle crew searching for a boy who would have been dead for weeks. A group of old men sailing a doomed vessel, attempting the impossible, attempting to sail around Cape Horn against the prevailing winds." He turned back to the fire. "She never returned."

"So, she was lost around the Horn?"

He was staring fixedly into the flames.

"She never returned," he said again.

"And you think that's the way he wanted it?"

"Some claim to have seen her," he was speaking softly now, and I was beginning to wonder just how far he got into his own stories, "sailing close by the Horn. There were sightings of her from other vessels, reliable sightings by trustworthy men. Always in heavy weather, always sailing in the wrong direction. Sailing back into the prevailing winds."

"Like a ghost ship," I said.

"Yes, indeed," he murmured. "Like a ghost ship. They all said the same thing. She sailed close on by them, all canvas raised, nobody on deck. A single light in an aft cabin and the sound of a violin rising up over the roar of the wind and water."

"What was the name of the boat?"

He looked up at me for a long moment, but then turned away and stared back into the fire again.

"I'm not sure." He murmured. "It's an old story."

"And that's …" I began, but he was still talking.

"He's been sighted too, or so they say, in seaports around the world. Sightings by men who had sailed with him, men who knew him well. Still dressed in his captain's uniform, forever asking after a lost boy." The old man stood up suddenly, looking up at the roof as if looking up at the moon. "It's late," he said. "I must be on my way."

As he pulled on his cap, I ventured: "How old are you?"

"And why would that be important?" He turned towards the door. "You do ask the strangest questions, do you not?"

Chapter 19
Letters

After the old man had gone, I closed the shed doors and climbed on my bike, images of my own son returning to haunt me as I rode back home along the darkened lanes. I considered stopping as I passed the pay phone at the end of the quay then decided against it, but as soon as I got back to the cottage, I unpacked my notepad and sat down at the kitchen table.

I stared at the blank sheet of paper for some time, feeling awkward and not sure of how to begin, and then finally I wrote:

Dear Tristan,

I looked at that for a moment then crumpled it and began again.

Dear son,

That felt too stilted, so I tore off another page and tried again.

Hi Tristan,

I drew a line through that immediately, angered that I couldn't even get past a clichéd beginning, then I got up and put the kettle on.

When the tea was made, I went out into the backyard and stood there for a long while looking out over a shadowed sea. A sliver of silver moon, easing its way past a dark cluster of clouds, was rising up towards the heaven's way out across the water, and as I watched its ascent, I felt an emptiness I hadn't experienced since childhood. I thought of the old man's story, wondering if any of it was true, knowing that I didn't want it to be.

It was a quiet evening, a soft westerly breeze coming in over the ocean carrying with it a smell of salt and wet seaweed. The peace and calm around only serving to increase my sense of isolation. I looked up at the night sky for some time wondering how it was that I couldn't put two words together to address to my only son, then I went back inside and sat down to the next blank sheet of paper.

Giselle,

I hope things are going better with your Mum. It must be tough for you. I looked after my own mother for almost two years, and I know how hard it can be. Give her my love and tell her I'm thinking of her.

I've been trying to write to Tristan, but for some reason the words just won't come out. I'll try again later this evening.

I've been working on an old sailing boat that my grandfather built here years ago. It was left to me in Grace's Will along with a cottage and some money. As you know, the company's finished and our unit is on the market. Once it's sold, and the mortgage settled, the remaining funds will go into our joint bank account. I want you to take it. It's yours, you earned it.

Giselle, I'm not sure how to say this but I'm beginning to realize just how far off track my life has been these past few years. I don't know how we got to this point, but I know that it wasn't your fault, I've no one to blame but myself. Things are different here; people talk to each other. I've been working with an old boat builder and he's been showing me the ropes. Once the boat's finished, I'd like to visit you in Brittany. I miss you,

Love,

Conor

I read through the letter a couple of times, then turned the page and tried again with my son.

Dear Tristan,

I hope this finds you well. I'm in Ireland now as you know. I've been thinking about you a lot recently and I really do miss you. My grandmother left me an old sailing boat here that I have to do a lot of work on, but as soon as the job's finished, I'm going to sell her and come to see you in Brittany. I know I've made you a lot of promises in the past that I haven't kept, but when we get together this time, I promise we'll go fishing, okay? Just you and me.

I love you,

Dad, XXX

I went outside and stood there gazing across the darkened sea, ashamed of the stilted words, cursing myself for not being able to write a decent letter to my only child, terrified that I might never see him again.

Tristan had been a blessing. The first few years we took him everywhere with us. We were inseparable. Sometimes, when Giselle was too busy to come, I'd take him off up the coast, just the two of us. There was a little motel whose grounds ran straight down to the beach, and we'd spend a night or two there. We'd fish, run on the beach, watch TV way too late, and eat McDonald's every day. Secret men's business, Giselle called it.

I sat there in the dark, remembering his smile, his trusting face, his innocence, and his tears at the airport that final day.

And then the feelings came to me, across the night dark tide

A stone-cold breath of loss and pain, like the time my father died

Images from another world, a coffin draped in snow

A father lowering to a grave, the King now down below

Standing by a mound of earth, mother cold alone

Standing stiff and silent, wondering where was home

Staring out across an ocean, not knowing the death was shared

Listening to the things she'd said, wondering had I heard,

'Forget about him now', she'd said, 'forget about this place

Forget about this island, this is not your home or race ...'

Yet still in splintered memories, he'd returned to me at times

His shoulders wide and willing, his hands with rope entwined

His voice the deepest cadence, my heart would ever know

His body turning in a field, his smell fast in my bones

His calm dark eyes beside the fire as he told the mythic tales

Images slumbering deep within, dark origins concealed

The grief of losing that first man

The wound that never healed ...

Chapter 20
Gifts

When I arrived at the shed the following morning, the old man was already there, the tools laid out on the bench, the kettle whistling away on the hearth.

"Maidin mhaith," he greeted me.

"Conas ata tu." The words came easily, as if lying there, waiting to be said.

I watched as he poured the water into the teapot, wondering if he ever took the greatcoat off.

"You slept well?" He was standing with his back to me, clouds of steam run through with rays of sunlight rising around him in the cold of early morning.

"No, not really."

"I was here from the dawn," he continued. "We'll need to make a start on that paint, it will take time. But first, the tea."

"Not for me thanks," I told him. "I just had breakfast."

He nodded and sat down in his chair.

"We have our work cut out for us now all right, every bit of that old paint will need to come off."

“I’ve never done that sort of work,” I told him.

“Don’t be worrying about that. Sure, it’s in your blood.”

“So you think being an O’Rourke makes me a boat builder?”

“I said it was in your blood. There’d be other things there too, no doubt.”

“You mean the gift you were talking about?”

“That’s right,” he nodded.

“And you think mine’s tied up with boats?”

“Boats may well be a part of it.” He took a drink of his tea. “I’d have thought your gift would have been clear to you by now.”

“You mean you know what it is?”

“Perhaps, but that’s not for me to say. That’s the very nature of the problem right there, people telling others what they should be doing with their lives. Parents, teachers, friends. Well-meaning people no doubt, but still mostly people who had no idea what their own purpose was in life.”

“But you think you know what mine is?”

“Perhaps.” He stood up and carried his teacup over to the bench. “Now then, let’s see what we have here.” I watched as he sorted through the tools, selecting out two scrapers and a few sheets of sandpaper. “There we are now. Why don’t we a make a start.”

Most of the old paint came off easily, flaking away before each thrust. But there were hard places too, lumps set like concrete that would bring the tool to a sudden, wrist-jarring halt.

I stood back and watched the old man working. He never paused. Paint flying off around him in all directions as if he knew some secret formula of which I was completely unaware.

"Look." He took my wrist in both his big hands and began sliding the scraper backwards and forwards along the length of the planks. "Always with the grain boy, never against it. Go after what's risen, don't be worrying about the bits that stick. We'll come back to them later. There now, do you see? It will rise of its own accord. She's been drying out here for years. That's it, leave the hard bits be, don't let them slow you down. We'll deal with them later."

Soon I was scraping away steadily, following the planks along, one after the other.

"See the layers?" He was pointing out the different colors. "See that? Half of that old paint's just falling off. Look at it: black, grey, green, any old color. Cheap paint, splashed on. No preparation, no pride. See there?" He was pointing with the edge of his scraper. "See the bottom layers? Still there after all these years. But it all has to come off now, inside and out. We'll take her back to the original *Erin* and see what she's made of." He looked up at me. "It's the same as yourself. You've no need to be asking me what your purpose is. Strip away everything that's not you. Take away all the old paint jobs that were done to you. The schooling, some of the old ideas the family may have put into you, the jobs and grandiose things you've dreamt up yourself. All your old nonsense. Strip all that away and what will you find? You'll find yourself, boy, that's what you'll find. And your purpose will be there underneath it all, still eager and ready to express itself."

"But I have no idea what it would be."

"Look to your gifts." He was smiling. "There's the clue right there. Follow your gifts. Follow your heart!"

"I don't think that would've worked for me," I said. "I had to earn a living too, you know."

"Ah now, sure people have an endless array of excuses. Not many of them would hold water."

"Look, I've worked hard for the last ten years. Work wasn't an excuse for me. I had a family to look after."

"You've been separated from your family for a year." He was looking across at me, his eyes steady. "Is that where the fancy career took you?"

"Why don't you give it rest," I told him. "You're jumping to a lot of conclusions."

"Perhaps." He nodded. "Perhaps I am."

We worked away steadily for the next few hours, scraping and sanding, the paint stripping off to reveal the solid oak planking beneath. We didn't speak again for a long time, but my mind kept going back to what he'd said.

"I'm going up to the store," I told him. "Do you want me to get you something for lunch?"

"I'm grand," he smiled. "You just look after yourself."

On the way up the road, I called in at the post office. A century's old, whitewashed cottage with a heavy thatched roof set back a little from the road. A small brass bell on the doorframe heralding my arrival.

"Good day to you, sir, and a fine day it is."

A small, wiry little man was observing me, stony-faced over the top of the counter.

"Is there such a thing as priority post on Inis Mór?" I said.

"There is indeed, sir, believe it or not. Ever since the Celtic Tiger reared its unlovely head, we've been getting involved with all that type of thing."

"I want to send these letters to Brittany."

He stared at them for a long moment and then put them back down on the counter.

"You have no return address on them," he nodded as if agreeing with himself. "And that's needed for the priority."

I scribbled *Tír na nÓg Cottage, Kilmurvey. Inis Mór. Eire* on the letters and gave them back to him. He examined them again for a moment or two and then looked up.

"You'd be Con Rua's boy so."

"Yes," I told him. "Conor O'Rourke,"

"You know there's a phone up there in the cottage now, don't you? It's just that Grace has it well hid." He winked at me. "Take a look in the cupboard under the stairs. You'll find it in there if I'm not mistaken." He held out a hand. "Timothy O'Sullivan. Postmaster, post sorter, postman and, according to my good wife, God bless her cotton socks, post just about everything else too. I knew your father well; he was a decent man."

"Thank you," I told him. "How long will it take for those letters to get to France?"

"No more than a day or two with the priority on them." He stamped the envelopes before putting them away in a heavy canvas bag. "You're working on *Erin* now, I believe, and a fine little thing she is. Kieran O'Rourke converted her from a fishing boat to a cruiser just the last few years of his life, God rest his soul. He was a great man with the boats altogether."

"So, I've been told. We should have her ready in a month or two." As I turned to leave, I remembered Wesley. "Oh, and by the way, I've been expecting a parcel from Dublin. Some coffee. Could you let me know as soon as it arrives?"

"The moment there's anything here for you, I'll have it up on your kitchen table in no time. You may rest assured of that." He nodded across the road. “Now you know there’s plenty of Nescafe over at the store there now, don’t you?”

Chapter 21
Wounds

When I got back to the boatshed, the old man was sitting by the fire, Boson curled up at his feet as if he'd known him all his life.

"There are some sandwiches there if you'd like," I told him. "Ham and cheese, there wasn't much of a choice up there."

"Just the tea would be grand, thank you," he indicated. "It's ready there on the hearth." As I filled the mugs, he reached for the leather pouch. "Will this disturb you?" He was holding up his pipe, eyebrows raised.

"No, not at all."

"We must maintain one vice." He was packing tobacco into the dark brown bowl, tamping it down with a thumb. "One vice and one vice only." He put a match to the pipe and, as I sat there watching, he puffed it into life. "Struggling with that reminds us that we are so much less than the gods." His eyes were studying me through the drifting strands of smoke. "And be careful which one you choose, some of them would kill you, given half the chance."

"And the pipe won't?" I said.

"No, the pipe won't kill you, or at least, not as quickly." He settled back into the armchair, smoke curling around his head like a mystery to be solved. “No, it’s generally people’s wounds what spoils their lives.”

“How do you mean, wounds?”

“Well, you’ll find that most people carry wounds of one sort or another. Some are wounded in the family, an abusive mother or father. It doesn’t have to be violence that does it, there’s plenty harmed just by being criticized too much. Or it could be a tragedy, like a death or a divorce.” He paused. “Wounded by our way of life, you could say, betrayed by a culture that has forsaken its traditions and beliefs.” He paused for a moment before continuing. “When people are damaged in that way, they tend to lose touch with their souls.”

“And so, what happens to them then?”

“Well, that’s easy enough answered. Once you’ve lost connection to your soul, you’ll have no idea as to who you are or what your purpose is in life. How could you? It’s your soul that carries the gift.” He was watching me intently. “That’s when the big house, the big car and the big salary become more important than your family or friends. It comes down to a loss of soul, boy, a loss of spirit. You’re not the only one, sure Jaysus, it’s an epidemic!”

“What do you mean by loss of spirit?” I said. “You mean loss of religion?”

“I’m not talking about religion. I’m talking about people losing their connection to their own spirit. That’s when all the other problems begin. First, they forget what’s important in life. Then they lose the passion for the things they once loved. Eventually they lose enthusiasm for life itself.” He looked up. “Some go off seeking comfort in a bottle. It’s no coincidence that alcohol is called a spirit. But it’s a false spirit of course, a pale substitute for the life force. The drugs are as bad, if not worse. Why do you think they call it heroin? They put it up their arms trying to become heroes, *hero-in,* do you understand? Why? Because they can't face the pain of not knowing who they are anymore. The pain of not having any real purpose in life. The pain of being alienated from their own souls. Others become obsessed with food, work, sex or money, forever looking for something that might help fill the hole in the soul. Others run from one romance to another." He paused and looked across at me. "What about yourself? What do you struggle with? And don't go telling me there's nothing for I'll not believe you. So, what is it? The drink, the drugs, fancy women, money, work, gambling? Come on now, there's a hundred others. What ails you? Name your demons."

I was feeling trapped. It wasn't something I wanted to get into.

"Well, I drank a bit in Sydney," I offered.

"Sure Jaysus, there's nothing wrong with taking a drink now and again. We all do that. Unless, of course, it's the Irish *bit* that you're talking about?"

"Well, I probably drank a bit too much at times. At least, Giselle thought I did."

"And that's it, that's your only vice? Holy Jaysus, it must be a saint I'm talking to!"

He was smiling across at me, his eyes twinkling.

"Well …" I hesitated. "Look, I did a few recreational drugs occasionally, okay. Nothing too heavy, just the light stuff."

"Ohhhh, Conor!" It came out like a sigh. "You must be seen as a terrible loss to the advertising world. Recreational drugs! What a lovely expression … and nothing too heavy … just the light stuff. Now, isn't that reassuring? Sure Jaysus, I'm starting to feel deprived myself just sitting here listening to you." But then he sat forward in his chair. "And what were they called?" he demanded. "Do they not have names?"

I hesitated. He was an old guy; he probably wouldn't understand.

"I understand well enough, just answer the question!"

"What …?" I said but he continued straight on.

"Their names boy, they must've had names."

"Well," I hesitated again, "I smoked a bit of marijuana sometimes, not much, and maybe a little coke now and again, you know, just enough to get things started."

He was peering at me intently through the wisping trails of tobacco smoke.

"Anything else?"

"No. I've been on antidepressants for a year or two, but I told you about that."

"And you're still taking that stuff?"

"No, not at the moment. I haven't had any since I left Australia." I was beginning to wonder where he was headed. "Look, I don't have a problem with drugs, and I stopped drinking over a year ago."

"I have no judgments to make of you, boy, none at all." He was shaking his head. "I'm way too old for that. My only interest is to help you understand how you lost your way." He went quiet for a while then, puffing away on his pipe, the wispy clouds wafting around his head like a half-formed dream. "There's a poem," he said finally. "Taken from the Irish, it would go something like this:

Blame not your kin, hold not to grief, no matter what was borne

Your Purpose lies within your reach and with your Soul was formed

Those childhood days you choose yourself, your soul intent on learning

But unless you rise to meet this Call, you will go forever yearning

"Why do you always talk in rhyme?" I said. "And how come it rhymes anyway? If you're translating it from Irish, how can it rhyme?" He was sitting there motionless, observing me, as smoke curled up in lazy swirls towards the rafters above. And then suddenly it dawned on me. "You just made that up, didn't you?" And immediately another realization. "You make them all up, don't you?" We stared at each other for a long moment. "Who are you?" I said. "You're not from the island, are you?"

"Do you understand, or not?" His voice was calm in the silence of the shed.

"I'm not sure. You're saying that our childhood prepares us for our purpose in life, is that it?"

"That's correct." He nodded. "The circumstances of childhood, whether good, bad, shapes and molds our gifts and our talents and in doing so, prepares us for our calling in life."

"So, you're saying that losing my father when I was seven was a good thing. Is that what you're saying?"

"I'm not saying that at all, as well you know. What I'm saying is that, without the exact circumstance of your father's life, you would not be the man you are today. I'm saying that the pain you endured in those early years molded and shaped your character, your gifts, and your purpose in life." He stared at me for a moment before going on. "But for you to appreciate that, for you to integrate that into your being, you would first need to honor your father's life." He paused again. "And also, of course, his death."

"Meaning what?" I didn't want to hear any more.

He leant forward in the chair.

"I've never heard you speak of him. His name never crosses your lips." He spoke quietly, but the words cut into me. "You return to Inis Mór after thirty years of silence, carrying another man's name, bringing with you all the emptiness of the new world. You talk of selling Tír na nÓg, the cottage of your ancestors, as if it were nothing to you. You speak of *Erin* here as if she's just something to be exploited for profit." He paused and I sat there, unable to break his gaze. "When your father died," he continued softly, "did you grieve his passing?"

"I don't remember," I said.

"You were old enough." His voice was deep in the stillness of the shed. "There would be memories."

"I don't recall," but tears were welling in my eyes.

"Some part of you remembers," he nodded. "That's plain to see. Open your heart, boy. Let him come to you."

Suddenly, I found myself struggling to contain emotions I'd suppressed for thirty years. Disowned images of my father's face flickering across my mind like clips from an old black and white movie.

"Can you see him?" The old man's voice was coming in again. "Where is he, boy?"

"In the car." I was struggling to control my voice. "In the front seat of the car." I stopped abruptly, unable to continue.

"Go on." He said gently. "Go on, if you can."

"I thought ..." I stopped, a surge of grief choking off my voice. "When my mother told me he was dead, I didn't believe her. Even when I saw the coffin, I didn't believe her. I made up a story that he was hiding in the boat somewhere, pretending to be dead. I guess I just couldn't accept that he'd left me." I stopped again, overwhelmed by grief and shame.

"Con Rua didn't leave you." He was shaking his head. "Your father would never have left you, not while there was breath in his body, not this side of the grave. Con Rua died in the car that night and you've never forgiven yourself for leaving him there."

I stared down at the cobbled floor, struggling to control my emotions.

"Did you ever grieve that night? Did you ever weep over his death?"

"That all happened thirty years ago," I said. "Weeping about it now is not going to bring my father back."

"No, it won't," he said quietly. "But it might bring Tristan's father back."

The words hit me like a blow, scattering my thoughts and taking away my breath as some internal barrier that had held back an age-old reservoir of guilt and grief collapsed, and I put my face in my hands and began to weep, an uncontrollable sobbing that shook my entire body. I don't know how long it went on, but when it finally subsided and I looked up, the old man was watching me.

"That's your wound right there, Conor." His voice was barely audible in the quiet of the shed. "The wound that separated you from your soul. Your mother denied her own broken heart and, in doing so, made it impossible for you to own yours. You lost your pain, but you lost your Self along with it." He stopped for a moment before going on. "And for you to come back from where you are now, that wound would need to be honored. To weep for a lost father is a noble thing. Con Rua is dead. Take flowers to his grave, he has waited for you these many years." He paused. "Talk to him, make your atonement with him, set him free, release him from the prison of the past and let his strength come into you. Honor your father, take in his spirit. Then and only then will you know who it is that stands behind you."

"Stands behind me?"

"Yes, stands behind you. We all need to know who stands behind us. Our fathers, our mothers, our grandfathers, our grandmothers. You can't waste your life blaming your parents. You come from a long line of ancestors, as do we all. There'd be poets, prophets, Seanachaís, warriors and Kings amongst them, no doubt. Men and women of courage and integrity. And they all hold a meaningful place in your lineage. You're an O'Rourke. The blood of your ancestors runs through your veins. For centuries, your family has built boats on this island and given Seanachaí to the world." He leant towards me. "You've been lost for a long time, boy. Lost without a father, lost to yourself, lost without a purpose in life. How could you possibly become a decent father?" And suddenly he was speaking in rhyme again.

"May it be your own dark footprints he follows in those early snows

May your shadow be the one he seeks, when his courage is running low

Let it be your own voice singing, when he goes searching for the truth

May your heartbeat be the truest he remembers from his youth

Let him feel the life force in you, let him know the sacred sign

Let him look back through the ages to own his name and line

Let him harbor his own passions, let him use the gifts he bore

Have your love support his purpose as you uphold the ancient lore

So he knows then at your passing there are things that have no cost

Then he will grieve a loving father that he knows he never lost."

We sat there for a long while, not saying anything.

"I never really felt like a man." I spoke it into the silence without thought. "I always felt as if there was something wrong with me, something missing. You know, as if I wasn't enough somehow."

"You have a wound, Conor. It's a common enough thing."

"I never knew how to be a father," I said. "Where do you start?"

"You start with yourself." He pointed the stem of the pipe at me. "We teach best by example. Find your own purpose in life and follow it. Lead the way. You don't need any of that other old nonsense. Mercedes Benz, nightclubs, drink, pills." He was smiling again. "Recreational drugs, indeed! Drink, drugs and illusions, trying to fill a hole in the soul that can only be filled by meaning. You have a gift, make good use of it. Find your purpose in life and give your heart to it. You come from a race of heroes, Conor O'Rourke, stand up and take your place among them!" He got up and began knocking the bowl of his pipe on the brick hearth surrounding the fireplace, the grey, white ash scattering down across the orange red flames. "*Erin* awaits us." He was heading back towards the ladder. "Let us not disappoint her."

Chapter 22

Cú Chulainn and the Banshee

We finished sanding late that day and as I went around the shed tidying up, the old man stood by the big double doors, looking out across the harbor.

"It's a fine evening for a walk." He was tapping his pipe out against the corner of the limestone wall. "What do you think, are you up for it?"

"Yes, I could do with some fresh air."

We closed the double doors at eight, a tiny sliver of silver moon rising quietly over a dark ocean, stars set as intense bright specks on an ink black canvas, winking down quietly as we walked back along the deserted quayside.

"We'll take the sea road," he said. "It's longer, but it's a nice walk."

We turned off at the end of the quay. A low stone wall running alongside a narrow winding track. A thatched roof cottage standing whitewashed and alone in the night, lights slanting down sideways through half-drawn curtains, glimpses of children's faces around a kitchen table, an old horse standing thoughtful by a wall. Straight lines of potatoes dug into a nearby field. The ruins of an ancient church, haunted and austere in its own private enclosure. The lane twisting its crooked way along by the shore. The old man walking at a steady, even pace. The sound of his stick tapping occasionally on the stone path.

"Grace dreamt of having the boat rebuilt for years." He glanced at me sideways. "She had a young fella over from Galway for a while, you know. Now there was a disaster if ever there was one." He was shaking his head. "He had no idea at all what he was about, the poor lad. Just needed a job, I suppose." We continued on for a while and then he added: "She fell ill then, that put a stop to all that."

"You said she was warned of my father's death," I said. "Who warned her?"

"She was sung to, forewarned of a loss in the family. She paid no heed to it. She blamed herself for that for the rest of her life."

"How was she warned?"

"She was sung to," he said again, "by the Banshee."

"The Banshee? The Banshee's a myth, isn't it?"

He stopped in the middle of the track and turned to me, the moonlight reflecting softly in his dark green eyes.

"You know nothing of the Banshee?"

"I've heard of it, but I've no idea what it actually is. My mother used to say it was a female hare, crying out at night, and people turned that into a ghost story somehow."

"No, that is not true." He said the words quietly, then pointed with his stick. "Why don't we turn up here towards Kilmurvey? You may feel inclined to offer an old man a cup of tea and a place by your fireside."

We walked in silence for a long time, a gentle breeze murmuring across the fields, moonlight shining down softly over a dark, heaving ocean, the lights of Galway glimmering in the distance like a thousand tiny candles blowing in the wind.

As we entered the cottage, he took off his cap, hanging it on a hook by the side of the door as if from long habit.

"I'll get the tea," I told him. "The fire's already set; you just need to put a match to it."

When I came back in from the kitchen, the old man was kneeling by the hearth, adding small pieces of kindling wood to the rising flames.

"There's cold ham there," I told him. "I could make up some sandwiches, if you like."

"No, thank you." He shook his head. "Just the tea for me."

When I came back from the kitchen, he was sitting on the edge of the armchair, a poker clutched in his big right hand.

"There we are now, that should do it." He was adding lumps of wood to the fire, smiling into the rising flames. "There's nothing quite like a good fire."

I watched as he settled back in the chair; he seemed to draw pleasure from the simplest things.

"So, what were you saying about the Banshee?" I said. "Do you really believe there is such a thing?"

"Well, there's some would deny it, of course. Your own mother might well have been one of them, but there's a lot more will swear that it's true, and then there's plenty more again that would have seen her for themselves." He took a sip of the tea. "Accounts of the Banshee go back in this country for over two thousand years. Her song has been heard from one end of Ireland to the other. Traditionally, of course, she was known to signal the death of a family member, although others believed that she'd sing to warn of impending misfortune."

"What sort of misfortune?"

He'd taken out his leather pouch and was fingering through the dark brown leaves, rolling the tobacco between his fingertips, separating out the fibers before filling the bowl and tamping it down firmly with a thumb.

"Well, I was told many a time that just before the famine struck Ireland, the cry of the Banshee was heard everywhere. They say the countryside was alive with her song, wailing away night after night. Now whether that was to forewarn of the famine itself or the deaths that followed, who could say?"

"Have you ever heard it?"

He paused to put a match to the pipe, puffing away for a moment or two before continuing.

"Originally, of course, there were only five of the oldest Irish families that had the Banshee attend them. The O'Brien's, the O'Grady's, the O'Neill's, the O'Conor's and the Kavanagh's. But that list has grown a lot with intermarriage." He took another long draw on the pipe. "One of the first times the Banshee was ever mentioned in Irish folklore was the day Cú Chulainn rode out to his final battle." He paused, squinting across at me. "Now, you do know of Cú Chulainn, do you not?"

"Yes. He was one of the great Irish warriors, wasn't he?"

"He was indeed, although I wouldn't feel right calling Cú Chulainn *one* of the Irish warriors." He glanced at me again. "Cú Chulainn was the greatest of all the Irish heroes. His statue stands to this day in the post office in Dublin. A reminder of all the men and women who gave their lives fighting for the Irish cause."

"That's right. I saw a picture of him in the hotel at Dublin. I didn't realize its significance."

He turned away, looking back into the fire as if seeking out inspiration in the rising flames.

"Cú Chulainn," he declared finally, "The Hound of Ulster. He gave his life fighting for his people."

"So, he was an actual person?" But he continued on as if I hadn't spoken.

"There was great nobility amongst the Irish warriors in those days." He took another long draw on the pipe, his eyes half closed as if remembering. "They were skilled in all forms of combat. Cú Chulainn himself was trained by the warrior woman, Scathach, trained in the ways of war but trained also in music, storytelling and poetry."

"Why was that?"

"Well, it was believed in the old days that until a man had embraced that side of himself that is woman, until he had found within himself the Second Heart, he could only ever be a soldier, never a warrior."

"And Cú Chulainn achieved that?"

"He did indeed. Although not as you might expect. You see, the tragedy of Cú Chulainn's life was that he killed his only son in battle."

"How did that come about?"

"Well, it's a common enough theme, fathers destroying their sons. Many of the old legends tell of the same thing. The story has it that Cú Chulainn was tricked into the battle by the boy's mother, Aoife. Cú Chulainn first met up with her on the Isle of Skye whilst he was training there with Scathach. Their affair was a passionate one and soon she had borne him a son they named Conloach. Now, Cú Chulainn loved the boy well enough but he was a restless soul and before long, he told Aoife that he must return to his homeland to serve his king. Before he left, however, he gave her a golden ring bearing the insignia of the Hound of Ulster. 'When his thumb will fill this ring,' he told her, 'send him to Ireland to seek out his father.' Now it is said that at first, Aoife was well enough pleased with the arrangement, but later, when she learnt that Cú Chulainn had taken himself an Irish wife, she went into a rage and then plotted her revenge against him."

The old man took another few puffs on the pipe before resuming his story.

"Young Conloach was trained in the arts of war and, as time went on, he became one of the fiercest warriors of his day. As soon as he was old enough, his mother arranged a passage for him to Ireland, but before she let him go, she put upon him three sacred *geasa,* sacred vows not to be broken, even under pain of death. First, that he could tell no living man his name, the second, that he never refuse a challenge, and the third, that he should die rather than surrender in battle."

The old man was shaking his head.

"With that, she sent the boy away to meet his father. Well, the moment the young warrior arrived in Ireland clad in the garments of war, he was confronted by soldiers from the court of King Conchobar. They enquired as to his name and mission and when he refused them answer, they sent a messenger to the palace. When the king heard the news, he had Cú Chulainn brought to him and summoned him to address the problem. The Hound of Ulster rode to the shore immediately but was dismayed when he saw that the intruder was but a youth.

"'My King demands to know your name and mission on these shores,' he told Conloach. 'Think well before you answer. I have no wish to challenge the life of one so young.' But the young man, bound as he was by his mother's spells, could tell him nothing.

"'If I could give answer to any man, great Cú Chulainn, I would surely give answer to thee. But I cannot, lest I lose my honor before you.'

"Again, Cú Chulainn warned him. 'You speak of honor, yet I hear nothing in your words save trickery. You must tell of your name and purpose now, or meet me in battle. Think well before you answer, young sir, for you will not live to see another dawn if I come upon you.' But Conloach, bound fast by his oath, could tell neither his name nor refuse the challenge and so was forced into taking up arms against his own father." The old man was shaking his head again.

"Well, Conloach gave a fierce account of himself, but he was no match for his father, and soon he was down on the ground from a spear thrust that had torn open his side. Now, the war fever was upon Cú Chulainn but, as he moved to finish his opponent, he caught a flash of the golden ring bearing his own insignia on the boy's thumb and knew in that instant that it was his own son that he had slain.

"'Conloach! Why did you not speak? What darkness held your tongue that you would die rather than confess me as your father?'

"'Father, before I left to seek these shores, my mother had me swear an oath to tell not my name to any living man nor refuse any challenge. I could not speak, lest I show myself a coward before you.'Cú Chulainn held the dying lad's head in his arms.

"'Then thou art the warrior, Conloach, and I the less. Oh son, if we had stood together, who could have stood against us? I offer my life now to the gods to do with me as they would, to pay any price, to die any death, but have you live this day.' But the young man was already falling away into the agony of death and rather than see him suffer more, Cú Chulainn took his sword and put it through his son's heart to have him pass more easily." The old man shifted in his chair. "That was how the Hound of Ulster was opened to the Second Heart. On that day, Cú Chulainn came to understand the quality of mercy. On that day, he became a warrior, no longer a mere soldier."

"From a broken heart?"

"Yes." He glanced up at me. "When we come to realize that all the money in the world means nothing compared to the loss of a son or a daughter, or indeed a sacred cause, it is then that the Second Heart may open. The story of Aoife, Cú Chulainn, and Conloach is an age-old theme. A single mother, an absent father, and a lost son." He was staring back into the fire again. "Never give a man a sword until he's learnt how to dance. That's what they say. Until a man has found within himself the compassion of the feminine, he has no right to be carrying a sword. The brash young soldier knows nothing of that. That is the domain of the warrior. A warrior follows his conscience. A soldier is only capable of following orders." The old man was nodding. "Once you've experienced the Second Heart, once you've learnt how to dance, your life will take on new meaning. You will begin to live from out of your own center rather than following the ideas of others. Only then will you embark on your own authentic journey in life."

"But what has all this got to do with the Banshee?" I said.

"Well, as I was saying, the Banshee sang to Cú Chulainn the morning he rode out to his final battle. He was accompanied by Cathbad the Druid that day and, as they crossed by a ford in a river, they came upon a beautiful, flaxen haired young woman, standing alone in the shallows, washing clothes and singing. A high pitched, wailing kind of a song that pierced Cathbad's heart like a knife. He stared at her in wonder, knowing she was of the faerie people, but then, as they passed by, he saw that the stream around her ran red, for the clothes she washed were soaked in blood.

"'Cú Chulainn,' he called out. 'Turn back! Look, the clothes she washes are the clothes you now wear. Turn away from the battle or you will surely die this day.' But the Hound of Ulster had seen the blood and knew what was meant by it.

"'I care not if I die this day,' he told Cathbad. 'As long as my deeds live on forever." The old man was speaking softly now, his eyes half closed. "It is said that he went into battle that morning singing. You see, after the passing of his son, he feared neither life nor death. He knew his destiny and he followed that path to the end. He was mortally wounded later that same day but, rather than have the enemy see him fall, he put his back against a standing stone and strapped his body around with rope. He stood there for hours, the enemy too afraid to advance, until finally a great blackbird lighted down on his shoulder and pecked out one of his eyes. Only then did they know that the great Cú Chulainn was dead. Only then did they dare approach him." The old man was peering fixedly into the flames, held fast by some inner vision of Cú Chulainn's lifeless form. "Cú Chulainn was a warrior, that was his calling. He gave his life defending his homeland, and in doing so, he inspired the thousands of Irish heroes who came after him."

"Do any of these stories have a happy ending?" I said.

"Stories aren't about endings, boy, stories are about beginnings. Or at least, that's what they're about when we hear them right. Find your heart and follow it. Seek out the gifts you carry then find a way of expressing them in the world. Only then will your life have meaning." The old man stood up. "You're tired," he declared. "You need rest." He nodded at the sandwiches sitting untouched on the table. "And get yourself a decent meal, there's work to be done." He pulled on his cap. "I'll see myself out."

"Good night," I called after him. But he was already gone, out through the front gate, along the dark winding lane.

Chapter 23
Letters

I sat there for a long while after the old man had gone, finishing off my sandwich and thinking over what he'd said. Then I went back out to the kitchen table and opened the notepad.

Tristan,

I guess you've received my first letter by now. I'm not sure why, but I had difficulty writing it. I've met an old man here and he's been helping me with the boat; or maybe I should say, I've been helping him. He's a strange old man but he's been good to talk to. I know it's going to be hard for you to understand this, but I want you to know that I feel really sad that you're not here with me right now ...

I stopped abruptly, struggling with my emotions.

I've spent most of my time the last few years building up a business, and I realize now that, whilst I was doing that, I ignored you a lot. Well, the company's gone broke, son, and in a way, I'm glad it has. The boat should be finished in a month or two and I want to see you as soon as possible after that. I miss you, my boy, more than you could know, all my love.

Dad XXX

I hesitated for a moment or two and then turned the page.

Giselle,

A few lines to let you know how things are here on Inis Mór. The island's a weird place, it's almost as if I've travelled back in time. I've spent a lot of time thinking and it's made me realize just how lost I've been these last few years. I was talking to the old man today and I realized for the first time that I've never had any idea at all of what I wanted to do with my life. I also realized what a failure I've been, both as a husband and a father. You were right to leave. You probably should have left a long time ago. I paused, unsure of where I was going.

I know you told me repeatedly that I was ignoring you and Tristan. I heard you say it a hundred times, and yet I never heard a word you said. I guess in the long run, you hear it when you hear it. I have no excuse to offer, except perhaps to say that I've been so lost myself that I had little or nothing to offer to you or Tristan. All I can say now is how much I regret that, and I hope someday I may be able to make it up to both of you.

Love,

Conor

Chapter 24
Steaming Planks

When I arrived at the boatshed the following morning, a huge fire was blazing in the hearth, Boson lay sprawled out on the cobblestones nearby, and what looked like an oversize drain pipe hung across the rising flames, steam billowing out from one end.

"Good morning." The old man was smiling, obviously enjoying himself. "I found the pipe up there in the rafters alongside the mast. It would be the same old pipe that your grandfather used, no doubt."

"What are you doing?"

"Steaming planks." He nodded towards the fire. "That's the way it was done in the old days."

One of the planks we'd been working on was sticking out from the end of the pipe, almost buried in clouds of steam. "I never boil them, although some do. I prefer the steam. It leaves the oil intact and it gives them a great spring altogether." He was stuffing rags in the end of the pipe, sealing in the steam. "Not too much water is the secret, although you do need enough." He stood back. "Right, another hour or so and we'll bend her round the frames."

I stood there watching as he fussed about the hearth, stoking the fire and adding a little water to the pipe now and again through a small hole in the top end.

"Where did you learn about boat-building?"

"I worked in the shipyards as a boy." He spoke without looking up.

"On wooden boats?"

"That's right. I know nothing but wood."

"That must've been quite some time ago."

"It was indeed," he nodded.

"Was your father a boat-builder?"

"My people were seamen for generations." He looked up. "Gather up some of that old timber lying around there now, we need to keep the fire hot."

As I went around collecting up the off-cuts, I watched him stirring a long-handled poker into the rising flames.

"So, what were you then, a boat builder or a sailor?"

"I was both in my day." He turned the plank over in the pipe and adjusted the rags. "There were times I worked at sea, and times I worked on the land."

"I was thinking about what you said yesterday, about having a purpose. Do you think everybody has one?"

"They do of course. Sure, isn't that what life's about? Oh God!" He shook his head. "Where else in nature would that question need to be asked?"

"How do you mean?"

"Look." He stood back from the hearth. "We have a little while before that plank's right, why don't you put the kettle on."

By the time the tea was ready, he was sitting back in his armchair, Boson crouching at his feet like a guardian at the gate.

"Would you like a biscuit or something?" I said.

"No, thank you." He was reaching for his leather pouch. "Just tea and the pipe for me." I watched as he prepared the tobacco, pressing it firmly into place with a thumb. "It's the strangest thing when you stop to think of it. Of all God's creatures, only mankind has lost its way. Consider that, if you would." He said it quietly, gazing into the flames as if talking to himself. "From the tiniest little sprite crawling around in the Bog of Allen to the greatest of all God's creatures, all living things swim, fly and dance in harmony with the natural world around them."

He struck a match and drew the pipe to life before going on.

"Do you see? The majestic blue whale cruising the depths of the Southern Ocean sings her own sacred song to the music of the spheres as she ploughs her way towards the mating grounds of her ancestors. The snow goose, along with thousands of others, lifts her graceful form skywards each winter, following her heart, winging her way across half a world of uncharted skies, seeking out the breeding grounds of her kind." He looked up at me, and for the first time, I saw sadness in his eyes. "When and where did mankind lose its way?"

"I know," I said. "It's not just me. A lot of my friends have no idea what they want to do with their lives."

"That's it." He settled back in his chair and took another long pull on the pipe. "The further we stray from the natural world, the further we move away from our own souls." He nodded. "And it is your soul that carries your gift and your purpose."

"I've never really had any idea what I wanted to do with my life."

He looked down at my right hand. "And yet you bear the sign of the Seanachaí."

"It was my father's ring. My grandmother left it to me in her Will."

"Your grandmother wore the ring?"

"I was told that she wore it on Halloween."

"Yes." He nodded again. "She'd have worn it to honor the soul of her son, Con Rua O'Rourke. The Seanachaí of Inis Mór."

"How do you mean?"

He was staring back into the fire again, his eyes glinting softly in the reflected light of the flames.

"Halloween, as you now call it, is the night dead souls return to earth to draw close to the living. So close, you can feel their breath on you." He was sitting quite still, pipe smoke trailing around one side of his face, his eyes glazed as if peering into some other dimension. "You can sense them if you pause long enough. In front of you, behind. The Druids were known to receive messages from them on that night. Prophesies, warnings, and the like."

I could tell by his voice that he was going off again. It was as if he went into trances at times, carried away by his own imagination.

"It's imaginary only if you have no imagination." He turned away from the fire and looked across at me.

"What?" I said. "Where did that come from?"

"There's a great arrogance about you, Conor." He spoke the words quietly, without anger. "Although it does seem quite unconscious for the most part. I suppose, in a way, if your life was in any sort of reasonable shape, if you and your family were together, I mean, or if you knew who you were and where you stood in the overall scheme of things, or even if you had some profound belief in something other than your own mind, I could more easily understand that."

"I didn't mean to come across as arrogant," I said. "It's just that I've never believed in ghosts or Halloween or any of that stuff."

"Whether you believe in it or not is of little consequence. The Celtic world has known of these things for thousands of years. Your forebears were connected to their souls, their ancestors and to the life force itself. They controlled the entirety of Europe, believing in *that stuff,* as you call it. Go easy boy, neither ignorance nor arrogance gives you the right to dismiss what is."

"*What is*?" I said.

"Yes. *What is*." He was staring at me. "Who defines the spirit of Inis Mór? You? No, I don't think so. The spirit of this island came into being over countless ages. What was the truth here two thousand years ago is still the truth here to this day. Ignorance or disbelief of the other world does nothing to change that world, it simply leaves this world lost and devoid of meaning. Your father, your grandfather and your great grandfather before you knew and respected the lore." He shook his head. "These things were known long before the stranger ever came to Ireland. Long before the written word. Long before the Christian era." He smiled. "Try wandering abroad on Inis Mór one night. Go off up there to the far end of the island close by those rocky ledges. Go off to where the seven chapels lie. Go up to Dun Aengus alone, if you dare, and sit there past the stroke of midnight. Then come back here and tell me no other beings run abroad. Who is to say what is true and what is not? Sure Jaysus, didn't you have voices in your own head? Where did they come from? You label them intuition and then dismiss them as such without even inquiring as to their source?" He paused for a long moment. "When did you first hear the voices?"

"Last year, I think. In bed one night. Yes. It was a month or two before Christmas last year."

"Then I will tell you when you heard them." He leant towards me. "It was the thirty-first night of October, the night of Samhain."

I felt a chill run through my entire body, as if some ghostly hand had stroked a cold finger down along my spine.

"Samhain?" I said. "What's that?"

"Samhain is the Celtic New Year, the day of the dead. The end of the old and the beginning of the new. The day departed souls return to earth. The thirty-first day of October. What is now known in the Western world as Halloween."

His words startled me. He was right, it had been Halloween. I remembered the children coming to the door dressed up as witches and asking for treats and suddenly, I remembered my early days on Inis Mór, and a group of people dancing around a bonfire, and my father sitting in a darkened room telling us that we had to wait quietly for the morning so as not to attract the dark spirits.

"I'd forgotten," I said. "I'd forgotten what it was all about."

"You've been gone a long time and there are many like you. People who never left Ireland have forgotten. They've let slip their heritage. It's a terrible thing. It leaves their lives empty and devoid of meaning. What couldn't be achieved by a thousand years of war has been done with a few years of prosperity." He paused. "Not everyone, mind, there are still people here that honor the old ways." He was staring back into the fire again. "Con Rua was one of them. Your grandmother was another."

"So how do they appear? Have you ever seen them?"

"It's early," he said, shaking his head. "And it's forbidden to talk of these things until after the sun has gone down lest we bring them into the light of day. Come on." He stood up. "There's work to be done."

Chapter 25

Dancing

We began fitting the new plank after lunch. It was an awkward job, the gap in the hull close to the keel and difficult to get at. We cut the timber to size, drilled screw holes, cleaned out the old caulking and maneuvered the new plank up into place; the old man taking me through each step carefully.

"There you are now, that's it. Take into account the width of each frame, some are thicker than others. Do you see that now? Try to miss the old holes if you can. If you can't, then you'd need to be using bigger screws. That's it now, sure we'll make a boat-builder of you yet, so we will." I was lying flat on my back, squashed in between the crossbeams of the cradle and the bulge of *Erin's* hull. "Now, this is the awkward bit."

He was pushing the steamed plank up into place in the long narrow gap. "There we are now, sure Jaysus, it fits like a bought one. Drive a nail in there now, if you would. Halfway along. That's it. Quick as you like, whilst she's still hot. Not too far now, it's only there to hold her." I was banging the nails in, the plank pulling up nicely in a tight sweeping curve. "Back here now, see if you can't get another one in there. Easy as you go. That's it." The old man was pressed into the hollow by *Erin's* keel, two bronze screws in his mouth, a screwdriver in his big right hand, Bosun close by, watching his every move as he drove the fresh new plank firmly up into place.

Twenty minutes later, we were almost done, just the tail end of the timber sticking out close to the center of the boat.

"Get another nail in there now, if you would. That's it, there's still too much spring in her. Go on. Another couple of taps should do it."

I swung the hammer twice but missed both times.

"Easy now," he murmured. "Easy does it."

I tried again but as I drew the hammer back, I struck the timber prop behind me and immediately the whole side of the cradle began to collapse, *Erin* lurching sideways as I scrambled out from underneath, desperately trying to prevent her from crashing over on her side.

I heard the old man groan as the boat came rolling over and for a moment, I thought he'd been killed, but then I saw him turn his head.

"Are you right?" he gasped. I'd jammed my shoulder under the swell of *Erin*'s hull to prevent her toppling further, but the weight was crippling, and I knew that I couldn't hold her for long. "Careful, boy, she'll roll on you!" The words came choking out of him.

He was lying on his back, his chest and lower body pinned to the base of the cradle by the keel, one hand reaching out towards me, and suddenly I caught a flash of my father's face, trapped in the car that night.

"Steady now!" The old man was straining up against the side of the boat with his bare hands, attempting the impossible. "If we could raise her just a little, she might roll back on her keel. Come on, give it a try!"

I got my back square on to the hull. I did not believe that we could move her.

"Ready?" He was staring up at me, wide-eyed. "Come on now. One, two, three, push!"

I forced myself to lift, straining upwards with every ounce of strength that I had. At first, there was nothing but then, to my amazement, I felt her move a little.

"Get out!" His voice was harsh and tight. "Get out while you can!"

But the task was impossible, and the boat settled back down on both of us, forcing me sideways, almost buckling my knees.

"Conor …" His face was white. "Save yourself."

My ankle felt as if it were about to break, and I knew I was close to collapse. Thoughts were swirling around in my brain, wondering how it had come to this. One part of me was screaming to escape but another part of me was saying no. I'd never prayed before in my life but as I felt my ankle beginning to go, I said out loud: "Please God, I can't leave him …"

Suddenly, I felt him alongside me. A touch of a hand on my shoulder. A fleeting smell of saltwater, tar and tobacco.

"Steady now." The voice was deep and resonant. "Hold steady. We're going to lift her."

"But …"

He cut me off.

"Forget about your ankle! If we can lift her just a little, we should be able to get the end of that prop back underneath her. On the count of three, give it all you've got. Ready? One, two, three, push!"

I closed my eyes and strained upwards, praying to God above for the strength.

"Push!" There was a fierce determination in his voice. "Puuuush! That's it, puuuuuush!"

I was straining against the terrible weight with every fiber of my being, desperation adding a strength I never knew I possessed. The boat was rising, inching its way upwards, a fraction at a time.

"The prop!" his voice rasped out again. "Get the prop!"

I opened my eyes and was stunned. The old man was standing like a colossus. His feet wide apart. His white hair falling back from his broad forehead. His long arms reaching upwards. His big hands gripping the rubbing strake on the side of *Erin's* hull. His dark green eyes glittering as he strained upwards against the impossible weight.

"You can't hold her!" I gasped.

But he closed his eyes and bent his head, and to my astonishment, the boat lifted even higher. He was carrying the entire weight of *Erin* himself.

"The prop," he rasped out again. "For God's sake, the prop!" He looked like Samson in the temple, and for a split second, a flashing thought went through my mind that there was something wrong with the whole picture. But I grabbed the prop, jammed it in against the side of the hull, and slid in the wooden chock that held it in place.

"Hammer it home, boy." His head was bowed, his eyes tightly shut. "Quickly now, hammer it home!"

As soon as I banged the chock into place, the old man collapsed back down onto the cradle. His greatcoat had pulled open and for the first time, I saw the dark navy-blue jacket he was wearing underneath, two gold buttons close to the top.

"Are you okay?" I asked.

"Yes, I'm fine."

"I thought you'd been crushed."

"Not at all." He glanced at me sideways. "You don't get rid of me that easy. Sure, worse things happen at sea!" And suddenly we were laughing, hysterically perhaps, but laughing just the same.

"Holy Christ," I said. "When I saw her rolling over, I thought you were a goner for sure."

That set us off laughing again. The old man throwing his head back and roaring as if it were the funniest thing he'd ever heard, Boson pushing up in between his legs, his stump of a tail wagging his whole rear end.

When we finally came to our senses, we just sat there for a long time looking at each other.

"Thank you for not leaving me." He spoke the words quietly. "You're a good man, Conor."

I nodded. I didn't know what to say.

He got up and went over to the washbasin and I sat there staring at his broad shoulders as he tidied himself up, oak shavings still clinging to the back of his dark greatcoat.

"How did you lift the boat?"

"We both lifted the boat." He spoke without turning. "Is there tea?"

I was staring at the reflection of his face in the mirror.

"You lifted the boat," I said.

"We'll need to strengthen that cradle." He was nodding, as if agreeing with himself. "It should have been done at the start."

* * *

I watched him as we waited for the kettle to boil. He'd wandered across to the far side of the shed and was examining the gramophone, still sitting there on the saw bench, covered in dust.

"Does this old yoke still work?"

"I've no idea," I told him. "It was there when I arrived. Thrown in with all the other rubbish."

"John McCormack, God rest his soul." He was examining a handful of old 45's. "And Joseph Locke. Sure Jaysus, he'd be dead and gone for years." Then another one. "Ah now, that's more like it. Paddy Canny, one of the greatest fiddlers ever to come out of Ireland. Let me see now." He was winding away at the little handle sticking out from the side of the machine, adjusting the needle as he went.

Suddenly, the entire shed was filled with sound. Drums, fiddles, and the wail of the Uilleann pipes rising and soaring as the old man moved to the center of the floor and began to dance.

He started off in the traditional way. Standing stiff and upright, his arms down by his sides, his feet flashing in and out, front and back, his black boots tapping out the speed of the rhythm on the hard-stone floor. But then he broke away laughing and went sweeping around the shed like a young colt. Feet kicking up in the air in the Irish way. Skipping and turning, lifting and reeling. Letting out little yelps now and again as he spun around the floor like a man possessed.

I watched him, amazed. I'd never seen anything like it in my life. He danced with absolute abandon. Swinging around the shed without a trace of self-consciousness, reeling and twirling until I felt sure he was bound to collapse. One moment, both his arms held straight down by his sides, the next, his hands up over his head as he went spinning off again around and around the cobbled-stoned floor. When the music finally came to an end, I burst into a spontaneous applause.

"That was fantastic," I called out. "Incredible!"

"Ah, never mind standing there clapping. Get yourself up here now and shake a leg!"

"But I can't dance."

"Sure Jaysus, you're full of cant's," and before I could protest further, he'd dragged me to the center of the shed and put the record back on again. "Come on now. We'll see if there's any can's left in you, will we?"

And then he was off again. Dancing around the floor in front of me, tapping his toes and kicking up his heels, spinning and turning like a wild man.

"Come on now," he was shouting across at me. "Let's see what you have in you. Let her rip, O'Rourke, show us how it's done!"

And suddenly, I was dancing. Slowly at first, but then, with the madness of it all, I threw caution to the wind and got into it. Reeling around the floor yahooing, kicking up my heels in some crazed version of the River Dance, sweeping around and around the shed with the old man, the strains of the day forgotten and left behind in one mad Irish reel.

"Your arm." He was roaring over the din of the music. "Give me your arm!"

And then we were reeling together. Swinging each other around in tight circles. Arms locked, heels rising as we went. Boson barking and snapping each time we passed, chasing us around as if enraged by my newfound choice of partners.

When the music finally ended, we fell back down into the tattered armchairs laughing, the old man's eyes flashing with excitement.

We spent the rest of that evening talking and laughing, and later, myself and Boson sat squashed in an armchair as the old man told stories of Ireland and the sea.

It was a magical, mystical evening, and beyond a shadow of a doubt, the strangest evening I'd ever spent in my entire life.

Chapter 26
Giselle

I said goodnight to the old man at the boatshed just after eleven o'clock and rode the bike back home. I was exhausted and looking forward to sleep, but the events of the day had left their mark and as soon as I got back to the cottage, I picked up the phone and dialed Giselle's number. It rang for ages and then finally, just as I was about to hang up, Tristan came on.

"Hello?"

"It's dad, Tristan."

There was a loud crash.

"Mum, it's dad! Quick!" He came back on again. "Hello, are you there? I'm sorry, dad, I dropped the phone. Where are you? Are you still in Ireland?"

"Yes, I'm still on Inis Mór. How are things in Brittany, son?"

"All right, I guess, but I hate school. I want to live in Sydney with you and mum. When will you come to see us?"

"It'll be a little while yet. I'm working on an old sailing boat. As soon as I'm finished, I'll be coming to see you. It won't be too long now."

"Are you going to sail the boat back to Australia? Can I come with you?"

"I'm not sure, son, it's a long way."

"Mum's here, dad. She wants to talk to you." I could hear the disappointment in his voice.

"John?"

"Hi, Giselle."

"Do you know what time it is? We're all fast asleep here."

"I'm sorry. I had to call you."

"Where are you now? Are you still on Inis Mór?"

"Yes, I'm still here. How are you?"

"We're doing okay. What's happening over there? How long are you planning on staying?"

"Did you get my letter?"

"Yes. So, you've turned into a boat-builder now?"

"I guess so. It feels a lot better than what I was doing in Sydney."

"And you've gone back to Conor?"

"Yes. I was christened Conor. You know that."

"I know. It suits you. I told you that years ago. How's the boat coming along?"

"Good. I'm enjoying it. I've never worked with my hands before."

"So, what's the story with the old man? How can you afford him?"

"He's doing it for free. He seems to enjoy it."

"Sounds like you've landed on your feet again."

"It's not like that."

"How do you mean?"

"I don't know how to explain it. Something happened at the boatshed today. An accident. It made me think."

"Think about what?"

"I've been thinking about what went wrong. Between you and me, I mean."

"And did you come to any conclusions?"

"Yes, I did. What you said was right. I was putting the business before you and Tristan."

"And you're only just coming to see that now?"

"Yes, I am. Things are different here. Life's much simpler. People talk to each other. It's given me a chance to slow down. I've realized that a lot of what you said was true. My priorities were completely back to front." I stopped, trying to get myself together. "I'm not sure how to say this but … I'm sorry. I'm sorry for the way I treated you and Tristan."

There was a pause.

"I'm sorry, too. Particularly for Tristan. He deserved better."

There was another long silence and I stood there mute. All the things I wanted to say just slightly beyond my reach.

"How's your mother, any improvement?"

"She's stable, and that's a blessing. She's on a new medication, we're hoping it will improve things."

"How are you doing for money? Can I help?"

"No, I'm okay. I spend next to nothing here. We don't go out much." There was another pause before she came back. "So, what are your plans? He asks about you every day and I have no idea what to tell him."

"Look, I know I can't undo what's done." I hesitated. "I guess what I'm trying to say is … could you to hold off on the divorce for a while?"

I heard Tristan's voice in the background and then she came back on again.

"I can talk now. Look, I made an appointment with a solicitor, but I didn't keep it. That letter you sent. It reminded me of a guy I knew a long time ago."

"I meant it. I want to give our marriage another chance. You're the most important thing in my life, you and Tristan. I want another chance to prove that."

"How can I believe you, after everything that's happened?"

"I don't know how to answer that. I don't know if there is an answer. But I do know if you give me another chance, I will not let you down again."

"And what about the business? What about all that?"

"I'm through with advertising, Giselle. I've written my last jingle and I've told my last lie. I've been working on a derelict old boat here, clearing out sheds, stripping paint and shoveling rubbish and I've never felt better in my life, and I want our son to experience some of that."

"Some of what? How do you mean?"

"Giselle, why don't you come over here for a few weeks? You can stay at the cottage. Tristan could work with me on the boat for a while ..."

"No, Conor, no. I can't do that." She paused. "Look, I have to go. Mums on the mend, but she's still in a lot of pain, and dad can't handle her by himself."

"I understand." I stopped abruptly, cursing myself for my awkwardness. "What I'm trying to say is … I do love you, Giselle."

"I know you do, in your own way." Her voice came back, hurt but softer. "You never had any trouble saying it before, maybe that's a good thing."

Chapter 27
Keels

It took us nine days to strip the paint from *Erin's* hull. The last few hours I spent on the bowsprit, scraping and sanding away until the last wispy little flake fell in a curving loop to the dark cobble floor below.

"That's it!" The old man was standing by the bench, stirring a long-handled spoon into the teapot. "Come down here now and we'll take a look at her." I climbed down the ladder. It had been hard, dirty work and I was glad it was over. "There she is now, that's the boat your grandfather built right there." He was holding out a mug of tea. "Take a good look at her. Kieran O'Rourke stood back here sixty years ago and looked up at the same boat you're looking at today."

As we stood there staring up at *Erin,* I felt a great sense of pride. The old man had been right. We had needed to go back to the beginning.

"So, what now?" I said. "What's next?"

"Next we'll check her fastenings." He took a sip of the tea. "Every one of them. Every nail and screw. After that, we'll move on to the keel bolts, they wouldn't have been touched in years."

As soon as we'd finished the break, we began examining the fastenings. The old man was like a bloodhound. Probing and prodding with his little knife, squinting in closer at some of the more doubtful ones, drawing circles around any that had discolored the timber, chalking large crosses in places where the corrosion was obvious.

It took us all afternoon to go over the hull and deck, and as soon as he'd finished, we began pulling out the screws he'd marked.

"They'll be tight. They've been in there long enough. Not as tight as they could be, mind, the planks have dried. Some will be worse than others. I could be wrong about a few of them but, right or wrong, all those we've marked will need to come out. Look now." He was showing me how to turn a screw the wrong way to free it up. "Do you see that? That's a little trick I learnt as a boy." He was never happier than when he was teaching me something. "A quarter turn to tighten it, that breaks the grip, then back the other way, see?" He handed me the screwdriver. "That's it. Tighten it up a quarter turn, that's it. Then the other way to unscrew it, see?"

We worked, side by side, until well into the evening. Many of the screws we took out weren't all that badly corroded and, in the end, there were only a few dozen that had really needed replacing.

"You don't take any chances with fastenings." He was reading my mind again. "There's many a lazy sailor you'd find sleeping on the ocean floor."

* * *

The next morning, we drilled out all the old holes before driving in the new bronze screws, slightly longer, slightly thicker than the original ones. *Erin* was taking on a different feel. She felt stronger and tighter somehow, as if she were consciously responding to the attention we were giving her. With every new screw or nail I drove in, I could feel the planks reverberating under my hand, not trembling as they had at first, but reverberating, as if some lost integrity was striving to re-establish itself.

The old man examined the boat each evening before we left for the night, going over everything we'd done that day, checking each new fastening, running his hands over *Erin's* curves as if to reassure her that all was well and we wouldn't be leaving her alone again for too long.

* * *

When I arrived at the shed the following day, the kettle was hissing away on the hearth and I could hear the old man clattering about inside the boat. I made the tea and carried two mugs up the makeshift ladder.

"Maidin mhaith," he greeted me as I appeared at the companionway.

"Conas atá tú," I passed him a mug.

"There's a message there for you," he indicated with his head, "On the chart table."

As I read the note, he sipped his tea.

"Mary and Lorcan have invited us over for dinner Sunday evening."

"That was good of them, but I won't be here. I have things to attend to over in Galway. I'll be gone for a few days." He went down on one knee. "Give them my thanks, if you would."

"What are you doing?"

"The keel." He pointed a long-handled wrench at the cabin sole. "It's time to check her keel bolts." I watched as he struggled a large nut off one of the heavy bolts protruding up through the bottom of the boat. "They've been set in there for years. I'd be surprised if those weren't the same bolts that your grandfather put in." He indicated with his head. "Pass me that mallet there now. No, not that one, the other one, that's it." I watched as he began hammering away, driving the bolt back down through the heavy timber. "Go below and see if you can't pull that one out. I'll knock it down more if needs be."

I went below to find the head of the bolt jutting out from beneath *Erin's* keel, bits and pieces of caulking flying about in all directions as he pounded from above.

"I have it," I called out. "You can go on to the next one."

I jimmied the bolt loose with a claw hammer and then pulled it the rest of the way by hand. It was almost eighteen inches long and about an inch and a half in diameter. Still solid and smooth over much of its length but wasted away down to half its original thickness near the middle. When I took it up to where he was working, he held it up to the light of the companionway for a moment or two.

"There you are now." He was nodding. "That tells us everything we need to know. We'll replace them all. See that?" He was pointing to the wasted part. "That's where the lead joins the wooden keel. That's where they go first. There's nothing can be done about it, it's nature's way. Sure, it's a miracle they've lasted as long as they have." He nodded again as if satisfied. "We'll replace every one of them."

"How long would they have lasted, the way they are?"

"It's hard to say." He raised his eyebrows. "Five years, ten, fifteen at most. But you don't take any chances with keel bolts. The very last thing you need is your keel coming adrift in a blow."

"Can that happen?" I said.

"It can, of course! Sure, it's happened to many an old boat that wasn't looked after, and to some of the newer ones too that weren't built right." He shook his head. "And it always happens at exactly the wrong time. Always in desperate weather when the ship is pounding in heavy seas. Not too many live to tell the tale. Once your keel drops off, it's over you go boy, like it or not." He looked up. "The keel's a lot like your purpose in life. It holds you on course, gives you stability, and enables you to stand up straight in difficult times." He knelt again and began working on the next bolt. "Go down below there now and we'll get this done. Once we have them pulled, we'll make a list of what we need. They should be able to get everything over from Galway within a few days."

* * *

It took us most of the day to remove *Erin's* keel bolts. There were twelve in all, many of them badly corroded. After we had them laid out on the bench, we took measurements, made out a list of everything we needed and then I took a walk up the store.

"Good evening." Madge O'Neil was standing in the open doorway of the store, frowning up at a leaden sky. "Come in here now out of the weather. Sure Jaysus, aren't you just like one of the locals now? I see you up and down that road every day without fail. How are you doing with that old boat of yours?"

"It's coming along fine," I told her. "Another month or so and we should have her back in the water."

She nodded. "God willing, so you will."

"How's your sister getting on?" I said. "Is she okay?"

"Ah, she's grand, don't you be worrying your head about Brigid O'Neill. Sometimes I wonder if I'm the crazy one, looking after her all my born days."

"So how old is she then?"

She was staring at me across the counter, her eyes bright and alert.

"Ah sure, she'll never let on, but I'll be ninety-nine next month by the grace of God, and she was here waiting for me the day I arrived. She'd be my older sister so." She straightened up. "Now then, what can we do for you today?"

"I have a list of things," I told her. "Some of it will need to come over from Galway."

She picked the sheet of paper up off the counter, frowning as she read out aloud. "Twelve keel bolts." She nodded. "That's a dozen." She went back to the list. "Inch and a half diameter, galvanized iron, double dipped. Caulking compound. A roll of Great Southern Oakum?" She looked up. "Great Southern Oakum? Sure Jaysus, we haven't seen Southern Oakum here in an age."

"Why's that?"

"Are you serious or are you pulling my leg?" She was staring at me across the counter.

"It's for caulking the planks,"

"I know what it was for, but Great Southern Oakum hasn't been seen on Inis Mór for the past forty or fifty years. It was an old Yankee product. I doubt you'd find it anywhere in Ireland, outside of a museum."

"So, what's used instead then?"

"I could give you a roll of caulking cotton. There should be some left out the back. Now what else do you have here?" She was frowning at the list. "Tar? Sure, tar's not been used here for donkeys' years." She stopped suddenly. "Are you sure you're not having me on?"

"I'm not having you on," I told her. "If you don't have tar, what else could we use?"

"Who made out this list?" She was staring down at the piece of paper.

"There's an old man working with me on the boat," I said. "He told me what he wanted, and I wrote it down. Why?"

She was shaking her head.

"Look, I'll talk to one of the fishermen. I think someone might be having a lend of you. The bolts will take five or six days. As for the rest, come back in the morning and I'll see what I can do."

* * *

When I got back to the shed, the old man was standing by the big double doors staring out impassively across a slate grey sea.

"There are storms close by." He spoke with his pipe clenched between his teeth, the wind whipping the smoke away behind him as he talked. "Nor'Nor'West." He nodded his head, his eyes fixed far out towards a darkening horizon. "You'll know when you get out there why you need to be prepared." He turned and we walked back into the shed together. "There's tea there." He indicated with his head as we sat down by the fire. "What would we do without it?"

"They weren't sure what you meant by Great Southern Oakum," I told him as I filled the mugs. "They said it hasn't been used here for years. They have caulking cotton. Will that do?"

"What's in a name?" he shrugged. "Oakum, caulking cotton, call it what you will. Just as long as it does the job, I'll not be arguing about a name."

I sat there watching him as he took another long pull on the pipe.

"The woman at the store was confused by the tar as well. She said it hasn't been used here for years."

"So be it." He looked across at me. "So, what do they have in its place?"

"She's going to talk to some of the fishermen. They'll know." He nodded and took another puff on the pipe. "You're not from the island, are you?"

He looked up.

"When will the keel bolts be here?"

"They'll be over on the ferry within the week," I said.

"A week?" He shook his head. "I don't want *Erin* without her keel for that long. We'll put a few of those old bolts back in before we leave tonight. A boat and her keel need to be as one." He was staring into the fire again. "The keel on a sailing boat is a lot like your purpose in life. It might not be seen by anyone for much of the time but it's critical if you're to be of any use in this world. Your purpose gives your life meaning. It enables you to stand up straight in hard times and it helps keep you on track in heavy weather. Once you know what your purpose is, once you've found what you're passionate about, nothing on God's earth can take you off course for long."

He paused and took another puff on the pipe.

"After we have the keel right, we'll move ahead with the mast. The mast sits at the forward end of the keel, rising up through the deck-head towards the heavens above. It carries the sails that capture the winds that give power and direction to your dreams. And I'll tell you now, if your dreams come from the heart, those winds will come." He paused for a moment, staring across at me. "The life force will take you to the most wonderful places once you've given yourself over to your calling."

"Is that what you did?" I asked. "When you were a young man?"

"No, I did not, more's the pity." He was looking back into the fire again, his eyes half closed as if remembering. "No, I took a different path."

"You never finished telling me about the boat you built," I said. "What happened to her?"

He glanced across at me for a long moment and then away again, pausing for so long that I wondered if I'd offended him.

"That's another story altogether," he said finally. "And not one there's time enough for this night." He stood up. "We need those keel bolts in the next few days. You might call in at the store on your way down in the morning and tell them as much."

Chapter 28
Selkies

I arrived at the Reardon's cottage just after six that evening, an umbrella clutched in one hand, a bunch of red roses in the other.

"Come in out of the rain." Lorcan was standing just inside the doorway, shaking his head. "Jaysus, she'll be at me for weeks now, complaining I never bring her flowers."

"Ah, pay him no heed, they're lovely." Mary had appeared alongside him, pulling at his sleeve. "Although he is right, I must admit, he hasn't brought me flowers in an age."

"Now then, do you see? Breaking up the happy home." He was peering out through the doorway along the rain swept path. "Is your friend not with you?"

"No," I told him. "He went over to Galway Friday evening. He'll be gone for a few days."

"Ah, more's the pity. I was looking forward to meeting the man. No matter, we'll catch up with him one of these days. Come in now, I have a few things for you to sign, if you would." I followed him through to a dining room table covered in paperwork. "As soon as we get this sorted, we can sit ourselves down for the meal." He was sifting through a sheaf of papers, pulling one out occasionally and pushing it across the starched white tablecloth. "There you are now, that will need your signature." He passed me a fountain pen. "It's for the deed on the cottage. It has to be registered in your name. I'm going over to Galway tomorrow for a week or two. I'll take care of the registration while I'm there. Sign there. And again there, that's it." He went back to the pile. "Now, this one's for the boat. It's not essential but if you ever took a mind to insure her, you'd need some sort of proof of ownership." He was studying the remaining few sheets. "And then there's the bank account. Now, we could transfer the money into your bank in Australia if you like, or you could open an account at Grace's bank over in Galway. Then all they'd have to do would be to move the money sideways, as it were. That would probably be the simplest way."

"Well, we're only halfway through with the boat, so I'll be staying on here for the foreseeable future."

"That's fine then. You can sign both lots of forms now if you like and as soon as you decide, I could go straight ahead with the paperwork."

"Come on now, you two." Mary had appeared from the kitchen carrying a tray. "Get all that paperwork off the table quick or there'll be no dinner in this house tonight."

"We're nearly done." Lorcan was pointing a finger to a final x. "Just one more signature and that's it."

A few minutes later, I watched as they said grace. Mary's head bowed to the age-old prayer of thanks, Lorcan's soft Irish brogue stirring memories of earlier, simpler days.

* * *

"So, we heard you had your own little cheili down there at the shed the other night?" Mary was smiling at me across the table.

"How do you mean, cheili?" But then it dawned on me. "Oh, you mean the music. Yes, we did. It was a crazy day. The cradle collapsed. The old man was nearly crushed. I'm not sure how it happened but after we got it sorted, he put a record on and we ended up dancing around the shed like a couple of lunatics."

"So, you do have a drink now and again?" Lorcan inquired.

"No, it wasn't that, it was just a weird sort of day. How did you hear about it?"

"Paddy Flaherty was in on the high tide with his crew." Lorcan was studying me over the rim of his glasses. "They heard the music and looked in the window. They said you and Boson were having a great time altogether dancing around the shed. There's no harm in that, m'boy, sure everyone's entitled to a day off occasionally."

"I was dancing with the old man," I said, feeling a little foolish. "He started dancing and I joined in. Boson was chasing us around, barking. It must have looked pretty crazy."

"Well maybe they just didn't see the old man." Lorcan was smiling across at his wife. "That's easy done, it's a small window. Paddy thought it was just yourself and the dog. He thought you'd probably had one or two over the dozen. He said that Boson was dancing a lot better than you were mind, but that's easy understood, he's been at it for years." He winked. "There's no shame in that, we all enjoy a bit of craic now and again."

"Why don't we move by the fire?" Mary was gathering up the dinner plates. "It'd be a pity to waste it. There's tea and fruit cake for you. I made it myself."

"Can I give you a hand?" I said.

"No, you cannot." Lorcan was shaking his head. "You're the guest. We don't go in for any of that women's liberation nonsense here on Inis Mór. Isn't that right, Mary?"

"Oh, that's right enough, for to be liberated, you'd first have to be enslaved, and if it was slavery I was looking for, I'd have chosen a better-looking master than yourself. Now get up off your backside and take those dishes out to the kitchen."

"Ah Jaysus, you have my heart broke." Lorcan was rising to his feet. "If I was a younger man, I'd be better able to defend myself."

"Sit over there now, Conor." Mary was settling into a chair by the fireside. "It's a pleasure to have you with us. I only wished to God that Grace could have been here too."

"I know. I'd like to have met her again. You get separated from people and the next thing you know, your life's half over."

"Ah, don't be talking like that. Sure, God love you, you're still only a boy."

"There you are now." Lorcan was back, drying his hands on a small red checked tea towel. "They're in the sink, I'll finish them later. God forgive you, Mary, and me no longer master in my own home."

"Pay him no attention." She was shaking her head. "He was over in Galway too long; he was a good enough man before that."

"So." Lorcan was settling into an ancient brown leather armchair close by his wife. "Mary tells me you're well on the way with the boat."

"Yes, it's going well. We've stripped off all the old paint and taken her back to bare timber."

"Well, isn't that grand. That's exactly what was needed," he nodded. "Sure, Grace would be delighted with you. I was supposed to be doing the same thing myself, but I must confess, time got away on me."

"You knew there was a hole in her hull, didn't you?" I said.

"Yes indeed, there was a problem when we pulled her up on the quay. The tractor wasn't man enough for the job, but it was all we had, so we made the best of it. She was dropped at the last minute, that's what put the hole in her." He was staring across at me. "Will you be right to fix it, or will you need a hand?"

"It's already fixed." I told him. "We bent a new plank around her last week. The old man's been showing me how it's done."

"And he's a boat-builder himself, I believe?"

"Yes, he is, or at least, he was. He was a sailor for most of his life, from what I gather."

"Well, you found the right man for the job by the sound of things. Do you have a name for him yet?"

"Oh, god," I said. "I still didn't think to ask, but you must know him, he's down there most days. You can't miss him. He wears a long black coat and a seaman's cap. He's a big man, always carries a walking stick."

"Yes, so you said. How tall would you say he'd be?"

"Very tall, well over six foot. Probably six foot three or four."

Mary was sitting across from me pouring the tea.

"In all my born days on Inis Mór, I could never have put a name to a man like that. He must be over from Galway or maybe Doolin, sure he'd stand out like a Protestant at a prayer meeting on the island."

Lorcan was frowning.

"A seaman's hat and a walking stick, you say, and a long black coat?'

"Yes. I've never seen him wear anything else. Maybe he is from Galway. I never thought to ask."

"And he was a seaman himself at one time?"

"Yes, I believe so. Why, does that ring a bell?"

He was looking across at his wife.

"Do you remember the old man Con Rua used to talk about, the old Seanachaí?"

She looked puzzled for a moment, and then surprised.

"Oh God almighty, Lorcan, sure that was donkey's years ago!"

"Yes, but that was the exact same description, was it not?"

"Well, yes, I suppose it was." She seemed reluctant to pursue it. "Try some of that cake now, Conor."

"Who was he?" I said. "A friend of my father's?"

"I'm not sure that you'd call him a friend. More of a mentor, I'd say." Lorcan was staring across at me. "He was a Seanachaí, set in the old ways. Told a lot of his stories in Irish, I believe. I never met the man myself, but Con Rua had a great respect for him. He met him up at Dun Aengus the first time, I believe. The old man used to walk there in the evenings. We could never make out who he was. Sometimes we wondered, was he just another of Con Rua's imaginings, but then he gave your Da that ring you're wearing, so I suppose he was real enough, after all."

"But why would you call him a mentor?"

"Because it was the old man that gave your father the story that made him his name." Lorcan was nodding.

"How do you mean, gave him a story?" I said.

"Well you see, in the early days, Seanachaí were trained up in all the old myths and legends, but as time went on, many of them developed stories of their own making as well. Now, those tales were their own private property as it were, and it would have been considered bad form to go telling another man's story unless, of course, you were given the right. Well, that's what some of the old Seanachaí would do. If they met a young man on their travels and they felt that he had the gift, they would train him up with a few of their own tales, to get him started as it were."

"So, the old man taught my father to be a Seanachaí?"

"Well no, not exactly. Your da already had the gift, but it was the old man that showed him how to use it. Your father could fill a room anywhere in Ireland, God rest his soul. He had the gift all right, and the old man would have known that."

"So, he was telling stories before they met?"

"He was, of course. Storytelling goes back with the O'Rourkes for generations. Your grandfather was a Seanachaí as a young man, but he gave it up when Con Rua was born. No fault of Grace's now, but he was a proud man and he decided there wasn't enough of a living in it for the three of them. The O'Rourke's had always been fisher people, so he went back to the sea. That was when he built *Erin*. Oh, your da was telling stories right enough but in more of a natural sort of way. It was the old man that showed him what it was to be a real Seanachaí."

"He trained him?"

"Yes, you could put it that way. You see the role of the Seanachaí goes away back in Irish culture. Well before the written word. Back to a time when every King and nobleman had their own Seanachaí. They were the learned men who carried the history and legends of Ireland. You see, to become a Seanachaí in those days involved twelve years of training. They had to be able to recite one hundred and seventy-eight stories off by heart, a different story for each night of the Celtic winter. Stories about Cú Chulainn and Laegaire, the Battle Winner, tales of warfare and border disputes, of cattle raids and elopements. The more skilled amongst them were known as fili, or the filid, roughly translated, it would mean poets, another interpretation might have been, weavers of dreams."

He paused and took a bite of the cake before continuing.

"When a Seanachaí spoke, it was believed that he invoked the spirits of the gods of Ireland." Lorcan took another sip on his tea before continuing. "Oh yes, there was a lot more to it than just telling stories. Seanachaí were revered and their belief system was profound. They believed in the equality of mankind. They believed that man was mortal but that his soul was immortal. They believed that their stories came from the spirit world and that they themselves were merely channels through which these truths could pass. They carried our history and our legends to every town and village in the country, risking their lives at every turn when it was forbidden by the stranger to do so."

"You mean the English?"

"Yes, the English, but there were others too. The Vikings had a great fear of the Seanachaís' power and they put many of them to death for it. But it was with the English that the Seanachaí came into their own. There were hundreds of them all over Ireland, speaking only in the tongue, in those days, although it was forbidden by law to do so. They wandered the countryside, living in ditches, sleeping in barns, asking no money for their work. It was passion that kept them going. A passion for the story, a passion for our language, a passion for the history and culture of the Irish race. There are some great stories from the Seanachaís' own lives, as you can well imagine. They were heroic men and women, there's no denying that. They traveled with Irish soldiers at home and abroad, telling their stories in war camps around the world. Carrying our legends with them wherever they went. Keeping the light of knowledge and culture burning in some of Ireland's darkest days."

He paused again to take a sip of tea.

"You see, the Seanachaí straddles two worlds. It was believed that the great Seanachaí of old had traveled to Tír na nÓg and brought the wisdom of the gods back to earth with them. There's a legend from around the West Coast here about a man called Finbar O'Malley. Sometimes I wondered if it wasn't him that Con Rua was hinting at when he spoke of the old man."

"How do you mean?" I said. "Didn't you ask him?"

"Ask him?" Lorcan looked up surprised. "Sure Jaysus, you wouldn't question a Seanachaí. That was never done, or at least not in the old days. You took the stories with you as they were, or you left them alone. You know what they say, ask a Seanachaí two strange questions and he'll never tell you another story."

"So, who was Finbar? Was he a Seanachaí?"

"Well, yes and no. Finbar O'Malley came from a family similar in many ways to your own …"

"Oh God almighty." Mary was standing in the doorway. "I'm not gone from the room five minutes and you're starting with all that old heathen nonsense again. Finbar O'Malley, indeed. Holy Mother of Mercy, Conor, what will you think of us? I'm ashamed of you, Lorcan, so I am."

"Ah now, Mary, will you settle down now. Jaysus, I'm only after telling him about the Seanachaí …"

"And don't you dare go blaspheming in this house! You're too long away from your Mass, Lorcan Reardon. That's the foundation stone of all your troubles, as God is my judge. Don't you be listening to any more of his meanderings now, Conor, you can get up and leave him there talking to himself any time you like."

"No, I'm enjoying it, Mary. It's fascinating."

But she was gone, sweeping out of the room as Lorcan leant towards me.

"Pay her no heed, she's a good woman, but the priest up there has her by the throat. We'd be better off letting Finbar rest in peace tonight. I'll tell you the story another time. She gets far too excited with the old tales. She's gone worse since the cat died; it shook her up badly. I swear to God, she'd have them up there saying Novenas for the poor brute if old red socks would allow it."

He sat back up again.

"Now, where was I? Oh, yes. Well, you see now, in more recent times, the population here was scattered. There was over a million people starved to death in the famine with another million or more forced to emigrate just to stay alive. Well, they sailed off to the New World taking their beliefs with them. There were Seanachaí amongst them, of course. When they got there, they took jobs at whatever they could. Working as farmers, woodworkers and fishermen, toiling alongside the ordinary men in the fields or out at sea, recounting their tales on rainy days on building sites from London to New York, telling their stories as the fishermen waited to haul their nets. Some of them took to writing, adapting to the new environment, keeping our culture alive for men and women driven from their lands by starvation. Your father was one of them. Con Rua turned his hand to building when he was over there in Galway. I've seen him there myself on a rainy afternoon and all the men laid off for the day, sitting around him in the back room at the Eyre's Tavern, the whole place hushed and silent …"

"He's right." Mary was settling back in her chair again. "That was the last time we heard Con Rua telling a story, God rest his soul.

We went over there for a day or two for the school fete. Sure, the weather was fierce altogether, blowing a gale it was, it was a wonder we got there at all. We went in for lunch and there was your da in the back room. Well, you could have heard a pin drop. He was telling a story about the famine, do you remember?"

"Oh, I remember well enough." Lorcan was nodding. "It was a story of people lost to the immigration. How some of them would save their lives but go on to lose their souls. I'll never forget it. He sang then, at the end. There were grown men, weeping. Your da had a terrible way of singing when he wanted. Like the banshee he was, God forgive him. A keening, wailing kind of lament was what it was. Like the Seanachaí of old were known to do. God knows where he learnt it from. From the old man, I suppose. I've seen grown men break down when your father sang in the tongue. Men who hadn't a word of Irish would weep. He was a great loss to us all, was your da. They came from as far away as America for the wake. You see, someday, we all have to come to terms with who we really are. Beneath all the masks, that is. That's why the stories are so powerful. They not only tell us who we are, they tell us who we once were, and that reminds us that we can be so much more than we are today."

"So, what was the story that the old man gave my father then?"

"Well, it was a story about a family that lived here years ago called the Flaherty's ..."

"Ah, don't be starting on with that old nonsense now." Mary was shaking her head. "And you, a historian. You of all people should know better."

"He has the right to know, Mary. Sure, he is Con Rua's boy. Everyone else on the island knows the story, what right do we have to keep it from him?"

"Because it's nonsense, that's why. That story's been told so many times, you have no idea yourself which parts are true, and which are not."

"Well, a lot of it's what Flaherty told the Gardai, so it's a matter of record. I've seen the reports myself. Now, whether Flaherty was telling the truth or not is not for me to say."

"What happened?" I said. "I'd like to hear the story."

"Well." He was frowning as if trying to recall the details. "There was a family called the Flaherty's that had lived here on Inis Mór for generations. They were decent enough people with a little patch of a farm up the road there over towards Killeany. Not much of a place now, but big enough to feed them all. They were well known to be good people with the cattle, and they bred some of the finest angus that ever came off the island. They only ever had the one child, Liam. He was a strange one from what I remember of him. Awkward in company and never mixed much with anyone at all. It was said of him that he was born in the wrong place at the wrong time, and that can happen, of course. But his father and grandfather before him had worked that patch of land and it was all he ever knew. The only time you'd ever see him was when he'd be taking a few of the cattle off on the ferry to Galway, or maybe you'd catch a glimpse of him occasionally down at the store in the wintertime."

He settled back in his chair before continuing.

"Now, the mother died first, and then the father a year or two later, and the farm went to Liam. Well, he stayed on there alone for a few years after that. We had an old matchmaker on the island in those days and there were some attempts made to find him a wife. But he wasn't what you'd call a handsome man and none of the local girls had the slightest interest in him at all. Well, he took himself off one summer, away over along the Connemara coast, and when he came back again, he had a wife with him."

Lorcan was shaking his head.

"And not just any wife. She was, without a doubt, the most beautiful woman I ever laid eyes on, forgive me, if you would, Mary. Sure, men and women alike would turn and stare as she went by." He smiled. "Well, that's when the stories began ..."

"That poor woman must have been driven stone mad by the gossip," Mary joined in. "There wasn't a girl on the island would give him the time of day and yet, as soon as he finds himself a wife, you have them all saying she's a selkie."

"What's a selkie?"

She stood up. "Ah, you'll have to talk to Lorcan about that old nonsense. Sure, I wouldn't be after wasting my breath on it."

"There was a time you would," Lorcan called after her. "There was many a time you sat there listening to Con Rua telling of the selkies."

"Con Rua was a Seanachaí," she snapped as she disappeared into the kitchen. "He had the right. You're an educated man. You should be well past all that old nonsense at your age."

"Pay her no heed," he said quietly. "Sure, there was many a night she'd sit there listening to your da telling the same story."

"So, what are selkies? I asked. "Are they faeries or something?"

"Oh no, nothing like that. Stories of the selkies go back for generations on these islands. They're seals. There's still plenty of them around Inis Mór to this day. There are stories of the selkies told in Scotland, all the way along the Welsh coast, across the water in Brittany and as far away as Nova Scotia. The tales vary from place to place but the theme is always the same, selkies come up out of the sea and take on human form."

"How do you mean?" I said. "You mean, they become human?"

"Well, yes and no. They're almost human but not quite. They're said to have a great beauty about them, almost like angels. The young girl seals will come ashore some nights, slip out of their skins, and then dance on the beach in the moonlight. Sometimes, if they get too carried away, one of them will forget where she's left her sealskin, and then she'll panic, for she can't return to the sea without it. To protect herself then, she'll go off into the nearest village and the next thing you know, she'll marry one of the local men."

He took a sip of his tea before going on.

"Now, she'll stay married for as long as it suits her, but she'll always be on the lookout for that skin of hers. Once she finds it, she'll be off back into the water in no time, leaving the poor man broken-hearted. There are different stories about them. Some say the selkies have great hearts and occasionally they'll take pity on a lonely man, sitting brooding by the shore. The man goes back there day after day until finally they fall in love. When that happens, a pact is struck between them. The seal will come ashore as a selkie to marry, but their first-born child must be surrendered back to the ocean or else the woman herself must go back, never able to return to the land in human form."

"Oh god almighty, will you stop!" Mary was standing in the doorway, one hand to her cheek. "Have you no shame at all? Have you ever heard such nonsense in your life, Conor? And don't go thinking you have to sit there listening to him, just to be polite. You're free to get up and leave anytime you like."

"No, it's interesting. I've never heard of selkies and it sounds harmless enough."

"It's harmless enough if you have sense enough not to believe it! But can you imagine the sort of life that poor woman would have had with the whole island thinking her a seal? Bog Irish nonsense is what it is. It's no wonder she disappeared. There's stories like that told all around Aran, God alone knows why."

"Because they're a part of our history, that's why." Lorcan was peering across at her. "True or false, Mary, there's accounts of selkies on Inis Mór going back for hundreds of years."

"Yes, indeed there is, and of banshees and ghosts and men with three heads down the back of the island. But I've lived here all my born days and I've yet to set eyes on one of them!"

"Well, a lot of this is a matter of record, you can't deny that."

"Ah, you and your records." She sat down next to him again. "Go on with the story, you're too far into it now to stop and you're doing better than I'd hoped you would, anyways."

"Thank you." He stared at her for a long moment before continuing. "Well, the truth of the matter is, that after the Flaherty's married, they never went near the sea again. That much is known. For the first few months they were back, you'd see her up at the church on Sunday mornings. I've seen her there myself. A woman of extraordinary beauty, was she not, Mary?

"Yes, she was a fine-looking woman all right, but that doesn't make her a selkie."

"Well, whatever she was now, people began to talk. They noticed she was unsure of herself at the Mass, never quite sure of when to stand up or when to kneel. Watching her husband all the time, taking the cue from him, as it were. And she never went near the sea, which was noticed of course, on a small island like this. So, the rumors persisted, and I suppose the Flaherty's would have known, for the next thing they began to miss Mass on Sundays. Well, that only made matters worse. Then a son was born, Rory Flaherty. He was delivered at home and the midwife said he had the saddest eyes she'd ever witnessed on a child. When the time came, he went to school with all the other children, but he was always seen as different, and the islanders can be very cruel about a thing like that.

"Now, things went along right enough until young Rory got a bit older and began to show an interest in the sea. It wasn't much at all at first, just a natural curiosity. Some of his friends were fishermen's sons and he took to going home with them at times after school. Flaherty didn't pay it much heed until one day the boy told him he wanted to go off fishing during the school holidays. 'Go fishing where?' he'd said. 'Just out,' the boy had told him, 'wherever they go.' Flaherty was troubled. The selkie rumors had started with the fishermen, and he knew that.

"'Stay away from those people,' he told his son. 'Farming and fishing don't mix. Stay with your own kind, there's plenty to be done around here without you running off in a boat somewhere.'

"Well, that was the beginning of the trouble. The boy's friends would kid him along about not being allowed out in a boat, and as time went on, he grew to hate the farm more. Before long, he was spending all his spare time down at the jetty. Talking with the fishermen, helping unload the catch, painting the hulls in between tides up against the harbor wall, working with them repairing the nets, and dreaming of the day he'd be old enough to choose his own path in life. Occasionally when the older Flaherty was busy on the land, Rory would spend a few hours out at sea in one of the little currachs, fishing just offshore from the island. Some of the boys said afterwards that whenever young Rory was with them, the boat would be surrounded by seals, big ones, small ones, young and old alike, all rising their heads up out of the water, staring in at young Rory."

Lorcan took another sip of his tea before continuing.

"You see, his parents never knew about any of this for they hardly ever came into town. He was fifteen years of age by then, keen to work but clumsy in a boat and unused to the ways of the sea. On one of those occasions, Flaherty had returned early from the fields to find his son missing. He'd gone down to Cill Rónáin looking for him and when he discovered the boy was out in a currach, he waited on the quayside for the boat to return. As soon as the boy came ashore, there was a row, and when one of the fishermen stepped in to speak up for the lad, it had come to blows. After that, things went from bad to worse. The boy was growing up fast and Flaherty knew he couldn't control him forever. He tried everything he knew with the lad. He told him the farm would be his one day. He told him stories of the sea and of the fishermen who'd been lost to the gales that lash the coast here each winter. He told him of the boats that had left Inis Mór never to be seen again, but to no avail. The more he tried to convince his son to stay away from the sea, the more the boy was drawn to it."

Lorcan settled back in his chair a little and glanced across at me.

"Now, that winter was the worst in living memory. Storms raged across the island one after another, almost without a break. Then, in the first week of April, one of the trawlers went missing. For three days, the fishermen's families waited down by the quayside, keeping a watch, hoping and praying. The boat limped in on the third night, battered but with all her crew safe. The fishermen had set up headquarters in our old boatshed, and once the men were safely ashore, a céilí started up of its own accord. You know, drinking, dancing and telling stories. It was meant as a celebration, but at some time during the night, a few of the younger lads got together and decided on an adventure. Now perhaps it was bravado, or perhaps they'd been allowed a drink too many, but three of them took a notion to row a currach out to the end of the pier and back. They'd done it many times before, maybe not in such bad weather, but they'd been brought up on the sea and they knew the boats well. Rory had wanted to go with them, but they refused, and he'd stood on the beach and watched as they rowed off into the stormy seas."

Lorcan looked across at his wife.

"That much is recorded. Tom Hagen was one of those boys. He swears to this day that was what happened."

Mary got up and began collecting the cups.

"I'll tidy things up now whilst he tells you all about the selkies, Conor. God forgive you, Lorcan, sometimes I think you're a frustrated Seanachaí yourself."

"Pay her no heed now." He was leaning towards me again, peering over the top of his glasses. "She's too much of a Catholic for her own good, at times." And then he went back to the story. "Well, no sooner had they set off, when Rory took a notion. He dragged one of the other currachs down from the beach and went after them. He got out to the end of the pier all right, but he was unaccustomed to the currach and the wind caught the boat and began pushing him offshore. The other lads saw what was happening and knew the danger he was in. With all three of them rowing, they managed to draw close enough to throw him a rope, but Rory lost an oar trying to catch it and after that, there was no hope. The other boys turned back for help, but by the time they reached the boatshed and gave the alarm, it was too late. Young Rory Flaherty had disappeared.

The seamen took the trawler back out immediately and spent the rest of the night searching for the boy, but it was hopeless. When they returned the following day, Flaherty was waiting on the quayside, beside himself with fear. He begged them to go back out again but the men were exhausted, and they knew there was no point. He pleaded with them, he offered them money and he threatened them, all to no avail. Con Rua always said that when Flaherty went back home to the cottage and told his wife what had happened, she'd immediately said that the boy was safe.

"'He sleeps,' she told him 'covered over by a sail, off the coast from Doolin. If he's to live, we must go to him now.'

"Well, perhaps Flaherty was half mad with grief, or maybe he'd known her secret all along. 'Go to him?' he'd asked. 'How?'

"'I will show you where he lies,' was her only answer." Lorcan was staring at me. "Now, those are the exact words on record. Even Mary will acknowledge that, or you can read them yourself up at the Gardai station. Now whether they be true or not is another thing, but that's what Flaherty told the Gardai after the whole thing was over."

"Did they find him?" I asked.

"Well, the fisherman refused Flaherty a currach. He'd never rowed a boat in his life, and they felt sure he'd be drowned, but he took one later that night against their wishes. The seas were rough, the winds still high. He told the Gardai afterwards that his wife was with him in the boat, but those that saw him swore he was alone. They still argue about it to this day after a few drinks. Some said there was a seal swimming alongside the currach, others said it was swimming out in front, as if to guide it. Well, that was where the legend began, but legends aside, what is true is that Flaherty came back two days later, rowing strongly, as if he'd been at it all his life. The son, unconscious on the bottom of the currach, and a seal trailing along behind them as far up as the beach."

"Quite a story," I said. "Is it believed here?"

"That's a good question. You see, there's them that say they believe it and don't, and then there's others that say they don't believe it and do. You might well ask Mary the same question. Of course, the church was always against the old ways. You can't have people believing in selkies and still be asking them for donations for a new steeple now, can you?"

“That’s enough of that now,” Mary called out from the kitchen. “Tell the story if you must, but don’t be blackguarding the church. I’ll not have it in this house.”

He winked across at me.

“Ah, I was just making sure you could hear right enough,” he called out. “Would there be any chance of a drop of tea, or would that be too much to ask?”

“I’ll get it,” I said.

“You will not.” Mary was walking back in with a tray. “You’re the guest, but you will be having the pleasure of watching Lorcan finishing the washing up just as soon as he’s done with all this nonsense.”

“So, what about Flaherty’s wife?” I said. “What happened to her?”

“Well, as Mary said, she disappeared that night and was never seen again.”

“She was lost from the boat?”

“The people who saw him rowing out said he was alone.” Lorcan was staring at me.

“Go on, Lorcan,” Mary said. “Finish the story. You might as well tell him the last bit now.”

“All right then.” He was settling back into his chair again, a cup of tea in one hand. “I believe it was the doctor that called up the Gardai. Young Rory was unconscious, but it was more from exhaustion than anything else, but Flaherty himself was in a state of shock. Doctor Shaw couldn’t get any sense out of him at all, but he realized enough from Flaherty’s ramblings that the wife was missing. That’s when he called the Gardai. Shaw only passed away here a year or two ago, but to his dying day he swore that Flaherty never once questioned the fact that his wife had gone back to the sea.”

"He told the doctor that?"

"No. It wasn't so much what he said, it was just that he showed no interest at all in either reporting her lost or having anyone go off looking for her. It was as if he knew she was gone for good. Dr. Shaw was concerned that Mrs. Flaherty could have still been out there in the other currach. That's why he called the Garda. We only had the one on the island in those days, Padraig Mulholland. He was a good lad, born over on Inis Oírr himself and used to the ways of the islands. Well, the way he tells it now is that he got the call shortly before dawn, and by the time he was dressed and on his bicycle, the sun was just coming up. He'll tell you to this day that halfway along the laneway up to Flaherty's farm, a mile or two outside of Cill Rónáin, he saw something up ahead of him on the road. Now at first, he thought it was a dead man, but then, as he drew closer, he realized it was a seal. He said it was right up on the top of the rise overlooking the far side of the island, lying in a pool of blood. At first, he wondered had somebody maybe killed the poor creature and thrown it off the back of a truck but then, as he looked around, he could see a trail of blood going away back down the hill."

"What?" I interrupted. "It had dragged itself up there from the beach. Is this a true story?"

"Well, he's retired over there in Galway now, so you could talk to him yourself, if you wanted to. What he said was that after all the rains we'd been having, the soil and mud had washed away leaving the rocks and gravel exposed. The seal had dragged herself over the stones all the way up from Cill Rónáin, and her belly was in bits. He swears to this day that she was just lying there staring over towards Flaherty's place, almost dead from the loss of blood. He said she took just the one look at him and then went back to staring over towards the farm. Mulholland said she had the saddest eyes he'd ever seen on any living creature ..."

"Padraig always said there were tears in her eyes," Mary interrupted quietly. "He was a decent young man. He stayed with her until after she died." She was dabbing at her cheeks with a handkerchief. "Now that's the last time I ever want to hear that story in this house. Do you hear me? Sure Jaysus, it's the most terrible thing I ever heard of in my life."

"And that's the story the old Seanachaí gave my father?"

"Yes." They were both staring at me, and I knew there was more to it.

"But you said you knew the Flaherty's, so what's the point? If it's a true story, why would it be so important to my father?"

"Oh, the story's true right enough." Lorcan was shaking his head. "But that's not the point. The point is that the old man told your father that story in every single detail five years before Flaherty ever met the poor woman."

Chapter 29

Curtains

When I called in at the store on Monday morning, Madge O'Neil was sweeping out the front of the shop with a long-handled broom, the dust from the floorboards swirling around an old pair of military-style boots protruding aggressively from beneath a faded denim dress.

"Good morning." She nodded her head in the direction of the counter. "I have most of what you wanted set out for you there now, although nobody's ever heard of that fancy coffee you were asking after. There's a roll of caulking cotton there that should do the job. If you're in need of more, you'd want to let me know. The paint will be in on the afternoon ferry, but the keel bolts won't be here 'till Wednesday at the earliest."

"Would there be any chance of getting them sooner?"

"Going across there yourself would be the only way known to man," she smiled across at me. "Take some of those bags with you, if you need to, but mind you bring them back when you're done."

As I turned to leave, I spotted Brigid, standing on a chair by the window, a measuring tape around her neck, a wooden curtain rod held like a staff in her right hand.

"Good morning, Con Rua." She was smiling down at me like a mischievous teenager. "You didn't see me up here now, did you?"

"No, I didn't," I told her. "What are you doing? You don't look too safe up there."

"Ah sure now, aren't I sick and tired of looking at these same old curtains year after year. I thought we might put up some new ones for the wake."

"So, whose wake is it?" I said, wondering if I was just humoring her.

"Pay her no heed." Madge was whispering close by my side. "She has it set in her mind there's to be a wake here next week."

"You were a long while gone, Con Rua, although I knew you'd be back. We'll take a walk up the cliffs together one day, will we not?"

"He's Con Rua's son, Brigid. Con Rua's dead these past thirty years as well you know."

"Oh, I know who he is, right enough." Brigid was smiling down at me as I moved towards the door. "Does he know who he is, would be more to the point."

As I wheeled my pushbike out to the road, I heard a woman singing. A high pitched, wailing kind of a sound that went on and on. I paused to turn back, but then for some reason, decided against it.

* * *

As I rounded the final corner, heading down towards the quay, smoke was already rising from the chimney of the old shed, and when I wheeled the bike in through the big double doors, I found the old man sitting there in his chair, Boson curled up at his feet.

“Maiden mhaith,” I said. “When did you get back?”

“Good morning. I was back on the last ferry yesterday. Has the paint arrived?”

“No, but it should be here this afternoon. I called in at the store on the way down. I have the caulking cotton and the sealant, but the bolts and the rest of the stuff won’t be here for a few days. You should have come over to Lorcan’s place last night, they were asking after you.”

“Ah, that was more of a family thing.” He stood up. “And besides, the ferry was late in.” He was knocking his pipe out against the red brick surrounding the hearth. “Come on now, let’s get started. We’re almost done, and we don’t have much time.”

* * *

It took us another four days to finalize the preparations. Filling in between the planks with the caulking, squeezing the long lengths of cotton up into the narrow gaps, tamping it into place with wooden mallets and short blunt chisels, the old man working away next to me, showing me how it was done.

“Good! That’s the way. Get it right the way up there now. Not too hard, mind, the planks will swell up again the minute she hits the water. If you hammer it in too tight, they’ll have nowhere to go. Firm but not too hard is the order of the day.”

I watched him as he worked. Feeding the long lines of caulking up between the planking, prodding it in as he went with his little knife, moving constantly from one end of the boat to the other then going back over it again with the mallet and chisel and tapping it all firmly up into place. It took a while for me to get the hang of it. I seemed to be either banging it in too far or not far enough.

"Don't be trying so hard." He was talking to me over his shoulder. "And don't be comparing yourself all the time. Just relax into it, it will come to you."

Once we'd finished, we filled the rest of the gaps with the caulking compound, squeezing it in on top of the long, pale strands of cotton.

"That will stem the water until the planks have taken up. Once they've swelled a little, she'll be right. You'll need to slip her again in a month or so to tidy her up a bit; after that, she'll be as tight as a drum."

The following morning, we went over the hull and deck area again. Filling in hollows, smoothing out irregularities and sealing any of the remaining holes we'd missed. I stood back at the end of that day and stared up at *Erin* in the evening light. She looked quite different now. Slim and graceful, her timbers sanded smooth, ready and waiting for the final touches of color to be reunited once again with her ocean home.

"There's a good drying breeze out there tonight." The old man was standing by the big double doors, looking up at a clear night sky. "If it holds good till the morning, we'll have the first coat on her by noon."

* * *

The next day dawned bright and clear, and as I rode my bike back down towards Cill Rónáin, I felt a great sense of excitement. The whole process had taken on a life of its own and I was looking forward to the day she'd be ready to launch.

The old man was by the fireplace when I arrived, down on one knee, cleaning out the grate.

"Good morning, and a fine morning it is." He nodded towards *Erin.* "The fire was going all night so she's as dry now as she'll ever be. We'll have the first coat on her in no time."

He handed me a paintbrush and soon we were working away together. I couldn't help watching him. Dipping his brush in the pot and then sweeping the paint across *Erin's* bare planks. Working the white undercoat into her timbers, first one way then the other. Long, even strokes, backwards and forwards, smoothing it all off along the grain, his body swaying to some internal rhythm of its own as *Erin* transformed into a thing of beauty before my eyes.

"You're doing well." He was smiling across at me. "It's not the first time you've had a brush in your hand."

"No, I painted the apartment a few times with Giselle. I find it relaxing."

"Yes, it's all that and a statement too, of course." He was smiling. "That's the foundation right there, the undercoat. After that's done, we'll sand her back again and put on another one, still white. But then, with the next two coats, we'll be showing our true colors: dark green superstructure with the white hull and the bronze portholes setting it all off. Once we're done, you'll be able to sail *Erin* into any port in the world and be proud of her."

"Tristan wants to sail her back to Australia. He's a bit of a dreamer."

"Well, you should be grateful for that," he nodded. "If the world's in need of anything right now, it would be dreamers. Dreamers are the visionaries; they perceive a different reality. They don't waste their time complaining about how things are, they dream of how things could be, and they help move us in that direction. Dreamers march to a different drum."

"But you have to be realistic, too," I said, regretting the words before they were out of my mouth.

"Sure Jaysus, there could be nothing more realistic than dreaming if it helps bring about a better world. It's the people who have no dreams we should be concerned about. They're the ones that squander their days. Stuck in jobs that destroy their souls. Throwing their lives away chasing money and prestige. Suppressing their life force and passion and trading what could have been for the illusory security of a few dollars in the bank. Sure Jaysus, did you not have enough of that yourself?" He didn't wait for an answer. "How's the depression been here on Inis Mór?"

"Depression? I haven't given it a second thought."

"Well, there you have it. Fill your days with work you love, and you'll never have to work another day in your life. Understand? When you're working at something you love, sure it isn't work at all, it's a blessing."

* * *

It took us four days to finalize the first two coats. The old man was tireless. First the outside of the hull and then up onto the coach-roof. Working from dawn to dusk. Inspecting the work each evening, making sure that everything was properly filled and sanded before applying the next coat. Watching the weather constantly, concerned about the moisture.

As we waited for each coat to dry, we attended to countless other jobs. Getting the mast down from the rafters, removing the bronze deck fittings for polishing, checking the gudgeon pins on the rudder, sanding her long, curved tiller, and installing the new galvanized keel bolts.

We spent the afternoon of the sixth day working in *Erin's* main cabin, applying varnish to the overhead grab rails.

"Tomorrow, we'll have the first topcoat on her." He was squinting along the length of rail, smoothing the clear varnish into the golden grain of the timber. "You're happy with the colors?"

"Yes, I want her the same way she was the day she was launched."

"Good. After we're done with the painting, we'll get the bow fitting and chain plates back on her." He looked around. "Don't bother sweeping up tonight. The dust will likely catch on the varnish."

* * *

The weather stayed dry for the rest of that week. Clear blue skies and a gentle breeze proving to be perfect weather for painting. We finished the final topcoat just before lunch on the eighth day and then we both stood back to take a look.

Erin sat still and quiet in the afternoon sunlight like a captive swan. Her snow-white hull smooth and graceful, her superstructure dark green, her brass portholes shining like burnished gold, her bowsprit jutting out in front of her, pointing away out towards the ocean, yearning to be set free.

"She's a fine little sea-boat." He said it quietly with a trace of sadness. "That little ship would take you anywhere in the world you had a mind to go." I didn't say anything. It was hard to believe that I'd wanted to sell her. "We'll need to get those deck fittings back on her. After that, we'll stiffen up the cradle. Once that's done, she'll be ready for the high seas."

Chapter 30
Finbar O'Malley

When I stepped through the wicket gate the following morning, there was no sign of life, the air still and cold, the cinders grey in the hearth, the boat standing quiet and alone in the gloomy half-light of the shed. I made up the fire, put the kettle on and then went over and stood there, admiring *Erin.* She was looking every inch like a proper little ship, and I was eager to get her back into the water.

I spent a solitary morning filling screw holes on *Erin's* mast, checking the galvanized steel fittings and sanding back the varnish; but just before midday, the shed door swung open and Lorcan Reardon appeared, followed by Boson, performing his usual spine-twisting rumba of a welcome dance.

"Holy Jaysus, will you take a look at yourself. You're covered in dust. Sure, I thought it was a ghost I was seeing."

"How are you doing, Lorcan? Watch your step, there's paint everywhere."

"Well, I take my hat off to you." He was staring up at the boat. "I never thought I'd see her like this again."

"We're launching her next week. We just need to stiffen the cradle up first."

He was walking around her slowly, running a hand along her gleaming hull. “You’ve done a fine job, Conor. Sure, Grace would be delighted.”

“When did you get back?” I asked.

“I was back on the morning ferry and glad to be home, at that. Galway’s a great little town but a week and a half of it’s about as much as I can stand these days.”

“I was about to make some tea. Will you join me?”

“No, I will not, but I will take you across to the hotel for a late lunch, if you’re up for it.”

“Sounds good to me,” I said. “I’ll clean up a little and be right with you.”

As I stood at the sink, washing, Lorcan was climbing the ladder to the cockpit. “You’ve replaced some of her old fastenings, I see.” He was studying the new work.

“Yes. We pulled out anything that looked corroded. The old man’s pretty thorough.”

“Well, he’s a boat-builder, right enough, I’ll give him that.” He was examining the varnished wooden trim on *Erin’s* coach-roof. “Bronze screws, countersunk in deep. All the slots turned in the same direction. Wooden plugs over the screw heads in the teak. You don’t see much of that work nowadays.” His eyes were roaming around the shed. “He’s not here today?”

“No, he skips a day sometimes.”

He turned back towards me. “You said you had some trouble here last week?”

“Yes. The boat almost rolled over on top of us.”

“And you said he was dancing. What was all that about?”

"Well, it's a bit of a story. The cradle collapsed. It looked bad for a while. He was trapped underneath but then we managed to lift the boat back up and get a prop …"

"How do you mean, lifted the boat?" he broke in. "Sure, *Erin* weighs four tons or more. Ten strong men wouldn't lift her, never mind yourself and an old man."

"Look, I know it sounds weird, but he lifted her. Maybe she was off balance or something. I don't know. But he lifted her. I saw him do it. After that, we sat around talking for a while, and then he put a record on and started dancing. I know it sounds crazy but that's what happened."

"Come on." He was coming back down the ladder. "That's clean enough. It's not a wake I'm taking you to."

We walked up to the pub sharing a single umbrella, the sky overcast, the rain scattering down in intermittent showers, the sea concealed by rolling banks of mist, dense and impenetrable as clouds, Boson strutting on ahead proudly as if to herald our approach.

The hotel stood on an outcrop of rock close by the ocean, its thatched roof hanging low across the small square windows. An old wooden sign bearing the legend "*Food and Drink"* hanging from a rusting iron bar.

As we passed through the entrance, I felt as if I was stepping back in time. The building was ancient. Heavy black wooden beams propped up by thick timber pillars supported a ceiling, stained and clouded by centuries of tobacco smoke. Flintlock pistols, circular steel-rimmed shields and a variety of vicious-looking cutlasses with solid brass handles hung on the grey stone walls. The smoke-hazed inner sanctum vaguely reminiscent of a medieval pirate's hideaway.

"So, what will you have, a Guinness?"

"No. I'll have a Coke thanks, no ice."

As he went to the bar, I settled into a chair by a window overlooking the sea. The mist was rolling in across the heavy, grey green swells, clearing occasionally in patches to allow beams of sunlight to play for a moment or two over the white-crested wavetops before closing back in like fine lace curtains drawn silently across a troubled seascape.

"There's beef and pickle sandwiches there for the both of us." Lorcan was back with a tray. "It was either that or cheese and onion. The cook must've had a heavy night of it." He handed me a large glass of Coke. "Slainte!"

"Cheers," I told him. It never felt right without a proper drink in your hand.

He took a long pull on his glass, sighing like a man suddenly relieved of misfortune.

"Ahhh, that's a great drop there now. Flannery worked at the brewery in Dublin for years. I swear to God, he does the best pint of porter on the West Coast of Ireland." He was frowning. "So, you don't drink at all, Conor?"

"No," I told him. "I can't handle the stuff. Once I get started, I can't stop, so I stay away from it."

"That's very wise of you. My youngest brother had the same problem. He died drunk at thirty-three, the poor man."

"I'm sorry to hear that," I said. "How's Mary?"

"Ah, she's grand." I watched as he settled into a chair. "Mary's one of the finest women you'd meet in a long day's march. Although, I must admit, she can be difficult at times." He winked across at me and took another pull on his pint. "She's a fierce one for the church altogether."

"So, I gathered. And you're not?"

"No, not really. I never was. I've studied the history of Ireland these past sixty years and I often wonder if it wouldn't have been better if St. Patrick had sailed right on past us and taken his notions elsewhere."

"So, you're not a Catholic, then?"

"Ah now, that's not a discussion I'd choose to get into. I have my own beliefs, put it that way, if you will." He was looking out the window, down towards the quayside. "So, you've made yourself comfortable enough at the shed?"

"Yes. I furnished it with all the bits and pieces that were left over down there. How did you go in Galway with the deeds to the cottage? Were there any problems?"

"No, none. It's done. We left it in the name of Conor O'Rourke. Anything else would have confused matters too much." He emptied his glass and set it back down on the table. "They'll have the papers sent out to you within the week."

"I'll get the drinks," I said. "Are you having another Guinness?"

"I am indeed. I've never refused a glass in my life and I won't be starting now."

When I came back to the table, Lorcan was sitting with his back to me, looking out through the rain-streaked window, Boson squatting on his rump in front of him, staring up patiently with his goldfish eyes as if awaiting some long overdue lecture. Over in the distance, partly obscured by the encroaching mist, an old square-rigged sailing ship was moving majestically along. Her sails filled and pulling, white water at her bow, a gentle, rolling, swaying motion as she cut through the grey green seas, heading in the direction of Galway.

"What would she be?" I said. "Some sort of training ship?"

"What was that?" He pulled himself upright suddenly, and I realized he must have been dozing.

"The ship out there. The square-rigger. Can you see her? Look, over there. A mile or so off the end of the jetty."

"Wait." He was fumbling with his glasses. "Where?"

"Over there, look. No, not there, over there." She was beginning to disappear, swallowed up by the rolling banks of mist. "Do you see her? Right off the end of the jetty. No, it's too late, she's gone." The boat had slipped away like a phantom, disappearing into the mist as if she'd never existed. I passed him a pint, jet black, solid white head. "I saw a square rigger the first week I was here," I told him. "It's probably the same one. I was up on the cliffs by Dun Aengus. What would she be, a training ship of some sort? Is there one based over there in Galway?"

"No." He was shaking his head. "Not that I know of. You'll see an old sailing boat going past every so often. We had the *Esmeralda* in here a few years back, the Chilean training ship. But that was something of a rarity. Just so long as it wasn't the *Galway Rose* you saw, you'll be right. Slainte." He raised his glass. "Good luck."

"So, what's the story with the *Galway Rose*? What was she, a ghost ship?"

"That's about what she was, right enough, a ghost ship." He was nodding. "I was telling you the other night about Finbar O'Malley. Well, she was his boat. He was her captain. More's the pity, some would say. Mary won't have his name mentioned in the house. God alone knows why. She has an extraordinary fear of ghosts. For all her Holy Roman Catholic beliefs, there's still a lot of pagan lurking down there somewhere in my good wife."

"So, what happened to the *Galway Rose*? Or is it that another one of the island's mysteries?"

"Well, it's an interesting story, right enough. But like so many of them, impossible to work out which parts are true, and which are not. You see, the O'Malley's were a bit like your own family, a mixture of Seanachaí and seamen. Not fisher people like the O'Rourke's, mind, but deep-sea men that took square-rigged sailing ships around the Horn. Finbar's father was a sea captain, but his grandfather was a Seanachaí. A Seanachaí of the old school. One of the greatest storytellers of his day, I believe. Old Patrick O'Malley had his home here on Inis Mór although he traveled a lot, of course, telling his stories. He was said to be well over the hundred mark when he died and that could easily be true. People do live to a great age here on the islands."

"I know," I said. "The two old girls up at the store must be close to a hundred."

"Well, yes and no." He took a bite on the sandwich and sat there chewing for a moment or two before continuing. "Madge O'Neil would be close to a hundred, but Brigid would be a hundred and five if she's a day."

"I've met her," I said. "What's wrong with her? Is it Alzheimer's?"

"Oh no. It's not like that at all. She's grand. Sure, she's been that way from as far back as I can remember. Don't be worrying your head about Brigid O'Neil; she'll outlive the two of us. Sure, wasn't she up at the cheili Christmas last, skipping around like a two-year-old?"

"She looked pretty frail the other day," I said. "I can't imagine her dancing."

"Well, isn't that the craic now with Brigid. She'll lie on that bed of hers for weeks on end, not moving a muscle and then, the next thing you know, she'll be up and off over the fields like a hare. Away off to Dun Aengus or the old lighthouse. Striding along, just as quick as you like. And don't go getting in her way when she has her mind set. She'll take that stick of hers to you in a flash, if she needs to. Sure, didn't she give a Garda a skelp only last summer? Madge had sent him up to the cliffs to bring her back when she lit into him with the blackthorn. He was supposed to be pressing charges, but he lost the heart. It wouldn't be a good thing to have on your record, of course, getting yourself laid out cold by a hundred-year-old senior citizen. He was running around here for a week with a lump on his head, the size of an ostrich egg. He never went near her again, and her only four foot nothing in her high heels."

"So, she is pretty crazy then," I said.

"Oh no, not at all. She's her own woman, that's all. Sure, you can't blame her. She has a right to be off over the fields, the same as you or me. She's a strange one, right enough, but I wouldn't feel right calling her crazy. She sees things. It was Brigid that warned Grace of Con Rua's death."

"How was that?"

"Well, from as far back as I know of, she's been giving out warnings, you know, prophesies and the like. They come to her from nowhere. She has no idea what they're about herself. There's those on the island say she's possessed, but I've heard of cases like hers before. There's a man in Dublin, I'm told, that can give you an answer to any mathematical problem you might have in no more than a second or two, yet he's not fit to tie his own shoelaces. They're retarded in some ways but then suddenly, they'll come out with the greatest truths for no known reason. She sees things. Ghosts and the like. It wouldn't have been thought of as all that strange here just a few years ago."

"But how did she warn Grace about my father's death?"

"In a song." He was staring out the window. The sky had darkened, the black rolling clouds that had been lurking out on the horizon moving in closer, as if considering whether or not to join in an assault on Inis Mór. The rain falling steadily, tiny streams of water like miniature rivulets coursing in zigzag patterns down the small square panes of glass. "Grace went up to the store there one day, for whatever reason. Con Rua had been over in Galway for a few years by then. Oh, he came home often enough, but it was never the same. He'd bring you along with him whenever he could." He paused and glanced across at me. "I won't speak ill of the dead, but your mother had no time at all for the island."

"I know that," I told him. "She said as much herself."

"Well," he began again. "Grace went in there one day and Brigid started on singing about Con Rua selling his gift and being lost to the world unless he came back to his own. She went on and on, I believe. Singing the same few lines over and over again …

Con Rua's gone a roving

To Galway and the shore

To sell the gift to strangers

Lost to his heart once more

The life force dying in him

Lest he return to Inis Mór."

"Well, it frightened the life out of poor Grace, as you can well imagine. Brigid can be fierce once she gets started. There's plenty of them laugh at her but there's not many would do it to her face." He glanced across at me. "Grace warned Con Rua, of course, but he took no heed. By that time, he was one of the best known of all the Irish

Seanachaí. He was wanted everywhere with his stories, always on the go. Over to Wales and Scotland, at times. Grace pleaded with him, but it was pointless. He had a mind of his own, did Con Rua." Lorcan paused, still staring out the window. "He died a few months later. That shook us all."

"So how does she come up with that stuff?"

"No one knows. Least of all herself. Some say it's a gift, others say it's a curse. God alone would know the truth."

"She said something about a fili. That's a poet, isn't it?"

"Yes. A poet or a Seanachaí." He was staring across at me. "What else did she say?"

"She said something about me asking the fili about a boat. It didn't make any sense. She told me to ask him about the men that were lost from a boat, or something like that. Her sister had no idea what she was talking about."

Lorcan took a pull on his Guinness, studying me across the top of the glass.

"Does the old man ever tell you stories?"

"Yes. He's told me quite a few stories."

"Stories of the sea?"

"Yes, why?"

He ignored my question.

"What else? What other things has he told you?"

"Well, we talk about the work, mostly. You know, about how to do things right."

"Is there poetry involved in any of this?" Lorcan was staring across at me. "Does he speak in rhyme at all?"

"Yes, he does. Why do you ask?"

"Did you mention to him anything of what Brigid said?"

"No. I don't think so. Why? Why all the interest in the old man suddenly?" And then it dawned on me. "Oh, give over Lorcan! You don't honestly think he's the same old guy my father knew, do you? That would make him over a hundred years old, wouldn't it? That'd be too much altogether. And why wouldn't he just say so, anyhow?"

"I have no idea; it was just a thought. What's the oldest you'd say he'd be? Could he be in his nineties? Ninety-five or more? Is it possible?"

"No, I don't think so. He'd be about eighty or eighty-five. There's no way in the world he could be a hundred years old."

"Ah, well," he shrugged. "People do live to a great age here, there's no doubt about that."

"So, what's the story with Finbar O'Malley? You were saying he went off to sea himself, is that right?"

"Yes indeed. You see Finbar came from a long line of seamen, but there were Seanachaí among them too. His mother had died giving birth to him, so he was brought up entirely in the male camp, as it were. When his father was at sea, he'd live with his grandfather, traveling with him all over Ireland, going from town to town as old Patrick told his stories. But then, when the father returned, he'd be off back home again to Inis Mór, to the family cottage, listening to tales of the sea and foreign lands."

Lorcan took a drink before continuing.

"You see, Finbar was a boy of thirteen when the famine struck Ireland. His father had been away for a year and a half at the time, and many thought himself and the boat were lost. Times were hard, but he managed to find himself work in a shipyard, repairing old boats and building new ones, but then that work fell away as the famine took hold and he signed on as a cabin boy on a square-rigged sailing ship running out of Galway. Well, that was how it all started." He finished off his pint and held out a hand. "You want another Coke? I have no idea how you can drink that stuff."

"Thanks." I slid my glass across the table and, as he walked up towards the bar, I happened to glance out the window, and there she was again, closer in this time. Her sails billowing, her spars towering up above the ocean, heeled over to the wind, bowing and dipping gracefully, stray patches of sunlight glistening off her wooden masts.

I stood up and pressed my face against the glass panes. She was much closer in now, only a half mile or so off the end of the jetty, and I wondered how she could have beaten her way back out against the tide without us noticing her. The visibility had improved a little, but I still couldn't make out anyone on deck. But then, as I watched, the gap in the mist began to close again, white clouds of vapor swirling around her once more as she gradually disappeared from sight.

"There you go."

Lorcan was standing next to me, holding out a glass.

"I just saw her again," I said, pointing in the direction of the jetty. "She's a lot closer in now. How deep's the water out there? Could she be in trouble?"

"Not from lack of water she's not." He was staring out into the mist. "There'd be plenty enough water out there for any size boat. Don't be worrying yourself about her now. She's probably one of those fancy American cruise ships you read about. They're made up to look old on the outside, but they're all mod cons down below. No doubt she'd have an engine in her that would put the Queen Mary to shame."

"No, she was under sail," I told him. "She had all her canvas up."

He peered across at me as I settled back in my chair

"There's not much of a breeze out there, Conor."

I felt completely stupid. It hadn't dawned on me.

"Maybe there's a bit more wind offshore," I said.

"Maybe." He nodded. "Now, where was I? Oh yes, Finbar O'Malley. Well, Finbar stayed with the same line for years. He was a big lad, over six feet in height with shoulders on him that would have embarrassed an ox. He took to the sea well. All the dreams he'd had of becoming a Seanachaí swept away through necessity. He was tested, of course, as young lads are at sea, but he'd been brought up in a hardy enough way without a mother and the other seamen soon learned not to press him too far. Well, within a few months of signing on, he was put up to deck hand, and within a year of that, he was made able-bodied seaman. He was never happier than when he was climbing the rigging of those hundred and fifty-foot-high masts, putting to shame grown men who couldn't keep up with his strength or courage. To cut a long story short, within five years of signing on, Finbar was appointed boson of a square-rigged sailing ship running out of Dublin around Cape Horn. Well, he never looked back. Two years after that, his captain died at sea and Finbar took over his first command. At twenty-one years of age, he was the youngest Irish captain afloat."

Lorcan sighed as if regretting the whole incident.

"A year or so later, he married a young Galway woman by the name of Connie Flynn. Now Connie was a music teacher, and many thought them mismatched, but others felt she'd be good for him, that she might soften him a little, as it were. Well, they were married less than a year when a child came along. Now, Aidan O'Malley was as different from Finbar as it was possible to be. Where his father was a tall, big boned, bull of a man, young Aidan was pale and slim. Where Finbar was bold and outgoing, Aidan was quiet and thoughtful. It was said of him that he was his mother's son, and I suppose that was true enough in many ways, for he took to the arts early, music, poetry and storytelling."

Lorcan smiled across at me.

"Old Patrick loved young Aidan from the very start, and it was said that he was more of a father to the boy than Finbar ever was. He'd have him sitting on his knee through the long winter evenings as he told his stories, traveling with him from the age of three to the fairs and gatherings around Ireland, watching, listening, and learning the ways of the Seanachaí."

He paused for a moment as if deep in thought before going back to the tale.

"You see, Finbar loved his son right enough, but he was awkward with the lad, and even when he was home, there was a distance between them. He'd wanted more children, but it was not to be, so he did the best he knew how with Aidan. Every time he'd sail back into port, he'd have his wife bring young Aidan down to the boat, hopeful that might inspire an interest, but in fact, it had just the opposite effect. The boy was frightened of the ship, almost as if he had some premonition each time he was taken on board. Aidan was ten years of age when Finbar resigned his commission and proceeded to build a boat of his own. Now, by that time he'd sailed the high seas for twenty-five years and was known to be one of the shrewdest seamen afloat. He'd worked as a boat-builder as a boy, he'd served as captain on a score or more of ships, he was familiar with every port and river in the trading world, and he knew exactly what sort of vessel he wanted. She was to be a three-masted barque, one of the fastest ships afloat. The day the *Galway Rose* was launched, he was the proudest man in Ireland and, as she slipped into the waters at Dublin,

Finbar bent down and whispered: "Remember this day well, son. One day, you will be her master."

Lorcan took a long pull on the Guinness before settling back in his chair.

"Well now, things went along right enough for the next few years but then, on one of Finbar's periods ashore, the subject of Aidan's future came up one evening over dinner. The wife told Finbar that the boy had a great gift for storytelling, and she felt he should be encouraged in that direction. She told her husband that their son had been attending wakes and weddings and was already recounting stories and songs of his own making. Well, Finbar was dismayed. He'd had no idea that the young lad had been following the path of the Seanachaí, and what had started out as an idle conversation soon turned into a bitter argument.

"'My son is to be a seaman,' he told her. 'His course in life is set. There's enough Seanachaís amongst the O'Malley's, as it is!'

"'But Finbar,' she persisted, 'our son has the gift. Sit and listen to him, if you would. Make your judgment then.'

"'There is no more judgment to be made,' he'd stormed. 'It's done. He's fifteen years of age. He sails with me on our next voyage. The time has come for him to become a man.' The wife had protested but to no avail. Some said it was Finbar's lack of a mother that had him so hard. Others said it was because he'd turned away from his own gift and therefore couldn't allow it in his son. Whatever the cause, young Aidan O'Malley sailed away in the *Galway Rose* the following month, bound for Cape Horn ..."

"Lorcan, this is a lot like a story the old man told me." But he just nodded and carried on.

"Now the boy was a bit of a dreamer and unused to the ways of the sea, but he made friends easy enough among the crew and he'd tell them stories in the evenings in his little cabin. Night after night, they'd crowd in there, young Aidan sitting cross-legged on his bunk, recounting the legends of Cú Chulainn and Fergus McRoach, stories of Tír na nÓg and poems that he'd learnt from old Patrick. Well, the early parts of the voyage were grand but, as the days went by and the ship drew close to the Horn, the weather began to deteriorate, and the young lad fell sick. The crew looked after him the best they could but soon he was incapable of doing his duties and he was confined to his cabin. He still told his stories each night for he knew the men loved them, and sometimes, he would sing for them or play the fiddle ..."

"Was it a fiddle or a violin?"

"No matter." Lorcan was too far into the story to stop. "As they approached Cape Horn, Finbar became convinced that his son was malingering. He couldn't understand how the boy could tell his stories to the crew each night and yet still be unable to fulfill his duties on deck. Well, the day it all came to a head, it was blowing a gale. The barometer had fallen to its lowest point. They hadn't sighted land in weeks, the sky above them was dark, both day and night. The waves sweeping along endlessly and forever around them. The winds droning on through the rigging like the sound of lost souls calling out for redemption. The seas breaking over the ship, as they do in those latitudes, washing along the decks in great waves as the crew clung on to the rope handrails, hanging on for grim life and praying to God above for mercy."

He paused and took another bite from the sandwich, staring out through the window as if seeking out the next piece of the story in the rolling mist.

"Finbar was exhausted that night," he continued quietly. "He'd been on watch for twenty-four hours, unwilling to leave the wheel through the worst of the storm. But as he stood there on the afterdeck, the elements raging around him, listening to his son's voice rising up over the sound of the wind and water, keening out some ancient Celtic lament for Cú Chulainn's lonely death, something inside him snapped and he went rushing below in a fury. He scattered the men from the cabin and raged at the lad about being a coward until the boy broke down and wept. Young Aidan was totally shocked. You see, he'd been of the notion that he was being of some use on the ship, telling his stories. Now he realized that his father considered his gift to be worthless."

Lorcan was looking across at me.

"It's a terrible thing. You see, all this part of the story is true, taken from actual records." He was shaking his head. "Well, the boy went up on deck later that same night. The crew said afterwards that he appeared to be in a trance. Not holding on to anything, as you would mind, but just standing there motionless on the deck as if his spirit had already left him. Well, the next thing, he was gone. Now, whether he went over the side by his own hand or whether he was washed from the decks by a wave, no man could say. After searching high and low, they woke Finbar and the order was given to turn the ship around, but it was an impossible task. As they swung beam on to the seas, the vessel began to founder, overwhelmed by the sheer force of the waters. Finbar tried again and again. They said at the inquiry that he seemed to have lost his mind altogether. Six men were washed from her decks that night before the crew mutinied. They refused his orders and tried to take control, but they said he was like a man possessed, cursing and swearing and fighting with the men on the helm. Finally, one of the crew took a belaying pin to his head and laid him out cold. Well, the next thing anyone heard was that the *Galway Rose* was limping into one of those South American ports close down by the Horn. The boat battered, the crew exhausted and the captain half mad with grief from the loss of his son."

"Lorcan, this is the same story the old man told me. The captain went off then looking for him with a skeleton crew and they were never seen again. Right?"

"Oh no. Nothing like that." He was shaking his head. "No, they came back home, right enough. There were some repairs done to the *Galway Rose*. They took on a few more crew, and then they sailed her back to Ireland. There was an uproar, of course, and an inquiry. It was a well-known case at the time, and it dragged on for months. Finbar didn't fare well at all. The crew who'd survived all spoke well of him, mind. They'd rallied around him after the death of his boy, but to no avail. The official verdict was that Finbar O'Malley had lost his son and his crew through negligence and bad seamanship."

"So, what happened to him? Did he ever go back to sea?"

"No. Sure Jaysus, he was fit for nothing after that. The wife left him after the loss of the boy, so he came back home to Inis Mór alone. Old Patrick had died during the inquest, of a broken heart they say, and all Finbar had left was a little cottage that used to stand up on the hill there by Kilmurvey. It's known that he wandered around the island like a ghost for months afterwards. There was no purpose left to his life at all. Most of the men that were lost overboard were from Galway, and he was shunned by many. People can be very cruel about a thing like that. The *Galway Rose* lay at anchor in Dublin for a year or more and then one night, she just disappeared. It was said to be the same night that Finbar threw himself from the cliffs up there at Dun Aengus. Well, that's where the stories began, I suppose. Legend has it that, when he arrived at the gates of Tír na nÓg, he was stopped by Brigid, the Goddess of poets and sailors, who was enraged by the way the boy had been lost, and Finbar was refused entry. He was told that he must return to earth by the gate of Inis Mór until such a time as he had made amends for his crimes. Told by Brigid herself that Tír na nÓg was forbidden to him until he'd saved the lives of fifteen young men, one for each year of the boy's life. All of them to be future Seanachaí."

I looked back out the window. It was almost four o'clock. The dusk of evening hastened on by an overcast sky. The horizon obscured, the rain falling endlessly across the shiny black cobbled quayside below.

"That was a long time ago," I said. "He must have saved quite a few by now."

"That's right." Lorcan was staring across at me. "It's said that he accomplished the task and was forgiven years ago. Finbar's tragedy was that he was never able to forgive himself. They say that's why he's stayed on here all these years."

"So, it's a ghost story."

"Perhaps."

"Is the cottage still there?"

"No, not anymore. It stood in ruins for years when I was a boy; people thought it haunted. These stories take on a life of their own. It was pulled down not long ago as unsafe." He paused and looked at his watch. "I'll have to make a move. Mary will be wondering where I am."

"Me too. I'd better get back and close up the shed. Thanks for the sandwich."

We walked out of the hotel together and stood there for a moment on the stone steps. The rain was beginning to ease a little, the first hopeful sign of a break in the weather.

"And don't be off looking for the *Galway Rose*." He was staring out across the darkening waters. "Legend has it that if she passes close enough by you, then either yourself or some blood relation will die within the month."

"Thanks for that," I said. "That's a nice cheerful little note to finish up on."

"It's a story," he smiled. "Slan go foill, Conor. Safe home."

We went our separate ways, and I strolled back along the quayside alone. The boatshed was in darkness and I decided instead to walk out to the end of the jetty. I pulled my cap lower, turned up the collar of my jacket and walked out to where the cobblestones met the sea. There wasn't a soul in sight. A couple of fishing boats tied up alongside the wall, rising and falling gently on the late evening swell, their hulls lifting quietly as the water took them and then sighing back down as the ocean breathed out once again. The mist was still drifting by, but as I stood there mulling over the events of the day, a glimmer of light caught my attention and I turned.

As my eyes took in the sight before me, my heart faltered. Out across the water, just a few hundred yards from where I stood, a huge, square-rigged sailing ship was cruising silently along. Her sails billowing like rope-tethered clouds. Her bow cutting effortlessly through the still, black water. Her three wooden masts towering high above her. The massive bulk of her hull rolling gently this way and that as she forged steadfastly along towards some unknown destination.

For a moment, it took my breath away, but then as I stood there staring, trying to comprehend what was happening, I remembered what Lorcan had said. "She's probably one of those American cruise ships." I scoured her decks, searching for some sign of life, but there was none, the boat appeared to be deserted. The big, timber spoked wheel high on her after deck moving a little, this way and that, clockwise a notch or two, then counterclockwise, as if some firm, invisible hand held sway. The only sign of life, a pale, candlelight glow coming from the stern cabin. I held my breath as she passed by, struggling to contain my fear. Desperately trying to believe that what I saw was real. Leaning forward instinctively, trying to catch a sound, but then, as I stood there staring after her, she simply disappeared. Sliding silently into the gloom of the star dark night ahead.

Chapter 31
Endings

I knew before I opened my eyes the next day that the weather had taken a turn for the worse. The wind that had been tugging at the thatched roof since the early hours of the morning, was now coursing in across the slate grey sea, wailing and keening over the rising swells like a requiem for lost souls.

I peered out the window cautiously, heavy, low-slung clouds, dark grey and ominous, were moving with a sullen tread towards the island, seething like cauldrons of boiling porridge, tumbling and writhing across an ever-darkening sky, bringing with them that sodden, pregnant menace that always precedes the worst of the storms.

I lay there in bed remembering. I'd dreamt that the old man had been telling stories down at the boatshed, sitting on what looked like a medieval wooden throne, surrounded by a throng of people. My father had been there with Mary and Lorcan, and my grandfather too, and the postmaster, Tim O'Sullivan. When the old man had finished the story, everybody had clapped, and then he'd had gone around the room, shaking hands and talking in Irish, but when it came to my turn, I couldn't speak the language, so he just smiled at me and passed on by without a word.

The rain continued falling as I cooked breakfast, silver shards of water driven sideways by a resentful wind, vicious torrents slashing in against the kitchen windows, hammering down remorselessly against the cottage roof and walls as if determined to wash away all traces of human habitation.

I wasn't sure if the old man would be down to the shed or not, so I worked around the house all morning, studying charts and waiting for a break in the weather. The radio kept assuring me that the rain would be easing later on in the day but, by three o'clock, it was still pouring down, so I called Pat Donovan's number and, fifteen minutes later, I was running for the shelter of his cab, a child's yellow plastic raincoat flapping uselessly around my head and shoulders.

"How are you doing, Pat?" I slammed the door shut behind me. "We're headed for the boatshed, if you would, mate."

"The boatshed!" I'd smelt the Guinness as soon as I'd opened the car door. "Well, aren't you the lad! There wouldn't be a decent, god-fearing man working on these islands today." He threw the taxi into a tight sweeping curve, heading back down towards the village. "Why don't I take the two of us up to Flaherty's for a jar? Sure, the craic's fierce, the music's going strong and there's fire up there that would burn the arse off a donkey!"

"No thanks," I told him. "It's a bit early for me."

"Ah, Jaysus, don't give me that." He was swinging the taxi into tight little corners with that unquestioning faith in providence given only to the very drunk. "Sure, haven't I been at it myself since nine o'clock this morning." He looked at me reproachfully over his shoulder, the whites of his eyes shot through with red, the cab somehow finding its own way along the rain-washed, storm-darkened lanes. "Give yourself a break from that old boat of yours. Sure Jaysus, you're obsessed!"

I paid him off at the quayside, still complaining about my abstinence, and made a run for it. There were no lights on at the shed, but I knew that the old man was there by the smoke billowing from the crooked chimney, and sure enough, as I stumbled in through the wicket gate, he was sitting there in gathering gloom by a roaring fire, Boson stretched out snoring at his feet.

"Good day to you. If I can say such a thing on a day like this." He smiled. "The electricity is gone. You might well have stayed home for all the good we'll be doing here today."

"I didn't think you'd be here," I said.

"Ah sure, it would take more than a drop of rain to ground an old seadog like myself." He was looking around. "Are there candles?"

"Yes."

He watched as I placed various sized candles around the shelves, Boson still snoring away, his paws shuffling occasionally in some private, doggy dream all of his own.

"You slept well, boy?"

"Yes, the storms don't bother me. They're a nice change from Australia."

"Do you dream at all?"

I looked across at him.

"I dreamt last night that you were down here talking to a crowd of people. You know, telling them stories. I dreamt you were a Seanachaí." I was watching his face. "I guess I should have realized that before now."

He turned back to the fire.

"And what else did you dream?" He spoke the words quietly, his voice little more than a whisper.

"I don't know. I know I felt frustrated. I wanted to tell them a story too, but I couldn't speak, for some reason."

"So why not tell me a story." He was staring at me, stony-faced.

"How do you mean, tell you a story?"

"Tell me a story. There's not much else we can do here today. Tell me a story, that's easy understood."

"I don't know any stories."

"Tell me the one about the captain," he smiled. "There's a story you know."

"What would be the point of that? That's the one you told me."

"Why don't you just tell me the story and we'll see how it goes."

I was feeling awkward, like a little boy back in school again.

"I'm not sure …"

"Try," he nodded. "Begin in the traditional way if you would. It's always a good way to start …"

The sky outside was leaden, the rain battering down hard against the roof of the old shed, flashes of lightning flickering uncertainly across the windows as we sat there still in the candlelight.

"Well …" I hesitated. "A long, long time ago, but then again, not so long ago at all, in a place known to few, yet frequented by many, there lived a certain ship's captain …"

Within minutes, I found myself describing the captain in the greatest detail. How tall he was, the color of his eyes, the cut of his jaw, the uniform he wore, and the way he walked. All details the old man had never mentioned and yet as clear to me as I spoke as if I'd met the captain himself a hundred times. We sat there beside the crackling fire, rain hammering down rhythmically, lightning bolts quivering intermittently across the night dark sky, probing down onto the earth's surface like ghostly, gnarled fingers from some other world, transported a century away to the wilds of Cape Horn, carried into a world of myth and legend by the power and imagery of the story.

He sat with his eyes closed, taking a puff on his pipe now and again and nodding occasionally.

I told the story without thought or effort. It was as if someone else was speaking through me. A clear, strong energy coursing up from my heart, carrying the old story forward into its next incarnation.

"'We're coming about!' the captain was roaring over the sound of the wind and water. 'Hard down on the helm, Master Boson, we are coming about,' but the men knew that he'd lost his senses and realizing that he'd kill them all in his madness, they overpowered him, locked him in his cabin and swung the ship back on her course."

When I finally drew the story to a close, the old man sat there staring at me for a long moment before speaking.

"You didn't miss a part of it," he said. "You added color of your own, and I felt the sadness in my heart as you spoke."

"So, you think I'm a Seanachaí?"

"You have the gift," he nodded. "There's no denying that."

"But where does that leave me? I can't make a living telling stories."

"You're a Seanachaí, living in the shadow side of your calling. Squandering the gift over there in Australia, writing silly jingles and telling people lies. That's the reason your life fell apart." He looked back into the fire again. "What you need will be given to you if you have the courage to be true to your destiny. If you're to put money first, then one day you will lose everything, including that money.

You've traveled that road already; have you not? You fear poverty?" He shook his head. "The worst form of poverty comes from squandering your life. That is true poverty. Open your eyes. There was never a time when the earth was in more need of our help. Every human being living in their calling adds something of value to the world. Some Seanachaí will stay with the oral tradition. Some will write out their stories for others to read. Perhaps you will do both. Tell the truth, your experience will help others. Without a vision, the people perish. Create stories that will inspire others and bring hope to the world."

There was a flash of lightning as he spoke that lit up the whole room, followed immediately by a deafening roll of thunder that shook the shed to its foundations.

"But I've never done anything like that before," I said. "I wouldn't know where to start."

"That's not true." He shook his head. "You've been telling stories for years. All that advertising nonsense, all your old blarney, living in the dark side of the gift. These would be stories of a different nature. Stories that would bring hope to people's hearts and meaning to their lives." He took a puff on his pipe. "And by the way, if any of the stories I told you along the way could be of use to you, feel free to use them. I give them to you now with my blessing."

I stared at him for a moment, unsure whether I could ask.

"You gave my father a story once, didn't you?"

There was a long silence, then he stood up and went across to the boat.

"You do ask the strangest questions, boy."

I got up and followed him over to where he was standing.

"And you have the strangest way of avoiding them. Do you realize that I don't even know your name?"

He was running a hand over *Erin's* hull, stroking her sides as if she were a living thing.

"She's a pretty one. The same as the day she was launched." He was staring up at her. "That's *Erin* right there, your grandfather's legacy to you." Flickering shades of light, thrown up from a dozen candles, were casting a warm glow over her white hull. "She needs two more coats of varnish on her mast, but you know about that. Finish the paint right, and she's ready for the open seas."

There was something in his voice.

"You are going to be here for the launch." I said.

"There are things I need to attend to over in Galway." He was staring up at the boat's rubbing strake.

"So, when are you going over there?"

"I'm booked on the morning ferry."

"There's a gale blowing out there,"

"We're on the edge of it." He wasn't looking at me. "It will have blown itself out by morning."

"So, you're leaving tomorrow?"

"I am," he nodded, "God willing."

"How long do you think you'll be gone?"

"It's hard to say. I have a few things to attend to, but I'm sure there'll be time enough for everything. You go ahead with the mast. I'll be back as soon as I can."

He'd gone back to stroking the hull.

"Are you going to be here for the launch or not?"

He turned away from *Erin* and walked past me. "You don't need me to launch a boat. My work here is done."

I stood there for a moment, not sure of which way to go.

"I have no idea how to thank you."

He'd gone across to the bench, and was collecting his things, putting them back in an old, brown leather bag.

"Thank me for what?" He looked up, smiling. "For doing what I love?"

I followed him across and stood behind him, not sure of what to say. Suddenly he turned.

"Come here, Con Rua," and before I knew it, his arms were around me, enveloping me in an embrace that buried me in the folds of his black greatcoat. For a moment, I almost pushed him away, but then I relaxed, a smell of tar and tobacco and saltwater enveloping me like some ancient dream of the sea. "You're a good man," he said, his deep voice reverberating throughout my body. "Look after yourself, and look after that boy of yours. Show him what it means to follow his heart."

"Why did you call me Con Rua?"

"That's what you were known as here as a boy." He was staring down into my face. "That's what it means in the Irish. Con Rua, Red Conor. You were both red heads. Both yourself and your da."

There was a deafening thunderclap directly overhead as he spoke, and I took an involuntary step backwards, and almost fell. Something had dawned on me when he'd called me Con Rua, something I could hardly believe. I looked up at him, confused, and as I did, I realized that he looked older and frailer somehow.

"Are you all right?"

"Yes," he said. But I knew that he was not.

"Sit down," I told him. "I'll make us some tea."

He nodded as I went to the hearth, but I know that I saw him sit down in the chair. I busied myself with the tea things then, setting out the mugs, getting the sugar. I was feeling sad and confused, but stronger somehow too, and suddenly I knew, for the first time, that I could finish the boat by myself if I had to.

"Look," I said, turning around. "If you have to go over to Galway ..."

But the chair was empty, the old man had disappeared. I went to the doorway and peered out along the quayside through the teeming rain, but there was no sign of him. I stood there for a long while, thinking over what he'd said, until the whistling of the kettle brought me back to the moment. As I walked back into the candlelit shed, I couldn't help wondering if I would ever see him again.

Chapter 32
The Wake

I woke late the following day and lay in bed thinking over the conversation of the previous evening. The wind had died overnight, and the rain was now no more than a gentle murmur falling softly against the bedroom windows. I thought of the old man and, for the very first time, it struck me as odd that I didn't even know his name.

After a while I got up, went down below, and made coffee, and standing by the back door looking out across the ocean, I thought of my father. The times we'd had together, the memories I'd suppressed, the years I hadn't even given him a thought, the unconscious selfishness of a wounded child, and the isolation of never knowing who it was that stood behind me. And I knew it was time to revisit his grave.

After leaving the cottage, I bought red roses at the little store at Kilmurvey, then walked up along the crooked laneways towards the graveyard. The day was still and overcast, a soft, gentle rain drifting in like heavy dew across a dark rolling ocean. The fields sodden and silent, blank-faced cattle standing stoic and mute behind their limestone enclosures. An ancient, sway-backed white horse, looking like a leftover prop from *The Man of La Mancha*, staring at me hopelessly over the top of a low, crumbling wall.

As I entered the main gate, I saw that Grace's new headstone had been erected. A simple, oblong monument like many of the others. The inscription standing fresh and clear. The sign of the Seanachaí cut deep into the center of the stone.

Grace O'Rourke 1915-2003

Loving Wife of Kieran O'Rourke

Mother of Con Rua O'Rourke

The Seanachaí of Inis Mór

He feared not life, he feared not death

He feared the place between

The place there is no passion

The place we lose our dreams

I knelt, placed the flowers on her grave and said a prayer, knowing at last what it was she'd wanted of me. "There's nothing to forgive," I told her. "You knew it wasn't my father. You knew that I was the Con Rua that Brigid sang of. I was the one that left the shore. I was the one that would sell the gift. I was the one lost to the world …"

I stayed there with her for a long while, talking to her, believing she could hear me.

Then I went across to where my father lay, and I knelt. His monument, still and expectant, in the grey light of morning. The soft, misted rain coming down like a blessing from above. Falling down across my face … down across my shoulders … down across his grave … the roses, blood red and green-leaved, against the black marble, drops of moisture gathering together before gliding down in silver streams across the stone, a silent communion, an enveloping of the spirit, a sense of relief and release, a reaching out and a reaching in, a whispering, breathing, soul song carried softly over the graves …

Sensing coursing spirits, my father and his kin

Still upon a hillside, yet strong their souls within

Around him and forever stretching back in time

My family through the ages each one had stood in line

A star dark, soul found memory, of race and home and blood

That I had sprung from this same soil at last I understood

To follow heart, to follow soul, to follow Spirit's ways

To tell the tales of days gone by, to remember whence I came

From the wet, the wild, the stony, the laughter and the pain

To seek Cú Chulainn in my own heart lest he died alone in vain

As I knelt before my father, I felt his spirit rise

Embracing me from Tír na nÓg where Irish souls reside

A laughing, singing presence, a story not quite told

A passing of an ancient gift, offered up for me to hold

A man I'd left behind in grief, a spirit long denied

When I stood at last to take my leave, I felt him by my side

I wept, but not in sorrow, the tears released in love

I felt his arms around me, a blessing from above

I know he stands behind me in unbroken Irish line

I know the gift he gave me came with an ancient sign

I felt his courage in my heart, I felt his strength and more

And knew I'd never lose again what I'd found on Inis Mór ...

* * *

As I walked back down the empty lanes, the weather trying to clear, fleeting patches of blue sky appearing occasionally from behind a slate grey horizon. The sun sparkling intermittently over a deep green, white-flecked ocean before disappearing behind the towering banks of cloud moving majestically and forever across the island's western shore. As I came down the final slope towards Cill Rónáin, I noticed a small group of people huddled together outside the general store.

"Conor!" Tim O'Sullivan, the postmaster, had detached himself from the group and was hurrying across the lane to meet me. "Will you look at yourself? Sure, you're as wet as a shag!"

"I was out walking," I told him. "What's going on?"

"Did you not hear? One of the old sisters died this morning. The doctor and priest are in there now, looking after her."

"I'm sorry to hear that," I said. "I knew she hadn't been well for a while."

"Oh no, it wasn't that." He was shaking his head. "It was a fall that killed her. She was putting up new curtains and came off the chair. The poor woman had her neck broke."

"Oh god," I said. "That's terrible. How's her sister taking it?"

"We're not sure. There's only the priest and doctor been allowed in. She'd be in bits, I'd imagine. They were together all their lives."

Just then, the store door opened, and Mary Reardon and the priest came walking down along the path.

"Good morning, Conor, and you too, Tim," she nodded to us as she took her leave of the priest. "It's a terrible thing, is it not? The poor woman was lying dead on the floor for hours before the sister even knew she was gone. Ah well, she had a good innings, you can't deny that."

"No, you cannot." Tim was looking thoughtful. "Although I must admit, I wouldn't mind going the same way myself. You know what I mean now. Nice and quick and clean, as it were. God rest her soul."

"Well, it was a merciful death in some ways, I suppose." Mary was shaking her head. "But it's not something I'd wish on myself."

"I have to keep going, Mary," I told her. "I have a lot on down at the shed. When will the funeral be?"

"Oh, it would be a few days away yet, but there'll be the wake first. You'd be expected to attend, of course; you were related, you know."

"Related, how's that?"

"Well, the two sisters were O'Neill's. You knew that. And Grace's mother was an O'Neill herself, so the sisters would have been cousins to your grandmother," she smiled. "Don't look so surprised, sure half the island's related. There's only nine hundred of us here for the past thousand years, so it's to be expected."

* * *

The wake was held in the front room of the store two days later. By the time I arrived, the place was already crowded. The men dressed up in their Sunday best, tight-fitting black suits and ties. The women bustling about in long, flowing dresses, in and out of the kitchen, chattering and smiling as they handed out refreshments. The coffin standing in the front window, propped between two wooden chairs. Laughter rising up occasionally as the drink took hold. An old man in the corner playing a squeezebox, a younger man with jet-black curly hair accompanying him on a fiddle, the priest moving around awkwardly as if he were somehow responsible for the whole thing, tea cup in hand, face flushed and red.

"And you're Con Rua's boy, or so I'm told." He was smiling at me cautiously as if unsure of himself. "Mary was just after telling me what a fine job you've been doing on Grace's old boat. We're all proud of you, so we are." His eyes were flickering around the room. "Now, if you wouldn't mind just reaching around behind yourself there and putting a little drop of that Jameson's into my cup, it would be much appreciated." He was nodding towards a whiskey bottle on the counter, smiling all the while. "It looks a lot better if it's proffered, of course." He smiled fixedly at my hand as I poured a generous tot into the cup. "A little more … a little more if you would … keep going …" and finally, as I filled it to the brim, "ah, that's it now. Sure, that's grand!"

"Would you like to try a drop of tea in that whiskey?" I asked. "Just to change the color a little, as it were."

"Ah, aren't you a great man altogether! Oh no, it's not the color I'm after, it's the taste that does it for me. It's a great pity it's an alcoholic drink." He winked at me, slowly. "If it wasn't for that, sure I'd be at it all the time."

He was still laughing at his own humor when I heard a voice over my left shoulder.

"Did you mention the *Galway Rose* to the fili, Con Rua, or were you too afraid to ask?"

I spun around, spilling my drink. Brigid O'Neill was standing behind me, a large glass of whiskey in her right hand.

"I thought you were dead!" I blurted out, "I …"

"Ah now, will you stop!" She stamped a foot down on the wooden boards. "It was Madge that went off the chair, not me. God almighty, sure half the island has me dead and gone and me just starting to enjoy my life." But then she quietened down again and took hold of my arm, staring up at me, her eyes clear and inquiring. "You saw her, didn't you? You saw the *Galway Rose*?"

"I saw an old sailing ship," I told her. "I have no idea as to her name."

She was smiling up at me, eyes shining. "That was the *Galway Rose,* you saw. There's no denying that!"

"What makes you so sure?" I asked, but she was off again on her own tack.

"She's a Barque, you know. One of the fastest ships of her day. Ask the fili about her. Ask him what happened to them what sailed on her. Ask him that, if you will."

"Now then, Brigid." The priest was reaching out a hand. "You have no right to be taking strong drink. Give me that glass there now and I'll get you a nice cup of tea."

"Tea is it!" Brigid turned on him immediately. "And you might well try a little yourself whilst you're at it. Sure Jaysus, you wouldn't even know what it looked like. And you, not drawing a sober breath from the day you arrived on Inis Mór. Away with you now or I'll put my boot up your backside!"

People were turning to the raised voices, Mary hurrying across the crowded room. "Come on now, Brigid, leave Father alone. He has enough on his mind now without any of this. Sorry Father. Come on now, darling, come on over here, if you will, and you can sing us all a song."

"He's not my father." Brigid was glaring sideways at the priest as Mary led her away. "My father was a decent man. Sure Jaysus, he needs to go out and get himself a right job. And I don't want him at my wake, either. Do you hear me now? I couldn't afford him. Dead or alive. He'd be the first to arrive and the last to leave. All he's good for is changing wine into water. He has the whole thing back to front. Sure Jaysus, he's a disgrace to the cloth!"

I watched as Mary led her away, propping her up on a stool in the far corner next to the musicians, the strains of Noreen Bawn rising up over the hum of conversation, the wake moving into another phase, the old man with the squeezebox smiling broadly, delighted he'd found himself a vocalist. Brigid's voice rising up loud and clear ...

"Come all ye young rebels, and list while I sing

For the love of one's country is a terrible ting

It banishes fear with the speed of a flame

And makes us all part of the patriot game.

They taught me how Connelly was shot in a chair

His wounds from the battle, all bleeding and bare ..."

Chapter 33
Tristan and the Selkies

I slipped away from the wake around nine that evening and rode the bike back home along the quiet winding lanes. The first thing I saw as I entered the kitchen was a pale blue envelope propped up against the teapot on the wooden table. I knew from the handwriting who it was from …

Dear Dad,

Mum told me that you might be coming over to see us in the boat. I hope you do but if you can't, Mum said I can come over and see you in Ireland. I'm sick of school and I don't have any friends here. If you want me to, I could come and live with you for a while. I know you're very busy, but I just want to be with you more than I am now.

I miss you dad.

Tristan xxx

I stared at the letter for a long time and then I went across to the cupboard and took out the phone. It rang twice and then Giselle was there.

"It's me, Giselle. I hope it's not too late?"

"No. It's okay. How are things over there?"

"Pretty good. How are you coping?"

"Apart from being tired all the time, I'm good. Dad took mum to the hospital today and the doctor was pleased with her progress. That cheered us all up. So, what are you up to? How's the boat coming along?"

"Good. I'm launching her tomorrow. I just got back from a wake, one of the old sisters died here a few days ago. They were something of an institution on the island, so it'll probably go on for another day or two." I paused. "I received Tristan's letter, how is he?"

"I didn't know he'd written you a letter, but he's fine. He's really looking forward to seeing you. For God's sake, don't let him down again."

"Of course, I won't let him down. That was a silly thing to say." The words were out before I could stop them.

"Silly?" her voice came back with a sharper edge. "You've done nothing but let him down for the past few years! Do you still not realize that?"

"Look," I began, but then I stopped, remembering all the times I'd called up to tell him that I couldn't make it that weekend, all the lies.

"Why should we believe you?" She was still talking. "You've broken more promises to Tristan than you've kept. I wasn't even sure whether I should tell him you're coming. Maybe it's best if you don't come. How do I know it will be any different this time?"

There was a silence then that seemed to drag on forever.

"You're right." The words almost stuck in my throat. "You've no reason to trust me."

"What does that mean?" she snapped. "You're not sure you'll be here? Is that what you're saying?"

"No, it's not that. I just realized that what you said was true. I have let you down, both of you, too many times. Why should you trust me? There's nothing to base it on." I hesitated. "Look, I know you're trying to protect Tristan, you're a good mother, you always have been."

"It's hard for me to trust you," her voice had softened. "I don't want to see him hurt again."

"Look, I'm not going to try to talk you into anything. I've done too much of that already. If you think it's too early, I'll respect that. But if you give me a time and a place, I will be there. It's up to you."

There was another long silence and I stood there knowing that I'd created this entire situation myself. All the broken promises, all the years of neglect, wondering if there was just too much damage done already.

"I feel as if I'm talking to a complete stranger."

The words came over the line quietly, all the anger gone.

"I told you …"

She cut me off. "No, I don't mean that. I mean there's something different about you. I'm not sure what it is. You've changed. You listen now." But then she said, "Look, Tristan's school holiday starts in a few weeks. Will the boat be ready by then? And don't tell me when you're setting off. I don't want to be wondering if you've disappeared at sea or anything silly like that. Just call me when you've arrived, okay?"

"Okay. And she will be ready by then, I'll make sure."

"The nearest harbor's Saint Malo. If you can make it to there, we'll come and see you." She paused. "But I don't want to spend the whole time talking about us. This is about you and Tristan. I'm tired, Conor, let's keep it low key, okay?"

"Okay, that's fine with me." I paused. "Can I talk to Tristan?"

"It's very late. I think he's asleep."

"I know, if he's awake I mean. Is there a phone in his room?"

"I'll take it in. Hang on."

I heard footsteps and muffled voices.

"Dad? Are you there?"

"Yes, I'm here son. Were you asleep?"

"No, I was reading. Are you coming to see us?"

"Yes, I'll be there in a few weeks. What are you reading?"

"Oh, it's a story about American Indians. It's a bit silly, really. It's about shapeshifting. Do you know what that is?"

"Yes, I've heard of it. Why do you say it's silly?"

"Well, people can't change into animals, that doesn't make sense."

"Maybe not, Tristan, but sometimes we need to go past what makes sense to understand the heart of a story."

"What do you mean, dad?"

"Well, the Irish have a long tradition of storytelling and although a lot of their stories might not make sense to the logical mind, they can still touch your heart if you're open to them."

"Do you know any Irish stories, dad?"

"I know a few. Would you like to hear one?"

"Dad's going to tell me a story mum ..." I heard Giselle's voice in the background and then he was back. "What's it about, dad?"

"Well, it's a bit like your Native American story, but this one's about the seals that live around the Irish coast."

"Is it a true story?"

"Well, that's the sort of thing you'd have to work out for yourself. You see, some people believe these things, and some don't."

"How does it start?"

"Well, this is a story about a man by the name of Liam Flaherty who lived on a small farm at Killeany. It wasn't much of a place, just a few acres and a cottage. But the family had lived there for generations and they'd produced some of the finest cattle that ever came off Inis Mór. Well, after his parents died, Liam lived there by himself for years but, as time went on, he became more and more lonely and eventually, he started thinking about a wife. Now, there was a matchmaker on the island in those days."

"What's a matchmaker?"

"Matchmakers introduce people to each other with the intention of marriage. You see, Flaherty was not what you'd call a handsome man, and he had no skills whatsoever when it came to courting a woman. He couldn't string more than a few words together without stuttering, and the young girls on the island avoided the poor man like the plague. He'd turn up at a cheili occasionally, but even then, he'd hide himself away in a corner and never once would he ask any of the girls for a dance."

"Was there something wrong with him, dad?"

"No, not really, son, but he was an awkward sort of a man, tall and thin with a long melancholy face and a twist in one eye. He just never seemed to fit in, that's all. People were fond of saying that he was born in the wrong place at the wrong, and that can happen of course …" As I continued, I began to enjoy the story myself. "Well, he must have got sick and tired of his life the way it was, because the next time he took a few cattle off to market in Galway, he didn't return to Inis Mór. Instead, he took himself off along the Connemara coast. Now, some said he just needed a break from the island, but others claimed he was so lost, he wasn't sure if he wanted to go on living or not. Whatever the reason, Liam Flaherty was gone from Inis Mór for the whole of that summer and when he returned home again, he brought with him a wife. And not just any sort of a wife. You see, this young woman was the most beautiful creature anyone had ever set eyes on. She was tall and slim with long, flowing, jet-black hair, her skin with a touch of colour to it, her eyes like golden almonds, almost luminous in their depth, her movements as graceful as a swan on the water. It was said that when she looked at you, man or woman alike, you would feel your heart tremble in your chest …"

"Was she a witch, dad?"

"Hold on now, son. Just listen to the story. You see, to confuse things further, she had eyes for nobody but Flaherty. She simply doted on the man. Wherever Flaherty went, there she was, alongside him. Working in the fields or walking up to the church on Sundays, arm in arm, they were like two lovebirds. He'd bring her flowers; she'd bake him cakes. He'd take her walking; she'd dance with him at night. They were totally infatuated with one another. Well, naturally enough, the islanders couldn't understand how such a woman could have fallen in love with a man like Flaherty, and before long, everybody on the island was convinced she was a selkie …"

"What's a selkie, dad?" Tristan's voice came across soft and quiet.

"The selkies are seal people, son. They're seals that take on human form and come up out of the ocean to live on the land."

"But are they real? Is it true?"

"Well, as I said, that's the sort of thing you'd have to work out for yourself. But look, you can't keep on interrupting, okay?"

"I won't dad, I promise."

"You see, legend has it that the young female seals sometimes get bored with living in the ocean, and they'll swim up on a deserted beach somewhere, slip out of their skins and dance and sing in the moonlight. Occasionally, one of them will get so carried away that she'll forget where she left her skin and she'll panic because she can't return to the sea without it. Well, the only way she can survive on land is to marry one of the local men, but before that can happen, a pact must be struck between them. They are allowed to marry but their first-born son must be returned to the ocean. If that is not done, they'll be haunted by misfortune until the selkie goes back to the sea herself, never able to return to the land in human form."

Tristan didn't interrupt again but I could hear his soft breathing as I continued. I told him how Rory Flaherty was born and of the events that led up to him being lost at sea in a small boat. And I went on to describe how his father had stolen a currach that night and risked his own life going after the boy even though the fisherman had told him that it was a futile quest.

"You see, son, the fishermen were convinced that there was no hope at all for the boy. They'd barely survived the gale themselves and they knew better than anyone that such a small craft had no chance of surviving those terrible seas. Nevertheless, they got on the radio to the Coast Guard and put out a distress signal for the two missing currachs. It was more of a formality than anything else. But to everyone's astonishment, twelve hours later, a deep-sea fishing vessel running for safety towards Galway, reported sighting a lone currach off their starboard bow, five miles west of Doolin. The ship's master spotted the currach amidst the worst weather he'd experienced in thirty years at sea. He said later that he thought he was imagining it, at first. A lone man rowing a tiny craft through the mountainous seas. No lights, no engine, no sail. The boat rising and falling in the towering swells. Well, he managed to bring the trawler about and hove-to close by the currach, but when they hailed him to offer assistance, he said that the man had ignored them completely, looking neither left nor right, rowing steadily towards Doolin as if in a trance. It was then that the skipper noticed a seal swimming a few yards out in front of the currach, as if to guide it. They hailed Flaherty a dozen times or more, but the seas were still rising and the skipper, fearing for his own life and the lives of his crew, had no option but to put the trawler back on course and abandon Flaherty to his fate …"

As the story progressed, I imagined Tristan lying in bed, listening.

"Well, to everyone's amazement, an exhausted Liam Flaherty rowed back into Cill Rónáin two days later, his son Rory unconscious in the bottom of the currach, a seal following along behind them as far up as the beach …"

I went on to describe how the fishermen had carried Flaherty and his son up to the quayside and from there, back home to their farm in Killeany, and I explained how the doctor had called a Garda when he realised Flaherty's wife was still missing, and how Flaherty had shown no interest at all in her disappearance.

"You see, son, there was only one Garda on the island in those days, a young man by the name of Podraic Mulholland, born and bred on Inis Oírr and well acquainted with the ways of the islands. Now, it's on record that he received the phone call just before dawn that day and he set off immediately on his bike for Killeany. Well, the way he tells it now is that a mile or so out of Cill Rónáin, he spotted something on top of a rise up ahead of him. At first, he thought it was a dead man but, as he drew closer, he realised it was a seal. Podraic said she was sitting, stiff and upright, still as a statue, her brown eyes unblinking as she stared down the other side of the hill towards Flaherty's farm. Mulholland said it startled him, but what shocked him even more was the trail of blood running all the way back down the hill. He said the road was red with it. You see the poor creature had dragged herself over the rocks and stones all the way up from Cill Rónáin, and her belly was cut to pieces. She'd lost so much blood that she was too weak to go any further ..."

The story had taken longer than I'd expected and as it drew towards a close, I decided to soften the ending a little.

"Young Mulholland felt a great pity for the seal, and he was still there with her when Dr. Swan came along a little later and together, they lifted her up into the back seat of the doctor's car and took her down to the surgery in Cill Rónáin. She was extremely weak, but the doctor stitched her up as best he could and then looked after her for weeks until she was strong enough to be returned to the sea. Well, that's where the legend began, Tristan, and to this very day, people will swear that, even as a grown man, whenever Rory Flaherty would go down to the harbor, a seal, scarred and battered with age, would swim alongside him, singing as he walked along by the water's edge ..." I paused, waiting for a response.

"You changed the end of the story." Her voice came across the line soft and warm. "The seal dies, doesn't she?"

"How did you know?"

"We're Celts too, Conor. I was brought up with those stories. A lot of them have sad endings. They're about life."

"Yes," I said. "The seal dies. I thought it might be a bit too much for Tristan."

"Tristan's been asleep for ages."

"Why didn't you say?"

"Because I wanted to hear how it ended. It was beautiful. Sad, but beautiful. That's the first time I've ever heard you tell Tristan a story." She paused. "I don't know what's happened to you, but whatever it is, I hope you can stay this way." She paused again.

"Look … I told dad you were coming over and he said it's okay to stay with us. There's plenty of room here. You'd have your own bedroom and maybe you could finish the story for Tristan, one night."

"I'd like that."

"But finish it properly. The seal died for her child, that's love. And the father dies a little too, you know. He sacrificed everything he loved for his son." Her voice changed. "Look, I'm sorry, but it's really late and I have to check on mum."

Chapter 34
Dun Aengus

After I hung up, I sat there for a long while, thinking of Giselle. It was close to midnight, but I felt restless, and on the spur of the moment I decided to take a walk up to Dun Aengus. I pulled on my leather jacket, wound a scarf around my neck and stepped quietly out through the front door. It was a cool, clear night, a few lights twinkling in the distance over towards Cill Rónáin, stars hanging heavy and bright overhead, waves below in the cove sighing in and out, as soft as an infant's breath as I moved along the deserted lanes towards a distant rise.

Once I'd passed through the village, I struck off to the west. The moonlight coursing down across the island, falling in patches over the rocks and grass. Cottages standing, still and silent in the night, white lace curtains drawn and sleeping. The surrounding fields lying quiet and separate as individual dreams within their age-old, stone-walled divisions. Moving up the hillside towards Dun Aengus, relying on the moon to guide me, surrounded on all sides by remnants of the past. The occasional squeal of an owl breaking through the trance-like quality of the night. Some unspoken need drawing me on.

As I crossed through the last line of the defenses, I was struck once again by the enigmatic solitude of the place. A sense of history. A feeling of loneliness and loss. Knowing that men had trodden this path before me carrying the tools and weapons of war. Remembering the old man's warning of Dun Aengus at midnight. Moving cautiously towards the half-seen entrance, the final gateway looming black, cave-like and ominous, in the shadows of the surrounding walls. Entering its dark maw, swallowed up instantly by a cold silence. Emerging on the other side into a totally different time and space.

I stood there motionless for a long moment, the craggy walls cast in faint silhouette against the starry night sky. A fishing boat's lights off Inis Mann winking gently in the cold night air. The stillness of the night reminding me of the first time I'd ever wandered into this ancient citadel.

I approached the cliff face cautiously and stood within a foot of the edge, staring down across a sea murmuring and shifting like some dark tethered beast below, disjointed memories as brief torn images flashing before my mind's eye. My grandfather standing next to me on the cliff top, one hand on my shoulder, looking down at a wave-flecked ocean. My father in a dark blue cotton shirt waving up to us from the cockpit as Erin *cut away out from the island, out to the west through the endless white-capped swells, her sails filled and smooth, her path fixed and true; gnarled brown hands twisting strands of rope in the soft glow of candles. A campfire burning in a ring of stones, the old man singing, his head thrown back, his eyes closed, a tall black Celtic cross, red roses at the base,*

Grace's whitewashed cottage, images in store

Bread steaming in the morning light, faces by a door

Men gathered for the digging, breath hanging in the air

Granda smiling with his eyes, my father standing there

Following down a stone-walled track, silent as we walk

Moving to the ready field, Con Rua glancing back

Sunlight slanting down on rain, across that wild Atlantic shore
Wind hard, grief-burnt faces, famine memories in store
Men turning in a field in spring, whose blood the shard rock tore
Bleeding out existence in the stony fields of Inis Mór ...

There was a sudden movement and I turned. Just a few feet away, an owl, head erect, eyes huge in the moonlight, stared back at me, curious and unafraid, from the edge of a darkened rock wall. We studied each other for a long moment, as motionless as statues. Then he made his decision, throwing himself forwards over the edge of the cliff, his great wings opening to catch his fall. Turning himself back in, angling upwards with the momentum, and then, the heavy, deep thrusts, lifting him back up over the edge, up above my head, before sweeping across the keep and melting into the anonymity of the star-speckled night beyond. It was only after he'd disappeared that I realized who it was I was looking for.

Chapter 35
The Launch

As I rode my bike down towards the shed the following morning, I was feeling low. I hadn't seen the old man for weeks, and it seemed clear that he wouldn't be attending the launch. The double doors were fully open when I arrived and Lorcan and another man were down on their knees, inspecting *Erin's* cradle.

"Morning, Conor." He stood up as I wheeled my bike in. "Come over here and meet Fergal. He'll be taking *Erin* down to the water for us."

Fergal was around forty-five years of age, a strongly built man of medium height, his dark brown eyes set into a face prematurely aged and weathered from too many years at sea.

"We'll need to have her down there by noon," he nodded. "The tide will turn just after midday so we can't be wasting any time. Once you have a few more bolts in that cradle, we'll make a start."

"Will that be enough?" Lorcan was frowning. "You know she was damaged on the way up?"

"Ah, you don't have to be worrying your head about that." Fergal was all smiles. "I've dragged my own boat down there a dozen times or more and I haven't lost her yet. Sure, didn't you have that young culchie from Connemara doing it the last time? What did you expect? Jaysus, it's a wonder he got her up here in one piece at all."

We began pulling *Erin* from the shed just after ten, the deep-throated roar of the tractor setting my nerves on edge as the cradle was dragged across the cobble-stoned floor, Lorcan running from one side of the tractor to the other, shouting orders above the roar of the engine, Fergal totally oblivious to it all. A small group of islanders gathered by the yard wall, laughing amongst themselves and calling out advice as the drama unfolded.

"Come on now, Fergal, do as you're told. You're not half the man your father was. Come on now, boy, get her down on the shingle, we don't have all day. That's it Lorcan, show him who's boss. One word from you and he'll do exactly what he wants."

Despite all the unwanted advice, the whole thing went off without a hitch, Fergal dragging *Erin* slowly along the roadway and then down the incline onto the dark pebbled beach, pausing occasionally to check the cradle, clearing away any rocks that threatened to impede its progress, easing the boat ever closer to the sea.

By midday, she was down by the water's edge, the tide just beginning to turn. Fergal unshackling the chains. *Erin* perched up above as if too nervous to look down. Watching and waiting as the water rose to cover the base of her cradle. Small rivulets washing along her keel, rising up, inch by inch, swelling around her timbers, higher and higher.

I looked over to the jetty but there was no sign of the old man, just a dozen or so of the islanders standing there cheering and waving as *Erin* rose on a swell and slipped free of her prison at last.

* * *

By the time we rowed ashore an hour later, only one figure remained standing at the end of the jetty.

"Conor O'Rourke?" He was smiling at Lorcan.

"No," Lorcan nodded across to me, "that's the man you're looking for."

"Patrick Finlayson." He held out a hand. "From Salthill, Galway." He was looking across the water to where *Erin* lay at her mooring. "You've made a fine job of her; I can see that. I was told you were launching her today, a friend of mine skippers one of the ferries." He straightened himself up. "Look, I'll get to the point. I have an old Galway Hooker here on the island that's in bad need of repair …"

"You're Tom Finlayson's boy?" Lorcan butted in.

"Yes. You knew my father?"

"I did, of course. Sure, everyone on the island knew Tom. He was the doctor here for years. I know the boat well, *Maid of Aran.* She's up in the shed there at the Reagan farm. She was a fine little Hooker in her day. Your father bought her off Regan's widow. He was to refit her, but nothing ever came of it. I know he passed on some years ago. He was a good man. God rest his soul."

"Yes, indeed." Patrick Finlayson was nodding. "He was a great loss to us. He left me the boat and it's been a dream of mine ever since to set her right. Her hull is mostly sound, although she may need one or two new planks. Parts of the deck will need replacing, I'm told, and of course, her paint work's gone altogether. All in all, she's in bad need of a refit. Michael Shaughnessy told me that your family used to build boats here on the island. Is that right?" And then, without waiting for an answer. "You spent some time in Australia, I believe?"

“Michael,” Lorcan interrupted, “it’s been a long day, why don’t we continue this chat up at Joe Watty’s place?

* * *

We talked for more than two hours in the front bar. Patrick Finlayson had dreamt of refitting his father’s boat for years.

“Well, do you have an answer for me, Conor?” He put his glass down on the counter. “Would you be interested in refitting the *Maid of Aran*?”

“What do you think, are you up for it?” Lorcan was smiling, obviously taken by the idea. “I’d be glad to lend a hand. She was a fine little sea boat.”

“I’m not sure what I’m doing after Brittany,” I told them. “It depends a lot on what happens over there.”

“*The Maid of Aran* is a bigger boat and she’s in worse shape.” Lorcan had turned back to the doctor. “The job would take six months or more, I’d say. Look, Conor will be gone for a week or two. Why don’t we take a look at that boat of yours when he gets back?” He paused. “You’d be needing a good size cheque book now if you want her to look anything like *Erin.*”

“I’m aware of that.” Patrick Finlayson was scribbling on the back of a business card. “That’s my home number. Call me when you’re back, if you would.”

We walked him down to the quayside in time for the last ferry, then I took the dinghy out to check *Erin’s* bilges. The boat was rolling gently in the evening swell and I sat on the foredeck for a while, watching the setting sun, remembering my father.

The last few weeks flew past. I worked late every night and rose early each morning with lists of things to do that seemed to get longer as the days progressed. *Erin* took on a little water the first week, as the old man had said she would. "She'll take a while to settle down," I remembered him sitting in the chair, puffing on his pipe, staring off into the distance as if picturing it all in his head. "Keep an eye on her bilge. The planks will need time to take up. Once that happens, she'll be as tight as a drum."

We stepped the mast one Tuesday morning at high tide, Lorcan and a few of the local fishermen helping to swing it up into place from a jerry-built crane rigged up on the quay. We adjusted the rigging that afternoon and the following day, took her out for sea trials on Galway Bay.

Erin sailed perfectly from the beginning, taking to the water like a salmon returned to the seas. I'd never skippered a thirty-three-footer single-handed before but, within days, I was tacking out through the islands to the open water beyond, changing headsails as Lorcan looked on, reefing down the main when the wind surged, and returning to Cill Rónáin under sail before dropping the anchor and settling back onto our moorings. We spent most evenings on board, talking and pouring over charts, working out the best approaches to the harbors of Brittany.

"I might give Saint-Malo a miss, if it's blowing too hard." I was hunched over the chart-table with a small torch. "It looks as if it could be difficult in heavy weather."

Lorcan was lying on the starboard bunk, tired from a long day's sail.

"That would be right," he said. "If it's any way rough, you'd be better running offshore until things calmed down."

He was nodding off, Boson sprawled alongside him, fast asleep.

"I'd probably get in easy enough on the high tide."

"Don't be worrying your head about that tonight." He was lying on his side, one arm around the dog. "There'll be time enough to work all that out before you leave."

Chapter 36
Erin go Bragh

I spent the last evening at Mary and Lorcan's cottage, talking over the final details of the trip.

"Now, I don't want you doing anything silly with that boat of yours." Mary was sitting in her armchair knitting. "You have a family to think of as well as yourself, you know."

"Sure Jaysus, don't you think he knows that." Lorcan smiled across at me. "He sails that boat better than his father did."

"It wasn't you I was talking to you. I was talking to Conor."

"I won't, Mary. Brittany's not far, and there's plenty of good harbors along the French coast. I'll be back in no time."

Erin was tied up in the deeper water by the far end of the jetty, and they walked me back to the boat after dinner, strolling along the quayside in the cool night air, Boson running on ahead of us, his demented goldfish eyes peering back over his shoulder every few bounds to make sure we were still following him.

After they'd left, I walked back along the jetty and stepped into the boatshed, half hoping that the old man would be sitting there, smoking his pipe. But the place was deserted. I was turning to leave when I noticed something on the bench and went across. A black walking stick lay on top of a pile of oak shavings, its silver head glinting softly in the half light of the shed. I reached out almost fearfully; I'd never touched it before. It was his blackthorn, there was no doubt about that. I turned on the light above the bench and peered closer. On the top of the stick, inlaid into the solid silver knob in intricate gold filigree was the sign of the Seanachaí. Engraved just underneath, the words: *Never give a man a sword until he's learnt how to dance.* I stared at it for a moment then looked around.

"Hello," I called out. "Are you there?" But the words just bounced off the walls, reverberating all around me in the silence that followed. I stepped back outside, still carrying the stick. The yard was deserted, just a solitary black cat slinking its stealthy way into the shadowed edges at the far end of the stone wall. I stood there motionless for a long while, then I pulled the gate shut behind me, feeling a great sense of loss.

* * *

I woke early the following day and after making coffee I carried a mug up on deck. The day was grey, patches of mist coming in from the west, trailing in across the water as soft and ethereal as dreams. I rigged a canvas cover over the boom to keep off the damp and then sat there in the early morning silence, sipping the coffee. The old man had missed the launch, now it seemed certain that he'd miss my departure, too.

"So, the big day has finally arrived."

I spun around. Tim O'Sullivan was smiling down at me from the quayside above. "Sure Jaysus, I didn't mean you to jump like that. I have a parcel for you from Dublin. It's your coffee. It was in on the late ferry yesterday." He was holding out a large package of Esperanza, encased in a transparent courier's bag.

"Thanks," I told him. "Just in time."

"Well, I'm glad I didn't miss you. I was talking to Brigid. She said you'd be away on the high tide."

"I'm heading over to Brittany for a week or two," I told him.

"Bretagne?" He grinned down at me. "Are there not enough Celts here on Inis Mór that you have to go off to Brittany looking for more?"

"My wife and son are over there," I told him. "Visiting her family."

"Safe home." He turned to leave. "Keep the mast up, the keel down and yourself in the boat. Good luck!"

Mary and Lorcan arrived at nine to say their final goodbyes, and after an impromptu breakfast of bacon sandwiches and tea, we spent the last hour going over final preparations.

By ten thirty, she was ready. Sails hanked on, the dinghy stowed, the portholes locked, ropes coiled on deck. I kept an eye out for the old man, hoping he might still show, but despite a couple of false alarms with fishermen in greatcoats, there was no sign of him, and eventually I just had to resign myself to the fact that he wouldn't be there. We were down below, going over the charts one last time when I heard someone shouting.

"Ahoy *Erin*! Are you there?" I stuck my head up through the hatch. An old fisherman in battered oilskins was standing on the quayside above, pointing out to sea. "The ferry's ahead of time, you need to get that boat out of here right away. Come on, now. Cast off those lines quickly or we'll all be in trouble!" I looked seaward through the drizzle and mist. The Aran Ferry was just offshore, bearing down on us at speed.

"Oh Christ!" But I needn't have worried. The whole thing went off like clockwork. As Lorcan helped Mary up the steel ladder to the quay, I went forward, cast off the bowline and hauled up the mainsail, pulling it up tight into place before lashing off the halyard. Then I hurried aft, caught the stern line from Lorcan and grabbed the tiller as we began to move slowly away from the wharf. As we cleared the end of the jetty, the wind caught *Erin's* sails and she surged forward confidently, as if eager to gain the open seas.

"Good luck." Lorcan was waving from the quayside, one arm around Mary. "Erin go bragh!"

A sudden gust of wind hit us, and *Erin* heeled over, white water spraying up from her bow as she picked up speed, her tiller trembling like a restless spirit underneath my hand. I held my course for as long as I could then I swung her over to give the ferry more room. She sounded two quick blasts of her horn in recognition, and as she slowed for her final approach to Cill Rónáin, the skipper leant out of the wheelhouse.

"Where are you bound, *Erin*?" he called out.

"Toward Bretagne," I shouted back. "God willing."

"Good luck." He shouted as he passed alongside. "Safe home."

I was waving back when I spotted him. He was standing on the upper deck just behind the wheelhouse. It was his clothes that caught my eye. A man about my own age wearing a dark blue suit of a kind you'd never see on Inis Mór. Two mismatched suitcases on the deck alongside him. Looking cold, alone and completely out of place as he peered through the mist towards the approaching island. It jolted me for a moment when I realized who it was that he reminded me of, and I turned instinctively and looked back towards Cill Rónáin.

The drizzle was still falling but I could make out a solitary figure standing at the end of the jetty. A tall man in a long, dark greatcoat, a seaman's cap and walking stick. I grabbed the binoculars and strained my eyes back through the encroaching mist. He was staring seaward towards the ferry, but then as I watched, his head turned a little and I knew in my heart that he was looking at me across the water.

For a moment, I went to throw the tiller across to follow the ferry back in, but something held me, and I paused. We stared at each other for what seemed like an age and then, as I watched, he saluted me slowly, in the old manner, his hand rising to his cap, pausing for a long moment before falling back down by his side. I stood there quite still for some time, then I straightened myself up and I saluted him back, as you would a Captain.

The End.

From the Author

Dear reader, I first visited Inis Mór as a young man and immediately fell in love with the island. My mother, who was born in Galway, had told me stories of the Inis Mór since early childhood and to me I was returning to a mythical place of dreams. Her family had hailed from the island a generation or two earlier, and she often spent her school holidays there as a child.

I have spent many wonderful times on 'The Mór' and some of the characters in this book are based on real people from there. The two old sisters, Brigid and Madge, I knew well and had tea in their kitchen many a time. No electricity, the water heated on an old, cast-iron stove top.

They were very much the island's historians and have only recently passed. As for the priest, I won't even hint as to his identity. I was fond of the drink myself for many years and am not in any position to judge!

A sequel to 'Passage' is planned, and I hope to have it out by late 2022. My website details, which has all my books listed, are below. Please keep in touch.

If you have enjoyed this book, I would be grateful if you took the time to leave a review, and any comments, on Amazon.com or Kindle.com. and for that, I thank you in advance.

Brian O'Raleigh

January 2022

brianoraleighbooks.com

brianoraleighbooks@hotmail.com

Brian O'Raleigh was born of wildly dysfunctional Irish parents and raised in the seaside town of Blackpool. After a troubled childhood, including being expelled from school at 14, recounted in his first gripping memoir, Brian fled alone to Australia at the age of seventeen, running from the law, his demons, and a growing dependence on alcohol. In 1967, he volunteered for the Six Day War in Israel, but later, disillusioned with that cause, spent the next ten years travelling throughout Europe and Asia. On returning to Australia, he worked for years at mining camps and construction projects in the outback. Finally, after coming to terms with his own alcoholism, he returned to Sydney, married, and settled down to raise a family.

Later, after a personal crisis, described in his memoir *Waking Walter,* he began studying philosophy and psychology, delving into the works of Plato, Carl Jung, Joseph Campbell, Bill Wilson, Viktor Frankl, and James Hillman, among others. During this period O'Raleigh experienced a profound, life changing epiphany, which dramatically altered his outlook on life and led him to create a modality, beyond therapy and beyond blame, that enables participants discover their innate gifts and talents and the actual meaning and purpose of their lives. He now conducts workshops in Ireland, Bali, and Australia, training therapists, counsellors, facilitators, and social workers. He began writing spontaneously in 2010 as a direct result of this awakening and has published five books.

Books by Brian O'Raleigh

The Boy in the Boat. A Memoir

Waking Walter. Memoir-Part 2. Available January 1st 2022.

Passage to Inis Mór. A modern-day classic set on one of Ireland's most beautiful islands.

Quest for Meaning-The Magical Power of Purpose. A groundbreaking work that explains the power of purpose and how readers can discover their ideal work or career.

Endor's Way-a compelling murder mystery set between Bondi Beach, Australia, and the island of Inis Mór, Ireland. Available October 2022.

Frank O'Shea of the Irish Echo.

"O'Raleigh writing is very much in the tradition of Irish storytelling, with strong, vibrant prose that reminds of writers such as Sean O'Faolain and Benedict Kiely".

brianoraleighbooks.com

brianoraleighbooks@hotmail.com

The Boy in the Boat

A Memoir

Growing up in his parent's hotel in Blackpool, Brian never knew why his parents fled Ireland. But he learned early to escape his father's demonic rages by slipping away from the Alexandra Private Hotel to the beach and the Kathleen R, the fishing boat that would become his refuge and his sanctuary.
At the age of eighteen, forced to flee the law in England, Brian travels throughout Europe, the war zones of the Middle East, and the mining towns of Australia, in a futile attempt to escape his own inner demons, the same demons that destroyed his father's life and caused his early death.

The Boy in the Boat tells the riveting story of Brian's violent childhood, his descent into alcoholism and crime, his dramatic and inspirational recovery, and his passionate search for meaning and purpose. A quest that would ultimately lead him to the profound realization that it is only in discovering our true purpose in life can we hope to achieve happiness, fulfilment, and success.

Australian New Idea:

"Brian is no angel. He's an infuriating drunk and an irresponsible brute, which is why this story of ultimate redemption is so powerful. It has its lighter moments too, where innocent humour offers respite from the cynical and wistful mood."

The Australian Irish Echo.

"O'Raleigh is a convincing writer, and this book deserves ranking with Angela's Ashes. He mixes dialogue, narrative and reflection in a story that is always gripping, often scary and sometimes funny. He is

searingly honest, and if this work can bring help to other tortured souls, he deserves great credit."

The Australian Woman's Day.

"From raw and compelling prose, a moving portrait emerges of Brian. From cowed child to fierce rebel and finally to an adult battling his own inner demons. This is a finely crafted memoir."

Endor's Way

Chapter 1

Bondi Beach

The body washed up on Bondi Beach around 3.am, the time of arrival established by its presence amongst the flotsam and jetsam that marked the furthest extent of the incoming tide. Empty beer bottles, old tennis balls, and multi-colored plastic thongs lay scattered recklessly along the high-water mark, intertwined with seaweed, bits of rope and the odd piece of driftwood. Rejected, along with Jameson, hurled back from whence they came by an angry, disillusioned ocean.

He'd been a handsome man, but as he lay there face up waiting for a saviour now long overdue, you could never have guessed that. The crabs and little fish that had escorted him on his long, slow drift from the foot of the cliffs at North Head to his final resting place on the beach at Bondi, had been pulling at the edges of the gaping chest wound that had terminated his life.

I arrived at the beach around eight o'clock it was a miserable day, grey clouds hurrying furtively across a darkening sky and the wind, coming in from the south-east, keening over the ocean swells like a requiem for lost souls.

The early morning jogger who'd stumbled across the body just before dawn was being questioned by the local police just out of the weather near the entrance to the surf club. I glanced at her as I got out of the car. She was around forty-five or so, tall, blond, and skinny, her arms folded tightly across a Spandex plated, anorexic chest, still pale and visibly shaken from her grisly find.

I nodded to the sergeant and moved past them towards the beach. Another half a dozen uniforms were on the windswept sands, close by the wading pool. Two of them were on their knees, securing the flapping yellow tape that determined where the public stopped and started; beyond that a small crowd of vultures in anoraks and track-suit pants hovered, drawn in by the scent of death, eager to be part of the unfolding drama.

As I approached the main group, the uniforms parted to reveal the kneeling figure of Carl Seagan, doctor, coroner, and if his detractors were correct, one-time abortionist to the Sydney social set. As he recognized me, his face took on a slight frown.

"Glad you managed to make it before the tide came back in, Harrigan," he turned back to the body.

Before I could respond, his assistant, a worried-looking young man just out of medical school, fumbled…

"I'm sorry, sir, it's your partner. It's Detective Jameson ..."

Email: brianoraleighbooks@hotmail.com

Website. brianoraleighbooks.com

Printed in Great Britain
by Amazon